Under the skillful stroke of his tongue, Calaine felt as if she were drowning, drowning in the desire that surged through her veins. A sigh escaped her parted lips and she felt herself leaning into him, giving in to temptation as she met his strokes eagerly. She welcomed the possession of his lips. She liked the pressure of her breasts pressed against his chest. She felt as if she had been waiting for this all her life. Heat surged through her and spread fast through her body. Her world was spinning like a top and all that mattered was being right here, right now with David. Her arms snaked around his torso and she clung tightly, afraid that if she let go, she would discover it had all been just a dream. She heard David groan and then his hold on her tightened, drawing her closer to his hard male body.

The need for air finally pulled them apart. They stared at each other, hearts thumping and breathing heavily.

HART & SOUL

Angie Daniels

Genesis Press Inc.

Indigo Love Stories

An imprint Genesis Press Publishing

Genesis Press, Inc.
1213 Hwy 45 North
Columbus, MS 39705

ISBN: 1-58571-0873
Manufactured in the United States of America

First Edition

Visit us at www.genesis-press.com
or call at 1-888-Indigo-1

Dedication

This book is dedicated in memory of two dear friends

Teresa (Reesa) Hill & Becky Lynn Estes

We never truly realize how much someone meant until they are no longer there

ACKNOWLEDGEMENTS

To my families, the Moores, Daniels, Andersons and Hills for their continued love and support.

To my sister Arlynda Daniels-Guyton for all the years she babysat for free. I love you gurl!

To my critics and dear friends Beverly Palmer and Sherrie Branch your opinions mean the world to me.

To B. Loehr Temporaries and Secretarial Support Services (SOS) for giving me the hands-on experience I needed to make my heroine's career believable.

To my mother Kathleen Anderson, if there was no you there would be no me. Thanks for always being there. I love you!

To Elizabeth Simon of Columbia for editing my submission package, and for helping come up with the title. Thanks for all your help.

To my fellow authors Gerald Malcolm, Toni Staton Harris, Doreen Rainey, Wanda Thomas, and TT Henderson. Thanks for your friendships and support.

To my homegirls Tonya Hill, Norma Rhodes, Kim Ashcraft and Novia Mearidy, your friendships have meant the world to me.

PROLOGUE

"Find your real mother…"

Calaine Hart bolted upright in bed with her palm pressed firmly against her racing heart. Sucking air into her lungs, she reminded herself it was only a dream, even though it was the same dream she'd been having since her parents had been killed in a hit-and-run accident three months earlier. She raised a hand to her damp forehead as tears of frustration flooded her eyes. *When would it end?* She couldn't keep battling the nightmares. Time would heal her wounds, but only one thing would erase the anger and resentment — answers to the questions that haunted her.

Throwing back the covers, she lowered her feet to the floor and slid them into a pair of pink terry cloth slippers. After taking another stabilizing breath, she rose and padded into the adjoining bathroom, where she splashed cold water onto her face. *You've got to pull yourself together.*

Staring at her disheveled image in the mirror, she took in the dark circles that had settled beneath her nutmeg-colored eyes, the result of too many sleepless nights. She shook her head in dismay. With a full day ahead of her, a good night's sleep was essential.

Calaine opened the medicine cabinet, reached for a bottle of sleep aid on the top shelf, unscrewed the cap and popped two tablets into her mouth. Before swallowing, she paused a moment to reflect on the number of nights she had required help to fall asleep.

Calaine shuddered inwardly when she realized that somewhere along the way she had lost count. Cupping a hand under the running faucet, she brought cool water to her lips. As the pills slid down her throat, despair assailed her.

Returning the half empty bottle to the shelf, Calaine caught her reflection again. *You look like crap.* Her thin face was tired and haggard. She couldn't remember the last time she'd used any make-up to enhance her cinnamon complexion. Even her chestnut curls were an unruly mess, long overdue for a trim. Calaine shut her eyes briefly as grief tore at her heart. She hoped the drug would kick in soon.

As the owner of her own employment agency, Calaine was scheduled to participate in a job fair the next morning. She was grateful for business because it was the only thing holding her together these days. There she found mindless solidity that helped camouflage the despair in her life. The fast-paced environment left very little time to think or to remember. However, at five o'clock, after the telephones had been forwarded and the front door locked, she had very little choice but to return home, where she found herself alone again and facing the agony of her loss.

"Find your real mother."

Only seconds before Katherine Hart had closed her eyes for the last time, she'd breathed those four words that had changed her daughter's life forever.

"C-Calaine, I'm so sorry."

Stroking her mother's hand, Calaine tried to comfort her the best way she knew how. "Mommy, there's no reason to apologize. The accident was not your fault."

"No...please listen." Katherine struggled to be heard, knowing the end was near. She signaled her daughter to come closer. Calaine leaned forward as her mother took another deep, shaky

breath. *"Promise me you'll find your real mother."*

Confusion swirled in Calaine's head before she finally man-aged to ask, *"W-what do you mean, find my real mother? I-I thought* **you** *were my mother."*

"I'm sorry..." Katherine gasped, struggling to catch her last breath. *"I couldn't go without...without you knowing the truth."* With that her fingers loosened their hold and she was gone.

Calaine swallowed hard as she wiped away the hot tears trickling down her cheeks. She constantly relived the traumatic scene that had changed her life. Since then, her thoughts had been consumed by too many unanswered questions regarding the two people she had known all her life as her parents. Not only did she have doubts about her relationship with her mother, she had begun to question her connection to her father as well. She had even considered the possibility that maybe she was adopted.

She rubbed her temple. Thinking about her parents made her head hurt. She splashed cold water on her face again and reached for a towel. Returning to her room, Calaine collapsed onto a mauve chaise and leaned her head against the cushion.

In search of a plausible explanation, she had broached the subject with both her aunt and uncle on two separate occasions. Not only had they told her she'd misunderstood her mother's last words, but they'd gone so far as to insist she was indeed the Harts' biological child. Still, a nagging voice whispered in her head, *Why would Katherine have told you to find your real mother if it wasn't true?* The uncertainty made it impossible to simply let the matter go.

Calaine hugged her knees to her chest as she realized that as much as she hated to admit it, a part of her had always known something was wrong.

The Harts had been tough, no-nonsense parents who had believed in preparing their child for the ugly world into which she

3

had been born. Consumed by her husband's political career, her mother had disdained emotional warmth. Calaine had, at times, wondered if her mother even remembered she had a daughter. Katherine had never been affectionate. Calaine could count the number of times she had bestowed a kiss or a loving word of encouragement.

Her relationship with her mother had been a tough one. She'd tried to do all the right things, such as staying out of trouble, getting good grades and graduating at the top of her class. She'd even waited until she was in college to date. However, it had never been enough. Her mother had been quick to judge and had rarely given praise. It wasn't until Calaine had opened her agency three years ago that her mother had finally told Calaine she was proud to have her as a daughter. For the first time she'd felt loved. Now she was alone. Or was she?

"Find your real mother." The echo of Katherine Hart's words slid around the edge of her mind.

If her mother had been telling the truth, there was another woman out there who might be looking for her. Maybe she would finally discover what she felt she'd been missing all her life. Maybe she would finally feel like she belonged somewhere.

A gush of spring air rushed through the half-opened window beside her bed. Feeling a slight chill, Calaine reached for a flannel blanket at the foot of the chaise and draped it over her shoulders. She'd spent so many nights in the very same spot crying, shaking with resentment at her parents for not telling her before...before it was too late to ask questions.

Katherine had been many things, dominating, outspoken, and strict, but she had never been a liar. If Katherine said she wasn't her biological mother, then Calaine believed her.

Then why was everyone else lying? The question stabbed at her heart.

Deep down she believed there had to be something no one wanted her to know, something they preferred to keep a secret.

By the time she finally drifted off to sleep, Calaine had made the decision to find out the truth.

CHAPTER ONE

Calaine moved through the double doors of the Holiday Inn Executive Center with her heels tapping lightly across the gleaming lobby floor. Wheeling a suitcase, she followed the signs directing her to a large banquet room at the back of the hotel. Once inside, she was met by a maze of partitions. It took her awhile before she found booth number twenty-two, where Office Remedies had been assigned.

"Hi, Calaine."

Turning in the direction of the familiar voice, she found Jennifer Salvage, a recruiter for Oscar Mayer, setting up at the next booth.

"Hey, Jen," she greeted with a warm smile. Maneuvering the suitcase behind the table, Calaine leaned it against the blue partition wall. She then turned and faced one of her most valuable customers. With humor playing at the corners of her mouth, she asked, "What're you trying to do, take money out of my pocket?"

Jennifer's blue eyes sparkled. "You know my boss still believes if I work harder we won't need your services any longer." She rolled her eyes heavenward and spoke with an exaggerated sigh, "I told her we've been trying to accomplish that for years, and it just isn't possible, but she still doesn't believe me. So here I am."

Calaine laughed aloud. Office Remedies had been supplying laborers to the corporation ever since she had adopted a temp-to-hire practice. No sooner had her staff filled a job then Jennifer was calling for another temporary. After two years, the local plant was now one of her largest clients. Like most employment agencies, Office Remedies did the background checks, drug testing, and handled the payroll. Then, in compliance with a disclosure in their contract, the temporary worker had the opportunity of becoming a permanent Oscar Mayer employee after sixty days. The program was a great success. However since her transfer to the Columbia plant, VP Karin Taylor had been searching for ways to cut recruitment cost in half by the end of the year, which would ultimately mean eliminating the program.

"As much as I hate to lose your business, it can't hurt to try. However, it won't be long before your plant has filtered through every male between the ages of eighteen and twenty-five in our little city," Calaine teased.

"Then I guess we'll have to start recruiting in the next town," Jennifer replied. The women erupted with laughter. Even with above average wages, the turnover rate at Oscar Mayer was still high. It also hadn't helped that the city's unemployment rate was at an all-time low.

The two continued to chitchat while Calaine prepared for the crowd that would soon fill the conference center for the annual event sponsored by the city. Applicants liked the idea of being interviewed right on the spot by some of the city's top employers. Last year's turnout had been tremendous, and it was anticipated that this year was going to be just as successful.

Calaine removed a large display, applications for employment, and several brochures, putting them on the table along with pens and a dish of peppermints. Several other recruiters arrived, and within the next half hour, all fifty booths were occupied.

An administrative assistant came around with a clipboard,

making sure everything was in order. She handed each of them a nametag. Calaine was pinning hers to her lapel when someone strolling through the door caught her attention.

The handsome stranger moved with an air of confidence. He was dressed in a tasteful charcoal gray suit with an expert cut that fit him perfectly. His powerful body stood well over six feet, exuding strength and class. Even from where she stood, she could feel the power that coiled within him, which rather unexpectedly made her blood tingle.

His good looks had also captured Jennifer's attention. She moved to stand next to Calaine and mumbled, "My, my, my. It's men who look like *that* that make being married so difficult."

Calaine nodded and murmured absently, "It's men like that who make being single a blessing." Her eyes followed him to where he stood near the front of the room, his stance emphasizing the force of his thighs. Watching as he spoke to one of the coordinators, she found something about his profile vaguely familiar. Where had she seen the fascinating creature before? The sunglasses shielding his eyes prevented her from seeing his entire face. Nonetheless, she noted that he sported short twisted locs while a neatly trimmed mustache accentuated his full, luscious lips.

She watched him pin his nametag above his jacket pocket, then reach for his briefcase. Turning, he began to move in her direction with a confident, bow-legged strut that caused her to gasp. Stunned, she opened and closed her mouth. When he removed his sunglasses, the blood drained from her face at the impact of those amazing eyes. It wasn't because of their penetrating shades of brown, gold and green. It was that she knew them all too well.

"David?"

Hearing his name, David Soul stopped in mid-stride to find two women looking in his direction. Drawing back, he focused on the woman standing to the right.

Calaine!

No, it couldn't be. Yet, he couldn't deny the familiarity in those striking almond-shaped eyes that made her appear almost exotic. How many times had he seen them in his dreams? Were it not for her eyes and the sexy mole on her upper lip, he might not have recognized her. Damn! The years had been good to her.

The Calaine he remembered had been a skinny and unsophisticated girl, while the lady staring across at him was shapely in all the right places. In ten years, Calaine had grown from a sweet little college girl to an incredibly attractive woman.

David noted that she was wearing a blue suit that hung on her body as if she'd recently lost weight. The jacket had a belt that emphasized a waist he could have easily wrapped his hands all the way around. The skirt ended mid-thigh, baring long legs clad in sheer hose that traveled all the way down to a pair of high-heeled navy blue pumps.

He remembered that she had worn her hair long in college. However, this short new look was very becoming to her lovely, heart-shaped face. Sleek and sophisticated, it added emphasis to her high cheekbones and succulent, magenta-painted lips.

He moved to where she was standing, his face lit with a mixture of surprise and recognition. "Hello, KeKe. What a *pleasant* surprise."

Her gaze was locked in the depths of his arresting eyes. "Same here," she managed to say, barely recognizing her own voice. The sound of her pet name on his tongue caused her body to respond in a way she'd rather not dwell upon. However, before she could pull herself together, David snaked an arm around her waist and pressed a tingling kiss upon a tender spot just below her ear.

Calaine quickly moved away from the heat his closeness

sparked. She groaned inwardly. Which stirred her more, the rough bedroom quality of his vibrant voice or the impact of his warm moist lips against her skin?

"How have you been?" he asked.

"Fine."

"I can see that," he purred.

Calaine didn't miss the glint of masculine appreciation as his eyes slowly perused her body in a way that made her skin prickle. She felt naked as his eyes roamed over her, and an excitement she hadn't experienced since college tore through her veins. For several seconds her heart throbbed and her nerves leaped. *Snap out of it!* At twenty-eight she was not about to react like a lovesick teenager.

"What are you doing back in Columbia?" she asked, breaking the silence that enveloped them. "Last I heard you were living in San Antonio."

"You've been checking on me," he teased.

"Not hardly," she snorted. David chuckled while she tried to ignore another delicious shiver.

He pointed to the banner beside her, displaying the University of Missouri's black and gold logo. "I've been back for almost a month. They made me an offer I couldn't refuse."

Glancing down at his nametag, Calaine read, *Director, Human Resource Services*. "I'm impressed."

"Thank you," he said with a husky sensual tone that sent her nerves into a tailspin.

Calaine had almost forgotten that Jennifer was standing beside her until she heard her politely clear her throat.

Stepping forward, Jennifer said cordially, "Jennifer Salvage. Pleased to meet you."

He looked down at the round woman who barely came to his shoulder. "David Soul," he said, smiling sweetly as he shook the proffered hand.

Jennifer fingered her hair that looked as if it had blown in the wind on the drive over and cooed, "So you're the new bigwig on campus. I interviewed for your job."

"So did half the city," Calaine interjected with a roll of her eyes. She hadn't, but she knew several people who had.

David pinned her with his gaze. Lips parting, he revealed a dazzling display of straight white teeth. "Then I guess I was the lucky one." He winked, then moved to set up his booth.

Calaine noticed Jennifer watching her with curious intensity. When David turned his back, Calaine wasn't the least bit surprised to feel Jennifer nudge her in the side. Tilting her head, Calaine met her gaze as Jennifer mouthed something she pretended not to understand. She knew what Jennifer was alluding to and she wasn't about to go there.

With a silly smirk, Jennifer strolled around her table and over to David's. "So, how do you know Calaine?" she asked.

Calaine's pulse skittered.

David stopped what he was doing and glanced across at her stunned face. His slow smile taunted her while his eyes twinkled mischievously like a little boy with a secret.

"I used to date her roommate," he replied.

"Along with the rest of the female population on campus," Calaine mumbled under her breath.

David chuckled. She had obviously whispered louder than had intended.

Jennifer tossed her long blond hair from her eyes and a knowing smile curved her mouth. "It sounds to me like the two of you have a lot of catching up to do. Feel free to take lunch together. I'll man all three stations."

Calaine gave an unladylike grunt. Jennifer must have read

something in their body language that had given her the impression they were friends, maybe more. At one time they had shared a subtle yet very strong connection, but that was before everything had changed. Now, a friend was the last thing she would call David. An associate maybe, but no longer a friend. There was no way she was spending any time with him. She had stopped caring for him years ago and definitely wasn't about to start that again. Before she could open her mouth to respond, the crowd started coming through the doors.

The University of Missouri — or Mizzou as they were referenced — was the city's largest employer, which guaranteed a continuous flow of interested applicants in their direction. Just as Calaine had hoped, the three of them were too busy handing out pens and applications for Jennifer to ask any further embarrassing questions.

In between prospective candidates, Calaine found her eyes drifting without her control over to the man who had left a bad taste in her mouth almost a decade earlier.

As her thoughts drifted back to the first time she met him, she realized she had been no more prepared to see him now than she had been then. David had been the first man she'd ever fallen for. What she hadn't expected was to fall flat on her face.

It was during summer welcome. Calaine was touring the student union when David came strutting down the hall with his hazel eyes and irresistible grin. At that instant, she knew he was the man of her dreams.

She remembered that he had worn a faint mustache and a short, faded haircut. Her body had acknowledged him with a shiver of excitement. There was something about him she liked. Something she liked a lot. She didn't know what it was, but at eighteen she hadn't cared. Only David had moved down the hall as if she hadn't been standing there. Not a smile, not a wink, nothing.

Since they had both majored in human resources they'd had several classes together. Though David took his education seriously, all his free time was spent running around like a dog in heat.

Calaine had fancied herself in love with him for almost a year before her feelings changed. She had been appalled as she watched him move from one female to the next. He had a magnetic charm that won him the hearts of women all over campus, not to mention their beds.

She remembered the day David had stopped her after class. Only instead of asking her out as she had expected, he had asked her to introduce him to her roommate, Donna Davidson. Calaine had refused, telling him to introduce himself but he had been persistent. David had badgered her incessantly until he finally wore her down with endless cups of Lakota's hazelnut coffee, her weakness. After the introduction, David had started hanging around their dorm hoping to run into Donna.

Donna had grown up Catholic and was determined to save her virginity for her wedding night. It would have taken a bigger man than David to wear her down. Calaine had to admit she had actually gotten a kick out of watching David trying to work his charm on Donna. Eventually she went out with him, and they dated off and on for almost two years before David realized that accounting was more important to Donna than dating. In all, he spent more time hanging around the dorm with Calaine than he had with her roommate.

Calaine blinked her eyes vigorously, returning to the present. She tried unsuccessfully to focus her attention on anything other than David. While he went through the routine of meet and greet, she continued to watch him out of the corner of her eyes. She definitely had not expected the rush of masculine awareness that had hit her right at her core when David had pulled her into his arms. For the first time in longer than she could remember, she was reminded of how long it had been since she had been with a man. *Too long*.

Desperate for a distraction, Calaine focused on the group heading in her direction. However, as soon as they moved on to the next booth, her vision shifted to David again. She noted everything about him. Things she needed to notice and things she did not. Like the way his dimples deepened when he said hello. The fullness of his lips as he spoke. The way he listened attentively as questions were asked, and the way he took the time to respond to each and every interested applicant with a level of professionalism that amazed her.

While David was handing out brochures and talking about career opportunities at Mizzou, Calaine wondered if he had married. *Not in this lifetime*. She seriously doubted he had learned the meaning of commitment over the years. Men like him never do, she thought.

She pulled her eyes away to greet another round of candidates. After providing each of them with an application, she moved behind her table to grab another stack of brochures.

Listening to David explain the University's application process, Calaine had to admit that he knew his stuff. Not that she should have been surprised. David had always strived to be the best at whatever he did. The more challenging the situation, the better. Unfortunately, he had decided in college to add women to that list. The rumor around campus had been that David was an excellent kisser and an even better lover. The kissing part she had personally experienced.

With a grunt, Calaine turned her back to him. She didn't want to remember the taste of him on her tongue or fantasize about what it would feel like to have him buried deep inside her. David might well be a wonderful lover, but that was one road she had never journeyed. Suddenly, however, images of him sitting in front of a fireplace with a baby on one knee flashed in her scrambled mind. Why was she thinking about sex, babies and David all in the same screwed up daydream? David Soul, married? Never.

She did however have to admit that he would have been everything Katherine and Geoffrey would have expected in a son-in-law—intelligent, confident, educated, career driven, and if he was still as tight with a dollar as he had been in college, then financially stable. Yep, her parents hadn't cared much for David the college student, but they would have approved of the man he had become, which in her book meant he was very wrong for her.

Calaine briefly closed her eyes, willing the painful memories away. Why did she have to think about her parents' ideas about her choice of men? She didn't want to think about her parents at all. Not today. Not in front of all these people. She let her breath out slowly, feeling the threat of tears. Knowing it was only a matter of time before they escaped, she asked Jennifer to watch her station. Calaine started for the bathroom. David intercepted with an iron grip to her wrist.

"Where are you running off to?"

She tried not to look directly at him. "To the restroom if you don't mind."

Tilting his head slightly, his devilish eyes flickered with amusement. "My bad. I thought maybe you were trying to sneak off to lunch without me."

Forgetting about the telltale signs, her head came up and met his direct gaze, their eyes fusing for several seconds. "I don't plan to have lunch with you, not today or any other day. Now if you'll excuse me, I have something more important to attend to."

David started to release her, then noticed the sadness in her eyes. Seeing a flicker of pain, his dark brow rose questioningly and his smile faded. "Is something wrong?"

She shook her head. She didn't want his kindness. Not now. Not when she was trying so hard to hold the tears in. I won't cry, Calaine thought with concentration, I won't. She tried to blink back the burn of tears that threatened to blindside her. She didn't want to give in to them. Not in front of David. Nevertheless, hot tears rose to the surface and clouded her vision.

David recognized the vulnerability she was trying so hard to hide. "You never were any good at lying." He signaled to Jennifer that the two were taking a break, then slid a possessive arm around Calaine's waist and guided her in the direction of the lobby. He escorted her to a pair of comfortable chairs in the corner and took the seat beside her.

Calaine hunched over with both elbows resting on her knees. Her body language told him she wasn't pleased he had seen her cry, which was why he was still holding onto her forearm. He was certain that if he let go, she would scurry away. At her sadness, David felt a protective pang. He wanted to lay her head against his chest, stroke her back, and tell her everything was going to be all right. Instead, he reached into the front pocket of his jacket, removed a white handkerchief and handed it to her.

"Thanks," she said as she dabbed under each eye.

David put his index finger beneath her chin and tilted her head so she couldn't avoid his speculative gaze. Unshed tears glistened in her eyes. For the first time he noticed the dark circles that indicated lost sleep. "Are you going to tell me what's bothering you?" he asked, genuine concern etching worry lines on his face.

Closing her eyes, she squeezed the handkerchief until her knuckles turned white, then took a deep breath and whispered, "My parents died a couple of months ago."

The deep sadness in her voice gripped him. In a sympathetic tone, he replied, "I'm sorry. I had no idea."

She swallowed hard, then opened her eyes again. Something in his warm expression encouraged her to continue. "They were killed in a car accident." Calaine stared off into the distance as fresh tears began to surface. She blinked them away. "It's still hard to believe they are no longer here."

When David reached over and squeezed her hand, she felt a surge of warmth. Years had passed, yet here he was sitting next to her treating her once again as if she were his little sister. At one time it had irritated her. Now she found his concern comforting.

Calaine told him about the hit-in-run accident with a drunk driver that had taken her parents' lives. Avoiding eye contact, she focused on the front entrance where several people had entered dressed in what appeared to be their Sunday best. As she spoke, David listened attentively. Feeling the heat of his watchful eyes, Calaine suddenly felt uncomfortable. She pushed a strand of hair away from her forehead. If she were lucky, David would go back inside and leave her alone with her thoughts.

No such luck.

He gave her hand another comforting squeeze. "How are you *really* holding up?"

Again, a glimmer of warmth flooded her body. Unable to look directly at him, afraid that he might see her reaction, she stared down at her shoes. "I've been taking things one day at a time." Calaine forced a cheer that she did not feel in her voice. Now that she had answered his questions, she hoped he was finally satisfied and would move on to the next damsel in distress. She didn't want his sympathy.

"I remember your parents," she heard him say. "They were

good people."

Tilting her head, Calaine could no longer resist looking him squarely in the face. The corner of her mouth ticked at the very memory of his brief encounter with her parents. "Good people?" she repeated with abrupt humor.

David wagged his brow suggestively and she started laughing uncontrollably. He too joined in.

Tears were streaming down her face again but at least this time they were tears of laughter. David wasn't sure why he had made such a corny statement. Death made him uncomfortable and he never knew how to react to someone's loss of a loved one. At least she looked pleased at the opportunity to dwell on happier times.

Calaine reached up and dabbed the corners of her eyes. "I guess you've forgotten that my father threatened to kill you." She giggled at David, who grimaced in good humor.

Her memory replayed the incident. David had come to the dorm looking for Donna. Calaine had just gotten out of the shower. Wrapped in a towel, she had let him in. They were sitting on her bed discussing midterm grades when her parents had come knocking at the door. Calaine would never forget the looks on their faces. She imagined it had looked suspicious to find her half dressed with a horny teenage boy sitting beside her on her bed.

Still laughing, Calaine turned and looked up into those beautiful eyes again. Big mistake. The air around them began to sizzle. Despite all the reasons she could come up with for not feeling attracted to him, she felt an intense ache in her chest that caused her nipples to bead as they rubbed against the fabric of her blouse. Thank goodness she was wearing a jacket.

David made her forget that she had been crying only mere minutes ago. His dimpled smile caused her heart to flutter slightly. Good Lord, the man was gorgeous! Then her gaze dropped to his lips and he licked them as if they were dry. It was something he used to do that drove her crazy. Now it caused a reaction in her that made her squirm restlessly on her seat. For a heartbeat she wanted to feel his lips pressed against her own. Breaking the magnetic pull, Calaine whipped her head around and stared toward the door again. Silence enveloped them. Nervously, she fingered the fabric of her jacket, hoping David would say something or just go away.

As if he could read her thoughts, David said, "I would like you to still consider me your friend. If you need anything, just let me know."

"Uh-huh. Sure," she murmured as her last attempt to resuscitate reason. Why was her body reacting in such a traitorous way to David?

"I mean it, KeKe," he drawled softly, giving her his full attention.

She glanced at him again and desire continued to course through her veins in hot spurts of awareness. She felt herself being pulled in by his charm, going all soft and warm inside. Her cheeks burned with remembrance of their last encounter.

Another wave of longing coursed through her. For almost a heartbeat, a part of her wanted him to take her in his arms and tell her everything was going to be all right. The other part of her knew better. There was no way she was going to fall into that trap. She had seen too many others who had fallen victim to him and she refused to be the next. The smartest thing to do was to put some distance between them so she could regain her senses.

"I need to get back inside," she finally said. In an effort to try to keep her mind on track, she rose. As she turned away, David reached out and gently touched her hand.

Hearing the underlying tone in her voice, he knew there was something else on her mind she had yet to reveal. "Why the rush?"

"Because I have a job to do," she murmured. His touch was making it almost impossible to get her body back under control.

Releasing her arm, he chuckled knowingly. "I see you're still running away from uncomfortable situations."

"I am not," Calaine defended.

"You are too," he retorted. "I can see that delicious pulse throbbing at your throat. I still make you nervous."

The expression on David's face told her he was thinking about the last time she had run away. Remembering, she felt her heart speed up, and she couldn't think of a retort to his comment.

"If you're not afraid, then prove it and have lunch with me." He smiled that wonderful, heart-melting smile she remembered. She had to look away to keep from returning it.

Her chin lifted aggressively. "I don't have to prove myself to you." How could she have only seconds ago thought she felt attracted to him? David hadn't changed a bit. He still had that same wolfish gleam in his eye. Once again, he had used a weak moment as an opportunity to get close to her.

She propped her fists on her shapely hips, unaware that the gesture drew attention to the fullness of her breasts. "I'll see you inside." With that, she pivoted on her heels and departed.

David watched the sway of her hips until she turned the corner and was out of eyesight.

Over the years he had dated a parade of women who'd aroused him. However, he wanted Calaine as he had never wanted any woman before. Watching her, David had experienced an emotion he hadn't felt in years—lust. Lord help him! She had felt good pressed against him, delicate and soft, and inhaling the sweet scent of her made his body...

He wasn't going to even finish that thought because what he was feeling was more than physical attraction. She used to be so sweet and…wholesome. He had at first thought of her as a nice girl, the type a big brother tried to protect. But his feelings hadn't remained that way.

Sweet Calaine.

He had always admired her in school. The way she had kept a level head and didn't allow his horny fraternity brothers to lead her astray. She had rarely dated and when she had, it was innocent. He'd made sure of it. Without her knowing it, Calaine had become like a little sister to him and he had made certain the other guys respected her virtue.

When he had begun dating her roommate, he ended up spending more time with Calaine than with Donna. He chuckled at the memories that were still pure and clear. Calaine had used every opportunity to scold him about his doggish ways.

From the beginning, he had known there was something special about her. After a while his feelings had changed and his motives were no longer as innocent as a brother's love for his sister. He'd wanted to get to know her on a more personal level but had stopped himself. Not because Calaine was Donna's roommate but because Calaine was too damn good for him. During college, he hadn't been looking for a commitment and knew she was not the type of girl to mess with. Besides, by then Calaine only thought of him as a womanizer. Then he'd made the mistake of taking advantage of a very vulnerable moment. Afterwards he had become one of her least favorite persons. It was obvious from her behavior today that Calaine was still holding it against him.

With another long thoughtful stare, David ran a hand across his locs. Seeing her again had made something in him come to life. By the widening of those lovely eyes of hers, he knew that Calaine had felt something too.

David saw something he wanted and it wasn't too often when

he didn't get it. Except for Donna and maybe even Calaine if he didn't play his cards right.

In one fluid motion, he rose from the chair and headed back towards the fair. David wasn't certain yet what his intentions were. All he knew was that he was eager to find out.

Calaine had been watching a Lakers' game for the past hour and didn't have the slightest idea what the score was. Any other season the team would have had her undivided attention but tonight her mind was a million miles away.

Lying across her bed, she found herself thinking about how much her life had changed in a year. The last two basketball seasons she had shared with her ex-boyfriend McKinley. They would spend evenings curled up on the couch with a bowl of popcorn rooting for rival teams. While Calaine was a diehard Lakers fan, McKinley's heart belonged to the Sixers.

She shifted uncomfortably, surprised McKinley had even come to mind. She hadn't thought about him in ages. Maybe it was because she was feeling so lonely.

Calaine reached for the remote and increased the volume, hoping the excitement of the game would drown out her thoughts.

So much for wishful thinking.

She was lonely but unprepared to do anything about it. Until she found out where she came from, she would never marry. Until she knew something about her maternal family's medical history, she would be too afraid to bring a child into the world. Nevertheless, the very thought of spending the rest of her life alone frightened her. She hoped to someday meet her soulmate and have many babies. At one time, she had even believed for awhile that she had found him.

Calaine had met Detective McKinley Clark at a policemen's ball shortly after opening her agency. The first thing she had noticed was that he looked impeccably handsome in uniform. It was love at first sight and it wasn't long before they were sharing an apartment. She had thought everything was going wonderfully until McKinley began to complain that she spent too much time at work. Because she was the boss, he didn't think she had to work quite so hard. As a result, her job had been the topic of several arguments. No matter how hard she tried to explain it, McKinley never understood that she had to work hard to get what she wanted, that she would not have gotten so far if she hadn't.

Trying to be sensitive to his needs, Calaine had decided one afternoon to leave work earlier than usual. After a quick trip to the grocery store, she'd rushed home to make McKinley a special dinner. She would never forget the look on his face when she walked in and found him in an compromising position with another woman.

Calaine chuckled lightly at the memory of the woman rushing out the house half dressed after she threatened to snatch the weave out of her head. It pleased her to know she could finally find humor in a once awkward situation. Her feelings for McKinley had died a long time ago. He had since relocated to Phoenix, and on several occasions had called, hoping to rekindle their relationship. But she had declined, finding that along the way she had gotten over the pain of losing him.

Since then, she rarely dated. Instead, she spent all her time and energy establishing her agency. She hadn't missed being in the company of a man until today. Seeing David stirred feelings she had thought long since dead. Damn him! She scowled as she reached for a pillow.

Against her better judgment, Calaine had been thinking about him ever since their encounter, and for the love of God, she couldn't understand why. It wasn't as if she were the least bit interested in him. Sure, David was gorgeous, but the man was a player, plain and simple.

Nevertheless, first-hand knowledge of his reputation did little to calm the desire stirring inside. She didn't want to remember the tender way he had kissed her a decade ago. Or the feelings of uneasiness after that night and all the other times they had run into one another on campus.

However, after today, it would be almost impossible to forget the feel of his hard body pressed against hers, his hot wet lips that brushed against her skin, the mustache that grazed her neck or the intense look in his sexy gold-green eyes. Even now her cheeks burned with the memories.

Clutching the pillow close to her chest, Calaine blinked several times, then made another attempt to watch the game.

She dismissed the emotions he had stirred as being the way any woman would have responded to a handsome man, David included. It was a physical attraction, nothing more. If she could help it, she would never see him again.

Nevertheless, when Calaine closed her eyes she could do nothing to fight the memory of his masculine scent that flooded her senses. Her lids sprang open and after quickly chastising herself, she tossed the pillow across the room.

The next time she decided to take a chance on love, it wouldn't be with a heartbreaker named David Soul.

CHAPTER TWO

It was late afternoon when Calaine pulled her Avalon into the circle drive of what she had once considered home. She stared out her windshield at the two-story Colonial style home. The prospect of going in gave her the chills. The house was large, formal, and lacking in warmth. She was certain that when her parents had the house designed, family living had not been in mind.

Calaine scowled at the newspapers scattered all across the front porch. She had contacted the *Columbia Daily Tribune* weeks ago asking them to cancel the subscription, but it seemed they were slow at getting around to her request.

After taking a ragged breath filled with the scent of newly mowed grass, she opened the door and climbed out the car. Her legs felt like Jell-O as she moved up the walkway lined with tulips to the stairs beneath a covered porch. She checked the mailbox and found several pieces of junk mail. The rest was being forwarded to her house.

Opening the door, she stepped into the two-story foyer that was centered by a graceful curved staircase. The faint odor of furniture polish reached her, a clear indicator that Merry Maids had made their monthly scheduled visit.

Moving to the right, Calaine entered the living room with its uncomfortable Queen Anne furnishings, surrounded a red brick fireplace, eggshell walls, and Persian rugs scattered over cherry floors. She dropped her purse onto a floral chair, then shrugged out of a brown sweater and laid it across a burgundy sofa.

Moving over to the mantel, she studied several photographs. With feelings of dismay, she wondered why she had never before noticed the lack of resemblance between her mother and herself. For the hundredth time, she asked herself why her mother had waited until her death to tell her the truth. Why?

Calaine looked at her reflection in the large mirror over the fireplace, looking for similarities between herself and her father. She and her dad shared the same complexion, the same widespread nutmeg eyes, and the same full lips. There was no doubt she was her father's daughter.

Calaine ran a nervous hand across her hair, then turned away. Mentally she had tried all day to prepare herself for this visit. She'd thought she could come here alone, but now she wasn't so sure.

You have to find out the truth!

Yes, she had to find answers; otherwise she would never be able to get on with her life.

After a few more seconds of coaxing herself, she moved back out to the foyer and followed another Persian rug that ran the length of the hall and up the stairs.

She stopped at the first door on the right and turned the knob. Staring at the large canopy bed and frilly pink curtains, her lips twitched. Dozens of stuffed animals were still in a net that hung in the corner. Several volumes of Nancy Drew mysteries filled a small white bookshelf.

The room had once been her personal refuge from a dysfunctional family life where having dinner together around a large formal table was nothing more than a pathetic ritual. Memories of being alone, talking to her dolls, or spending hours sitting in the window reading haunted her still. She remembered dreaming of turning eighteen and gaining her independence.

Her college years had been the best time of her life. When her mother had suggested that she live on campus, Calaine had jumped at the opportunity to escape the reserved life inside the house. Nothing had ever felt as good as that freedom.

Shutting the door, Calaine moved past the other three rooms to the end of the hall where her parents had slept. She stepped into the master suite and stood motionless in the doorway of the sitting room as she took it all in.

The room was still just as her parents had left it. Their former housekeeper, Maria, had worked that unforgettable morning as she had for almost ten years. The sheets had been changed and the bed made. Calaine looked at the handmade imported bedspread covering the king size poster bed, the matching draperies drawn over the windows, the chest of drawers, and the armoire standing in the far right corner of the room, all in the traditional style loved by her mother.

Calaine moved over to the large bed that stood well over four feet off the ground. Lowering onto the mattress, she remembered that when she was smaller it had taken the help of a footstool to climb in or out.

Next to the bed on the nightstand was her father's watch. He had forgotten it that morning. She reached over, picked it up and read the inscription on the back. *"I love you Daddy."* Tears flooded her eyes. She had given it to her father last year for his birthday. She swiped a forearm across her face, her cotton shirt wiping away the tears. "I can't do this," she whispered. Leaning over, she reached for the phone and dialed.

"Hello," answered a deep robust voice after the first ring.

"Uncle Thaddeus?" she asked in a tear-smothered voice.

"KeKe, what's the matter?" Thaddeus Hart knew her all too

well and immediately picked up despair in her otherwise even-tempered voice.

She swallowed back the painful lump in her throat. "I'm over at the house." She didn't even have to tell him which house. She heard him swear, then sigh.

"I thought we'd agreed that we would go there together?"

Even though he and her father were brothers, Calaine felt uncomfortable having someone else rummaging through her parents' belongings. "I know, but I needed to do this myself," she replied in a weak yet insistent whisper.

"Are you sure?" Thaddeus didn't sound totally convinced. He knew Calaine was stubborn and had a tendency to let her pride get in the way. She sounded tired. He had a strong suspicion she still wasn't getting much rest.

Closing her eyes, Calaine could picture the concerned look in his large brown eyes and the frown upon his full lips. She pinched the bridge of her nose, willing away the tears. "Yes...I'm sure. I just needed to hear your voice."

"You know you can call me anytime." There was a noticeable pause before he suggested, "Why don't you let me take you out to dinner this evening?"

Calaine sniffed. As usual, her uncle was trying to cheer her up. She shifted the phone to her other ear and replied, "All right."

He heard the thaw in her voice and sighed with relief. "I'll pick you up at your house around seven."

"I'll be ready."

"Love you," he said.

She smiled. Those two words meant the world to her. "I love you too."

Calaine hung up the phone, took a deep breath, then glanced around the room again. An antique clock on the wall had stopped some time ago. The time still read seven-thirteen. Its soothing chime had helped her sleep on numerous occasions.

She remembered the time when she was five that Grandma Graves had slipped and broken her hip. Katherine had gone to spend the weekend with her mother. There had been a terrible storm that night and Calaine had been too afraid to fall asleep. She'd raced into her parents' room and her father had lifted her up and onto the bed beside him. While stroking her hair, he had spent hours comforting her with stories — some of which he had made up — until she had drifted off to sleep.

That memory brought along her first smile all day. She had loved her father. Whenever Katherine wasn't around he had always seemed so much more relaxed and at ease. Her father had been her favorite. Calaine couldn't help wondering if that was why it had been so hard for her mother to reach out to her.

Because she wasn't your mother.

Calaine jumped up from the bed. She was on a mission. It was time to find out the truth.

"Now where do I begin?" she mumbled aloud.

Deciding to slowly work her way around the entire room, she moved to her parents' closet. She looked past a row of designer-labeled clothing and grabbed a stack of picture albums on the top shelf. Carrying them over to the bed, she took a seat and opened the first one. For the next hour, she went through album after album.

She was soon reminded of happier times when she, her parents, Uncle Thaddeus and Aunt Alma had vacationed together. They had gone to Disneyland one year, then spent several days on the beach in the Bahamas the next. Sitting cross-legged, she found herself laughing at pictures of herself in their backyard on her seventh birthday. Her parents had rented a pony that had ruined her cake.

Finally getting to the end of the stack, Calaine picked up the last album. It was large and old. With the back of her hand, she dusted off the cover and opened it. Looking inside, she realized she had never seen any of the photos before and was surprised to find captured moments of her parents together in their early years. She was amazed at how young and beautiful her mother had been with her mahogany long legs and shoulder length black hair. She was smiling and appeared happy. Calaine frowned. How come she never remembered her mother that way? Katherine had always been so serious and stern.

There were photographs of Katherine from childhood as a child all the way to her twenty-fifth birthday, which appeared to have been a large celebration. Calaine saw pictures of her grand-parents, who were all deceased, her mother's sister, Aunt Greta, and several cousins who had all taken part in the celebration. She studied a close-up of her mother dressed in a beautiful lavender dress. Katherine had been a beautiful woman when she smiled.

Turning the page, her hand froze as something clicked in her mind. Calaine flipped back to the inscription at the bottom of her mother's photograph. April 23, 1975.

She had been born a month later.

Quickly, she flipped back through all of the photos of her mother's birthday party again. Her dress was form fitting, revealing every curve.

She wasn't pregnant.

"Oh my God!" Calaine dropped the book onto the floor.

For the next two hours, Calaine combed every corner of her parents'room, frantically trying to find answers. Finally, in the bottom of her mom's dresser she found a small fireproof box that was locked. Heart pounding fiercely, Calaine raced downstairs with the box in her hand, then reached into her purse to retrieve a large ring of keys that had belonged her mother. Finding a small silver key, she nervously tried it several times before it opened the box. Then she lifted the lid and looked inside.

There were several pieces of costume jewelry, a hundred dollars in cash and numerous pictures. She skimmed through them, finding a picture of her mother carrying a baby wrapped in a blanket. *That must have been me.* On the back was scribbled 1975, confirming her guess.

As she thumbed through the stack, she found a picture of six young women in nursing uniforms standing in front of the school of nursing. She looked closely at the photograph to see if any of them looked familiar. They did not.

Freshman class of 1974.

There was something eerie about the photo being in the box. Who were these women?

She set it aside while she finished rummaging through the last of the items. At the bottom was a carbon copy of a cashier's check for twenty-five thousand dollars drawn by Uncle Thaddeus and made out to her parents.

Why had he given them so much money?

Calaine closed the box and leaned back against the couch. Sitting quietly for several seconds, she had the strangest feeling that she had stumbled onto something. She reached for the photo and stared at the six women again. They were all beautiful black women smiling proudly at the camera. *1974.* The year before she was born. Something about the picture kept drawing her to it. What was it? Flipping the photo over, in faint letters she found scribbled in poor penmanship, *"For Calaine."* A chill washed over her. Could one of these women be her mother?

There was only one way to find out.

The hostess escorted Calaine and her uncle to a table in the farthest corner.

She loved Outback Steakhouse. It had been one of her favorite places since she first tasted their coconut shrimp. Now whenever she needed a night to unwind she dropped in.

"How's work?" Thaddeus asked, trying to break the silence. Calaine had been unusually quiet since he had arrived at her house to pick her up. It upset him to see that she still looked extremely tired.

She smiled fondly at the handsome man across from her. Creeping onto sixty-five, Thaddeus had been aging slowly for years. His hair was completely gray now, adding character to his otherwise pale face.

Tilting her chin, she smiled at him. "Better than ever. I've had over fifty job orders this week."

"Sounds like business is good," he smiled, causing the fine lines around his brown eyes to crinkle.

She nodded. "Very good."

It wasn't until the waiter arrived for their orders that Thaddeus reached for his menu to study the selections. Calaine didn't have to. She already knew it by heart. She ordered the shrimp and a large house salad while her uncle order a fifteen-ounce steak.

When their waiter departed, Thaddeus grasped her hand from across the table. "I know going to my brother's house was difficult for you. That's why Alma and I want to help. We would be more than happy to help you pack up the house and put it on the market."

"I know and I appreciate your offer. I just need a little more time," she said reassuringly.

He nodded, deciding to leave it alone for now. "I'm very proud of you," he said, and as if an afterthought he added, "and so were your parents."

A slight frown marred her forehead. "They had a hard time showing it."

He squeezed her hand once more before he released it. "People express things differently. They may not have been very affectionate with you, but then how often do you remember seeing them show affection to one another?" he reminded.

Staring across at him, she took a moment to think about what he'd said. He did have a point. Her parents had rarely showed affection even to each other. She could probably count on her hands the number of times she had seen her parents kiss, usually only during the holiday season when several dozen guests were around.

She closed her eyelids briefly. "You're right," Calaine nodded, not trusting herself to say anything more until the waiter returned with her Margarita. She could smell the tequila before she brought the straw to her lips. She took several sips until she felt better under control. Then she reached into her purse and removed the piece of paper. "Uncle Thaddeus, can you tell me what this was for?"

He accepted the piece of paper from her hand, looked down at it, then frowned with surprise. "Where'd you find this?" he asked with a speculative glance.

"In my mom's drawer," she supplied, then waited for an answer.

Thaddeus was quiet for the longest time. When he finally spoke, his voice was so low she barely heard him. "It was a gift. I gave it to your parents when you were born to put towards your college fund."

"Oh," she answered, lips compressed with disappointment. Calaine wasn't sure why. For some strange reason she had expected the money to have been for something else, something that would have explained who she really was.

His eyes were fixed on the lines furrowing her forehead. "Why the long face? I'm your uncle. Since Alma and I were never able to have any children, you were all we had to spoil."

She nodded hard, trying to will away tears as she suddenly felt the need to cry. Reaching for her glass, she took a large swallow, then reached into her purse again.

"I also found this photo. Do you know who they are?"

Thaddeus stared down at the picture and the color in his beige face drained. "Oh, my!" he gasped.

Calaine tried to calm her excitement. "You know who those women are?"

Thaddeus rubbed his clean-shaven jaw as he spoke. "I-I taught all of them that year. The nursing school was still part of the medical school until around 1975 when it became its own separate entity." His voice suddenly sounded softer, almost far away. "Those were the most determined bunch of women I had ever met. This one here," he pointed to a medium brown-skinned woman on the end, "she was smart enough to go on to medical school." He paused. "What a shame."

"What do you mean?" she questioned.

"I was told she committed suicide the following year. I never heard why. What was her name?" He looked long and thoughtful, then shrugged. "Eventually they started drifting apart. I can't remember but I don't believe they all graduated. I think one or two of them even dropped out of the program." He continued to examine the photo until their food arrived.

Calaine stared across the table at Thaddeus as he carved his medium-well steak, her mind reeling with all of the information he had given her. After several seconds of deliberation, she shifted nervously on the bench, then launched into what was really on her mind. "Could one of those women have been my mother?"

Thaddeus nearly choked on his food. His expression held surprise. "What?"

Calaine repeated the question, even though his reaction was a clear indication that she was onto something.

Thaddeus lowered his knife. "Sweetheart," he began as he tried to regain his composure, "as I have told you before, Katherine was your mother."

A shadow of annoyance crossed her rather delicate face. He was lying and Calaine knew it. "No, she wasn't," she countered. "I've seen pictures of her twenty-fifth birthday party and she was not pregnant."

Thaddeus averted his gaze to his plate. She could tell by his silence that the photographs were never meant for her to see.

Glancing up again, he looked at her with somber eyes and said, "KeKe, you need to let this go."

She wished she could deny what her heart and mind were telling her, but she could not. "I can't," she persisted, then lowered her head and voice as if afraid someone at the next table might overhear. "I know Katherine wasn't my mother. I feel it in my bones. I think I have always felt it. So why are you lying to me? Please, Uncle Thaddeus, I have a right to know the truth."

There was another brief pause. When Thaddeus finally spoke, he had to clear his throat twice before he could get the words out. "Some things are better left alone. The past is the past. There's no point in stirring up memories that might be painful."

"So Katherine wasn't my mother?" she asked as if she hadn't heard a word he had said. She saw the struggle in his expression and felt it within herself. "Please tell me," she murmured then held her breath as if bracing herself against her worst fear.

Seeing the pain in her eyes, Thaddeus could no longer keep her from the truth. His eyes shadowed with concern as he tried to find the best way to break the news to her. Regretfully, he shook his head. "No, she wasn't your mother. After three miscarriages,

Katherine was too afraid to try again."

"Oh, my God! It was true," she gasped. His admission sent her blood pressure skyrocketing. Taking a deep breath, she tried to slow down the pounding in her chest.

"Katherine had loved you as if you were her own child."

"It was hard for her to love me because I was Dad's love child," she mumbled absently. Her disappointment was apparent by her tightly compressed lips.

"KeKe, just leave it alone," he pleaded.

There was no denying his concern. The worried look in his eyes was quite apparent, but she had every right to know the truth. "I can't." Toying with her salad, she knew there was no way she was going to be able to get anything down. Dropping her fork, she clutched her stomach, afraid that she might be sick. "Do you know who my mother was...is?"

Thaddeus hesitated before he finally shook his head and replied, "N-no, I don't."

Calaine breathed a sigh of relief. If he had, she would have felt betrayed by him also.

At her prolonged silence, her uncle leaned in close and said, "It takes a strong woman to raise another woman's child. She didn't have to do it."

Yes she did. Calaine didn't say it aloud but she was thinking it. As the wife of a prestigious member of the community there was no way Katherine would have given that up and faced the humiliation in front of her peers. Calaine should have felt grateful for that. Instead, she felt as if she had spent her entire life paying for her father's mistake. Had her mother agreed to raise her husband's love child just so she would have the pleasure of throwing it back in his face?

Calaine didn't know who she was anymore and the only people who knew the truth were either dead or not talking.

When their waiter returned, Calaine ordered another drink. A half hour later, she felt as if her load had been lightened slightly. Somehow, she had convinced herself that she was a step closer to finding the truth. "I want you to help me find her."

In the eyes he had grown accustomed to over the past twenty-eight years, Thaddeus read her determination. She wasn't going to budge. He sighed. "All right. I'll see what I can do."

David had been watching her from across the room since she had arrived with the distinguished-looking gentleman. Calaine was upset, that much was obvious.

Ever since Friday, he had been unable to get her full pouting lips out of his mind. Tonight they were outlined in a lovely shade of mauve that complemented her coloring. She was dressed simply in khaki slacks and a long-sleeved chocolate t-shirt. Her hair was brushed away from her face, showing off her delicately carved profile and high cheekbones.

"Why don't you go over there?" Caress suggested, breaking into his thoughts.

David looked across the table at his older sister who was staring at him curiously. "What?"

She waved her fork in Calaine's direction. "You've been watching her since we arrived."

He smiled at his sister. He never could put anything past her.

Caress had inherited their father's curly dark brown hair and tall slender body, their mother's beige coloring and hazel eyes. One of the benefits of being back in his hometown was being near his sister and her family.

David chanced another quick glance. "I'm just curious about who that man is. He looks familiar."

She patted her mouth with a napkin, then replied, "That's her uncle, Dr. Thaddeus Hart. He's a professor at the university."

He gave her an amused look. "How is it that you know so much?"

"Like you have to ask," she replied with an unladylike grunt. "This is Columbia. Everybody knows everybody and everything there is to know about one another. You haven't been gone *that* long."

David slapped his forehead and groaned. "How could I forget?" It was one of the reasons he had left right after graduation.

Being born and raised in a small town had its downfalls, the number one being that just about everyone knew him by name. He used to feel so closed in that he couldn't wait to escape, and he would have left right after high school had he'd not been offered a scholarship at Mizzou. However, as soon as he'd had his diploma in his hand, David had jumped at the chance to leave the state with the plan never to return.

He'd moved to Tampa, then relocated to San Antonio after his parents retired there. But besides his family, he'd never felt the same close knit feeling he'd had in Columbia. He'd found he missed people knowing his name and asking him how he was doing. When the position at Mizzou came open, he'd jumped at the opportunity to return. Now that he was home, he planned to lay down permanent roots. He had just closed on a large house on the city's Southside and was moving the weekend before his youngest sister's graduation. He was anxious to leave his hotel suite.

After swallowing the last piece of cheesecake, Caress pushed the plate away. "I feel like a pig." Resting her elbows on the table, she leaned forward and smiled. "So, big brother, now that you're back home and have bought that huge house, you have any plans of settling down and filling it with a wife and kids?"

Several years ago, he would have laughed at her suggestion. "I would love to settle down if I could find the right woman."

Caress smiled as she mentally scanned through several possibilities. "I'm sure that won't be too hard to do. Columbia is full of single women." The problem with her brother was that he was too damn picky. She wasn't sure if she had ever seen him with the same woman twice. Maybe he really was ready to finally settle down; however, it was going to take a great deal to convince her.

"Since you know so much about everyone, tell me. Is Calaine involved with anyone?" He had wanted to ask his sister earlier but hadn't wanted to appear over-zealous in front of the only woman capable of reading him like a book.

Her gold-green eyes widened until he could see their depths. "You're interested in Calaine?"

Looking away, David shrugged. "You never know." He would never admit it but after tossing and turning all night, being with her was definitely a strong possibility.

Her brow rose and a curious smile curved her lips. If her brother was interested in Calaine, he had made a wise choice.

As a volunteer coordinator, Caress had had the opportunity to work with her on several occasions. Calaine had been involved in numerous community service projects and always found additional time to pitch in. When a family lost their home to fire a year ago, Calaine had gotten a not-for-profit organization called Habitat for Humanity involved. After they had agreed to build the family another home, she had been right there pitching in. Despite her snobbish parents, Calaine had turned out to be a very caring and giving individual.

Caress leaned forward and rested her chin in the palm of her hand. "Calaine was engaged to a police officer a while back but I heard she caught him with Tonya Cook and, well,…it was nothing nice."

David shook his head. Was there anything his sister didn't know?

"Anyway, I haven't heard that she was dating anyone else."

David raised a glass of water to his lips and stole a glance across the room at Calaine again. She was blowing her nose. A frown marred his face. Whatever she and her uncle were discussing had her upset. He shouldn't care, but he did.

All the years they had known each other, he had dated every woman around him except Calaine. He had never even considered being romantically involved with Calaine until the night they had shared a brief kiss.

Now she was the perfect candidate.

Fat chance.

He would just have to figure out a way to get her to see past his playboy image. Otherwise, Calaine would never take him seriously.

It was after eight o'clock when Calaine returned home.

Her small three-bedroom ranch style home was nothing like the elegance in which she'd been raised. Her home looked lived in. Katherine had insisted on decorating the place for her, but Calaine had stood firm and refused. This was her house and it reflected her own personal taste. No Queen Anne furnishings or cherry woods, and no expensive artifacts or paintings.

Two floral overstuffed couches were in front of a big-screen television. A glass-topped coffee table was in the middle scattered with magazines she never had time to read. Everything else she had found either at a garage sale or had bought at Wal-Mart. The rest of the house was sparse but it was just the way she liked it. She believed furniture wasn't meant just for showcasing. If she didn't need it, she didn't buy it.

She kicked off her shoes, dropped her keys and purse on the coffee table and padded into the kitchen to put her doggy bag in the refrigerator. Closing the refrigerator, she looked over at the answering machine and saw she had one message. She reached over and pushed the button.

"Hey girl, this is Donna. Give me a call when you get this mes - sage. I'm going to be in town at the end of the month and I want to reserve your couch."

With a smile, Calaine reached for her cordless phone and went out onto a small wooden deck. She took a seat and propped her feet on the railing, then dialed. After several rings, Donna's husky voice came through the line.

"Hey, girl. I thought maybe you were out on a date."

Calaine snorted into the receiver. "Not hardly. I was out with Uncle Thaddeus."

"How have you been?"

"As well as expected." They hadn't seen each other since her parents' funeral. Donna had flown in and helped with all of the preparations. Feeling sadness returning, Calaine quickly changed the subject. "Guess who's back in town?"

"Who?"

"David."

Donna paused a moment as the name registered. "*My* David?"

"Yes, *your* David," Calaine chuckled, finding her possessive claim quite amusing. "You better stop talking so loud before Bruce hears you."

There was another brief silence before Donna replied, "He moved out."

Calaine gasped. "When? Why?"

"Irreconcilable differences. The two of us were disagreeing on a lot of different issues lately. Bruce was the one who finally decided it would be better if he moved back in with his brother. I agreed." When her explanation was met by more silence, she added, "Hey, it's better now than after we got married. Don't worry. I'm actually enjoying single life again."

Calaine wasn't convinced. Donna and Bruce had been together for almost four years and had planned to marry in the spring. The fact that Donna was being evasive proved that she really wasn't taking the break-up well. Nevertheless, Calaine decided to wait and broach the subject when the two were face-to-face. For now, she would just play along. "Maybe it's time to rekindle your relationship with David."

A feminine laugh came through the phone. "Hmmm, maybe it is. I can't wait to find out if he's lost that arrogant attitude."

Calaine grunted. "Not as far as I could tell."

"Good." Donna sounded pleased. "I always found it so sexy. A weekend of being wined and dined sounds quite appealing. Tell David I'm looking forward to catching up."

Calaine giggled. "I'll tell him. See you soon." She hung up feeling a great deal better.

The two had maintained a close relationship long after graduation. They shared just about everything.

Staring off at the diamond-studded sky, Calaine took a deep breath. She hadn't shared her discovery with Donna. She would, eventually. Right now, she needed time to get used to the idea herself. She also wanted to see what else she could find out first.

Even though it was an exceptionally warm evening, a shiver

spread through her as she remembered what the day had revealed. Uncle Thaddeus had confirmed her suspicions about her mother. Though reluctant, in the end he had agreed to help. Now all she needed were answers.

Calaine released an exasperated sigh. The dull ache of not knowing was killing her.

CHAPTER THREE

David eased his BMW into the small parking lot. After climbing out of his car, he strolled to the front of the building, where he was greeted by the aroma of grilled onions.

A hotdog vendor was to the left of the elevators with a line of customers eagerly awaiting lunch. David's stomach growled. The breakfast he'd eaten at Cracker Barrel had suddenly become history.

He exited the elevator on the fifth floor, then walked across the hall into Office Remedies' small reception area. A woman with long ash-blonde hair and green eyes smiled at him from behind a large oak desk. The nameplate on her desk read Norma Brown.

"Hello," she greeted with an inviting smile. "May I help you?" Her voice was soft, gentle.

Leaning forward, David returned her friendly smile. "My name is David Soul and I'm here to see Calaine Hart."

"Do you have an appointment?" she asked with an inquisitive glimmer in her eyes.

"No, I thought I would drop by and maybe catch her for lunch."

Norma gave him a warm motherly smile. In the three years she'd been employed at Office Remedies, she could count the number of times Calaine had gone out to lunch, not to mention with a man. Lunch out would do her boss a lot of good. "She's finishing up a meeting. Why don't you have a seat and I'll let her know you're here."

Returning her smile, he nodded. "Thank you."

David took a seat in one of the blue-cushioned chairs conversationally arranged around a large mahogany coffee table. Across from him was a professionally dressed woman filling out an application across her lap while the man next to her flipped through a magazine. Beyond a glass wall, he saw a woman in front of a computer, more than likely taking a typing test.

He looked around the room, impressed with the decor. The floor was covered with taupe and blue Berber carpet while the walls were cream with a blue border. A Calgon water cooler was in one corner and an industrial size coffee maker in the other.

Draping his ankle across his knee, he reached for a magazine and flipped to the featured article while he waited.

Calaine adjourned her weekly meeting with her sales team and headed down the corridor to her office. With her sales manager Debbie's persistence, they had finally landed a contract with State Farm Insurance, one of the city's top ten employers. She was excited at the possibilities. Office Remedies had already received an order from the claim's department for a receptionist. Since it was their first order, they had to make sure it was filled with their best employee. Sherrie, her staffing supervisor, was already on the job. Calaine had confidence in her ability to find the most qualified candidate.

She entered the last door on the left and crossed the rose-carpeted floor to her desk, then reached for her water bottle. It was considerably warm for late April.

Taking a seat in a large leather chair behind her desk, Calaine reached into her purse for something for a persistent headache. Her hands touched the photograph. Removing it from her purse, she stared down at the six women again. She must have looked at it a dozen times, trying to find some kind of resemblance between herself and one of the women. Unfortunately, each of them had something that she could identify with. One woman's hair, the other's eyes, the third woman's complexion. Calaine concluded that her mother could be any of them.

Why did my mother save this picture? She had debated asking her Aunt Greta but declined. She had been an emotional wreck since her sister's death and Calaine didn't want to bring up any painful memories. Her aunt had lied to her about her birth and Calaine wanted to know why but now was not the time to ask. She would give Aunt Greta a little more time to deal with the loss of her sister. Calaine gave a raggedy sigh. She had concluded that she was going to have to find out the answers on her own.

She picked up a pencil and gnawed on its end. She didn't know who she was anymore. Her entire life had been one big lie. She couldn't do it any longer. She had to know. Her life was in shambles and until she found out the truth, she would never be able to move on. She could have a brother, a sister or even both. The thought caused her to gasp. As a child, she had always wanted someone to play with.

The first thing she had to do was find out the names of each of the six women.

"Excuse me, Calaine." Her receptionist's voice came through the intercom, startling her. She had been so absorbed in finding her mother that she had almost forgotten she was still at work.

Calaine pushed the button on her intercom. "Yes, Norma?"

"A David Soul is here to see you."

The mere thought of the man standing in her lobby made her

pulse leap. What could he possibly want? The last time she'd seen him, he'd witnessed her in tears. He probably thought she was a blubbering fool. Part of her was anxious to find out what he wanted while the other part wanted him to stay as far away from her as possible.

However, she had to admit that David had changed. The other day, even as shocked as she had been, she'd sensed the changes ten years had made in him. David seemed to be a stronger, more mature individual. *Why do you care?*

"Would you like me to send him back?" Norma asked, interrupting her thoughts.

Before she had a chance to think any further, Calaine heard herself say, "Sure, go ahead." She smoothed the front of her salmon suit and straightened in her seat. Taking a deep breath, she reached for a pen and stared down at a report, pretending to appear busy.

A moment later she heard a slight rap on the open door. By the time she had raised her head to acknowledge his presence, David had already crossed the short distance and was standing over her desk, grinning and flashing even white teeth. Once again his startling good looks caught her off guard. She resented looking up those inches to his face and the tremor that went through her when she did.

She was a jumbled mass of nerves. Slowly as she regained her breathing, she took in the gorgeous man in front of her. David was once again dressed impeccably in a suit. This time his slacks were gray and pleated, and were accompanied by a black single button jacket that spanned his broad shoulders beautifully. She could feel his aura from where she was sitting. He had a male magnetism that seemed to reach across the desk and touch her. Calaine tried to shake it off, categorizing it simply as a woman's response to a handsome man, nothing more.

"Hello, KeKe."

His smile was warm and slow and his voice flowed through her blood like fine wine. If she were a lesser woman, she would have sat there drinking him in, losing track of the time. Instead, she quickly pulled herself together and forced her full lips to twist in an unwelcoming manner. "I would prefer your calling me Calaine."

David cocked a sexy eyebrow and gave her an appraising once-over, taking in her cocoa painted lips. "Why? Have you outgrown the nickname?" he teased.

"No." She briefly closed her eyes and sighed. *It just sounds so damn sexy when you say it.* "It just sounds unprofessional."

David seated himself in a leather chair across from her desk. "Tell you what. I'll only used it when we're alone." He crossed his left ankle over his right knee and gave her another irresistible smile.

Calaine picked up the double meaning in his words. Ignoring her heart which was pumping wildly against her ribs, she cleared her throat and asked as naturally as she could manage, "What can I do for you?"

"I have a proposition for you." David licked his lips, drawing her attention to his mouth. It reminded her of the time they had shared a pitcher of Jungle Juice and ended up rolling around on the floor of her...

She averted her gaze only to meet his direct stare as she asked, "What kind of proposition?"

"Subcontracting our secretarial pool."

Her slanted eyes widened. "What?" she gaped. She couldn't possibly have heard him right. Calaine had been trying for years to get her foot in the door at Mizzou. However, due to budget constraints, the only temporary employees purchasing would authorize were from their own in-house temporary services.

She blinked back her disbelief. "What happened to SOS?"

"Nothing. Secretarial and Office Support Services is still in full swing. However, until the hiring freeze is lifted on campus, we can't keep up with the needs of our departments. So in the interim, the department has decided to subcontract with any agencies willing to lower their billing rates to reflect ours."

Her eyes widened by his suggestion. Her mind was reeling at the amount of business the merger could generate. "I'm sure we can come to an agreement."

David stretched his long legs out in front of him, then leaned over and reached into his briefcase. Removing several sheets of paper, he held them out to her. "I've had a chance to look over your rates and —"

"How do you know what my rates are?" she asked in surprise after accepting the sheet of paper in his proffered hand.

"I have my ways," David stated confidently as he handed her another sheet of paper. "Here are the rates we are willing to pay, which would drop your current billing rates fifteen to twenty percent."

Calaine briefly glanced over rates classified in every category from an executive assistant to a medical records clerk. "I'm impressed."

David noticed that the lines around her mouth had softened. He gave a low confident rumble. "I thought you would be. We'd also like to include a sixty day liquidation clause."

She sat back in her chair. "Our current liquidation is no fee after ninety days."

Crossing his arms over his jacket, David smiled, "I know. But with the amount of business we can bring you, I would hope you would be willing to modify your terms as you have done at Oscar Mayer."

I just bet. Irritation sparked. Jennifer and her big mouth. He had somehow managed to wiggle out the details of their contract. It upset her because all of her contracts were supposed to be confidential. And David was still as cocky as ever.

"If there's a hiring freeze on campus, what difference does it make how the liquidation clause is written?"

"There are always ways around things. In a hardship situation we have authorized departments to fill vacant slots. However, that's handled on a case-by-case basis and only our vice chancellor can approve those requests."

She took a few minutes to glance through the report he had given her. This was too good to be true. Two major accounts in one day. Wait until her staff heard about this. "Shouldn't I be dealing directly with Joann? After all she is the manager of SOS."

"You should and you shall. Nevertheless, I'm the boss and she's so overwhelmed at the present, I told her I'd be more than happy to help her out," he replied.

Calaine glanced across at his confident smile. She wasn't about to be intimidated by his charm. The contract was like dangling meat in front of a hungry lion and he knew that every temporary agency in the city would jump through hoops for the chance to work with the University, Calaine included. Or so he thought. She folded her arms and tipped her head to one side as if she was still considering his proposal. "I'll have to give it some thought, then discuss it with my team. I'll get back with you in a couple of days."

Her response caused his jaws to sag slightly. "Very well. When you're ready I'll have purchasing put together a contract that we'll both be pleased with."

"Very good." Lowering the papers, she laced her fingers and smiled across the desk at him. "Thanks for considering me."

David found it to be the first real smile she had given him since their encounter last Friday. He allowed his eyes to roam down her.

Calaine looked lovely in a suit that she had accessorized with a silk, two-toned scarf draped around her neck.

"You're welcome. I've heard nothing but great things about your company. Your customer service values are commendable."

"Thank you," she said with a hint of pride. "I learned a long time ago customer services can take you a long way." Adopting a practice of customer satisfaction was essential to the success of any business. Office Remedies had an eight-hour guarantee. If a customer was dissatisfied, they were offered a replacement and the first eight hours not charged. "I'll have my sales manager schedule an appointment with you or Joann so that she can go over the proposal in more detail."

He heard the excitement in Calaine's voice and saw the sparkle in her eyes. Like him, she took a great deal of pride in her work. "Good."

David had been duly impressed from the moment he had stepped into the suite. He was just as impressed as he looked around her office. The walnut-paneled room, although small, was elegantly furnished. An entire wall of windows provided a scenic view of Mizzou's campus.

Relaxing in the chair, David didn't look in any rush to leave. Calaine needed to say something to break the silence that hung between them. "Well, I need to get back to work."

He glanced down at his watch. "How about lunch?"

"No, thank you. I've got a thousand things to do," she stuttered.

David flashed a half smile, pleased to know that he still caused her to stumble over her words. "I'm asking for a lunch between friends, nothing more."

"I can't." She had an appointment with a distributor, but didn't feel she owed him an explanation.

"You can't or you won't?" he asked with a wicked smile.

Her gaze moved back to her eyes. "Do we have to go through this again?" she tossed back with a frown.

"How about a business lunch? We can discuss the terms in further detail?" he persisted.

She intentionally avoided his gaze. "I really can't."

He leaned across her desk. "Are you afraid to be alone with me again?"

Oh for Pete's sake! Once David set his mind to something, it was easier to find front door parking at the mall than to change his mind.

She didn't like the way those brilliant eyes of his made her go all shivery inside. It was difficult enough trying to keep from squirming in her seat beneath his scrutiny.

"Why would you say that?" she finally managed to say.

David took a moment longer than she would have expected before answering. "It's just an observation. We used to be very close and then things changed." He paused, then continued hesitantly. "I was just wondering if it had anything to do with…" He purposely allowed his voice to trail off. There was no point in mentioning what they both were thinking. That much was obvious.

"Absolutely not. Now, if you'll excuse me…" When she tried to hide the nervous flutter of her hand by rearranging a stack of papers on an otherwise neat desk, she instead sent the pile sliding onto the floor. With a curse, Calaine reached down to pick the papers up.

David had moved around her desk to help despite her protest that she didn't need his assistance. He reached for a stack and underneath was the old photograph. David grabbed it and rose to his feet. Then, staring down at the six women, he asked, "What are you doing with a picture of my mother?"

CHAPTER FOUR

As a soft gasp escaped Calaine's lips, several sheets of paper slipped from between her fingers and fluttered back onto the floor. Even though her heart felt as if she were running a marathon, she couldn't move. As her mind registered the significance of his words, her body stiffened. There was no way she could have heard David right. For several seconds she stared at him mutely until she found her voice again. "One of those women is your mother?" she asked, barely above a whisper.

This is it, she thought. The photograph was already beginning to paint a story.

David nodded. "Yeah, this one here." He pointed to the fair-skinned petite woman in the middle. "Even though I have to admit with that Afro I almost didn't recognize her." He chuckled absently. Glancing up from the photo, his expression sobered at the look on Calaine's face. "Is something wrong?"

"No, nothing." The shock of another discovery hit her full force. She felt faint. With a shaky hand, she retrieved the photo from him and slowly lowered into her chair. Breathing hard, she found her throat suddenly dry. She reached for the water bottle and took a long swig.

David's eyes were glued on her. Calaine looked as if she was bracing herself against something terrible. He tried to remember the last time he'd seen her look that distraught and came up blank.

Whatever it was, it had her upset. Even when one of his fraternity brothers had dumped her and she'd later cried on his shoulder, her reaction had been nothing close to this.

"Are you going to tell me why you look like you've just seen a ghost?" he asked with obvious concern written on his face.

She didn't answer. She needed a few more minutes to pull herself together. Her pulse was racing. Talk about a small world. One of those six women was David's mother. One of the women she believed to be *her* biological mother was *his* mother. Strange thoughts continued to race through her mind; then she gasped inwardly as a possibility emerged. What if they were... No, she didn't even want to go there.

"Calaine," he called, breaking into her thought.

She blinked and found that David had returned to his seat. She studied his face and found herself searching for some similarities in their features. "How old are you?" she blurted out as she felt the screams of frustration at the back of her throat.

"What?" What did his age have to do with anything?

"Answer me, dammit!" she demanded with a hint of hysteria. "I need to know." She was practically pleading for an answer.

David hesitated a second longer, baffled by the complete turn-around in her behavior before answering, "I'm six months younger than you. Why?"

Her eyes narrowed suspiciously. "How do you know how old I am?"

"For crying out loud, Calaine! Have you forgotten we went to school together?" he barked with laughter that lacked humor.

While nodding, memories of Donna decorating their dorm room registered in her mind. She even remembered the cake she had bought in honor of David's birthday.

Calaine slumped back against her chair and sighed with relief.

Thank God for small miracles.

This was starting to turn into a nightmare. Her mind was working overtime again. First, she had found out that Katherine wasn't really her mother and now the only connection she had with her past, she had to share with David, of all people.

"I would like to help you." She heard him say.

"What?" she asked suspiciously. "Help me with what?"

"With whatever is on your mind. I could tell at the job fair that something other than your parents' deaths was bothering you. I have the same suspicion even now."

"How would you know?" she snapped. "You don't know anything about me!"

"I know more than you think. I'd know even more if you would just talk to me. Come on, KeKe. You still haven't told me why you have a picture of my mother."

She looked sadly over at him and wondered if she could share her dilemma with him. She needed to talk to someone.

"Please, Calaine, talk to me," he tried again.

She pulled in her lower lip and after a moment blurted, "I'm trying to find my birth mother."

"I thought…" David's voice trailed off, confused by her words, before his dark brow shot up with surprise. "Mrs. Hart wasn't your mother?"

She swallowed back an emotion so consuming she couldn't put a name to it and sadly shook her head.

David's expression was of awe and surprise. "How long have you known?"

Calaine blew out a shaky breath. "I didn't find out until a couple of months ago." Leaning back in her chair, she told him about her mother's last words, the photo she had found, and the conversation she had had with her uncle two nights prior.

David raked a hand across his locs. "I'm sorry. I couldn't begin to imagine what you are going through. You must really be having a hard time right now."

"You don't know the half of it." She leaned forward, folding her arms on the desk. "How would you feel to know the life you had lived was not really the life you were born to at all? It has all been a lie."

"How can you say that?" David gaped. "You weren't adopted. You grew up with your father."

She shook her head with dismay. "It's not the same. I never had a close relationship with my mother. I never felt loved and accepted. I never had long talks and shopping trips like all my friends had with their mothers." Her voice came off thick with a knot of emotion that clogged her throat.

David nodded, understanding. He remembered all the weekends his mother had spent at the mall shopping for hours with his sisters, even the times they'd spent painting each other's toenails and playing dress up.

"My real mother is out there somewhere. I might even have another family I know nothing about, a sister, a brother." She hadn't realized until now how alone in the world she really was. Sure, she had her uncle, an aunt and a few other distant relatives but that was it. There was no one else. Or was there? She reached for the photo and looked down at the women. "All I know is that one of these women is my mother."

"How can you be so sure?" David didn't want to shake her confidence but he didn't want to see her get her hopes up too high either.

"I feel it in my bones."

He saw the dejected slump of her shoulders. He watched her as she gazed down at the photo, lost in her thoughts. The glazed look in her eyes made him hope she was right. "Well, I can at least guarantee you that the woman with the Afro is not your mother."

She glanced up and grinned at his attempt to cheer her up.

He saw the relief in her shoulders. "You didn't think you and I could have possibly been brother and sister, did you?" Heaven forbid!

She shrugged. "I just had to be certain." If he were her brother, it would be more than she could handle in one lifetime. "You always did try to act like you were my big brother."

"Somebody had to protect you from the big bad wolf."

She felt warm at his comment, though sisterly love was the last thing she felt when she was around him.

The rich, deep gold of his eyes shone in the bright afternoon sun, pulling her into their depths. Her gaze drifted to his wide mouth, and the pink tongue that suddenly darted across his lower lip. That habit was driving her crazy! She felt the urge to rise from her seat, lean across the desk and entwine her tongue with his.

"Is there anyone else you can ask about your birth?"

Regaining her common sense, Calaine shook her head and glanced down at the photograph again. "Only my mother's sister, but I don't think she's going to be much help." Slamming a fist on the desk, she murmured, "They should have told me the truth!"

She looked so miserable David rounded the desk in two strides and came to her, placing a comforting hand to her shoulder. "There is no point in trying to figure out why. Your parents must have had their reasons. Maybe your mother wanted to make sure you never thought any less of your father or thought of her as anyone other than your natural mother. If you were your father's...," he cleared his throat, "love child, then I can understand why your mother never wanted you to know. How many women would put up with their man stepping out on them? Then, to make matters worse, bringing a child into the picture. Only a strong woman would raise another woman's child."

She nodded. Her uncle had said the same thing. "You're right." The warmth from his fingertips penetrated through her skin. She suddenly felt embarrassed not only by the contact but for spilling her guts. Why had she poured out her heart to him? She couldn't even imagine ever looking at him the same again.

"I'm all right…really." Calaine swerved in her chair, removing his hands. "I-I guess I better get back to work."

With his hands clasped behind his back, David was moving towards his seat when he stopped and swung around to face her again. "I want to help you find your mother," he volunteered.

She saw the pity in his eyes and shook her head "No, I don't want your help," she argued softly.

His silence gave her a moment of hope that he was about to give up.

"You need my help," David finally said as he lowered into the chair. His voice held a ring of command and his smile came slowly, as if an afterthought to soften his order. "That way you can talk to my mom. I'm sure she knows how to find the others."

"No, really, I can do this on my own," she assured him with cool poise intended to mask her own misgivings.

"No you can't." David locked firmly into the argument.

Calaine sighed heavily and rubbed the tension at the base of her neck. Common sense told her to refuse his offer but her strong desire to uncover her past prevailed. "All right, let me think about it."

David gave her a triumphant smile. "Good."

He wasn't quite sure why he had offered to help except that he still felt as protective of her as he had in college. He also had a hunch that there was more to his concern for her than that but he wasn't ready yet to explore those possibilities.

The phone rang. Before reaching for it, Calaine managed a smile and finished with, "I really do appreciate your offer. Now, if you'll excuse me, I need to get back to work."

David surged to his feet. "I'll talk to you soon."

David returned to his office still thinking about what Calaine had told him. He couldn't imagine how he would feel if he found out the Souls were not his biological parents. They were a close-knit family. Besides Caress he had two younger sisters, Daphne and Christie, and an older brother, Carlos. His parents were still alive and kicking. They had retired in San Antonio almost a decade ago, which was one of the reasons why he had decided to make Texas his home.

He couldn't explain why, but he wanted to help Calaine find her mother. He wanted her to find answers to all her questions, to have the family she had always dreamed of having. He wanted to see the bags fade from beneath her eyes and the brightness return. He was willing to do whatever it took.

Picking up the phone, he dialed home, certain that his mother was watching her soap operas. Ruby Soul picked up on the third ring.

"Hi, Mom," he said, following her greeting.

"Hello, Davie. You know I'm watching my soaps," she reminded.

He chuckled. "I figured as much." He had never understood her loyalty to the world of make believe. However, his mother had said time and time again it felt good to know rich folks had problems too. "How are you doing?"

"Much better if you'd let me watch my program," she stated.

He chuckled again. When he was a child, Ruby had never had to yell. Her tone had been sharp enough for her children to know she wasn't one to repeat herself.

David pretended to be insulted. "Mom, don't you want to hear from your baby boy?" There was a prolonged silence. "Mom, are you listening?"

"I'm sorry…okay, a commercial's on. How's my son doing?"

He smiled, pleased that he finally had her undivided attention. "Good, Mom, real good."

"Wonderful. I can't wait to see your new house."

"I can't wait for you to come up and see it. Mom, I want to ask you a question before your soap comes back on."

"Okay, but you better make it quick."

"A friend of mine stumbled across a photo of you and five other nursing students."

"Oh really, I wonder which one it is?" she asked curiously.

"It was taken on the front steps of the school."

She took a few seconds to think about it. "Hmmm, I don't remember that one."

David tried explaining the setting, but she still drew a blank.

"She's trying to find her mother and thinks that maybe one of those women might be her."

"That's interesting."

"Do you know anything about a student having a baby in 1975?"

"Let me see. 1975? 1975? I don't think so. I can't think who might be in that photo."

"Would it help if I had the names?"

"It would help if I could see the photo. The only person I remember is Coletta Ross. She always wore her hair in a ponytail. And there was a Eunice, I can't remember her last name, and maybe a Linda somebody. Your godmother should also be in that picture."

"Aunt Wanda?" he asked, stunned.

She chuckled with fond memories. "Yeah, since she had that good hair, Wanda always wore big Shirley Temple curls."

David laughed absently. "I can't believe I didn't notice her."

"Are you still coming home for Christie's graduation?"

"I wouldn't miss it for the world." He adored his baby sister. She would be graduating with a teaching degree in two weeks.

"Well, then bring your friend. Wanda will be here and if you bring the photo we can look at it together. You know two heads are always better than one."

"Sounds good, Mom."

"Oops! My soap's back on so I have to go. Give me a call this weekend."

"Tell Dad I said hi." David hung up feeling good about what he had found out.

By the end of the workday, David had decided he was going to ask Calaine to fly to San Antonio with him for his sister's graduation. During that time, anything could happen.

CHAPTER FIVE

Calaine went home that evening with her mind still reeling through a haze of fact and wonder that she had had another breakthrough. She was beginning to believe that maybe it wasn't going to take as long as she had originally thought to find her mother. Part of her was anxious to find her, the other half was frightened as to what else she might find.

On the way home she stopped for Chinese takeout. Setting the sack on the counter, she quickly went to her bedroom to change into a pair of sweatpants and an oversized t-shirt. Fixing herself a plate, she moved to the living room and sat in front of the television.

Channel surfing, she found herself drawn to an episode of *Unsolved Mysteries* about a mother who was looking for her daughter. By the end of the episode, Calaine had lost what little appetite she'd had.

Sighing, she curled her feet beneath her. What bothered her the most was the fact that her mother had walked away from her without a backward glance. What woman in her right mind could abandon her own child? The same questions kept running through her head. Why did she leave me? Why has she never tried to get in touch with me? She wondered if her mother ever thought about her. She had a sinking feeling she did not.

Calaine reached for a pillow and hugged it close to her middle. It was just too lonely an evening. Even though Uncle Thaddeus had called earlier to see how she was doing, Calaine still felt alone, though spending her evenings by herself was a norm. Some days she didn't mind, but lately, especially since her parents' deaths, being alone was starting to get to her. It was on days like this that she missed having someone special in her life.

She hated to admit that David made her miss that someone special even more. He was still as charming and convincing as ever. There was no way she could have said no to his offer to help if she had wanted to. She was looking forward to his assistance, but a part of her had other reasons for wanting him around. However, she wasn't ready to explore those ideas. After all, she was expecting to help rekindle his relationship with Donna.

Using all her energy, she forced thoughts of David from her mind and focused on an episode of *Cosby*. Calaine lay back on the sofa and before she even realized it, she had drifted off to sleep.

The sun had just begun to set when she heard someone knocking. Rolling off the couch, she rose and walked to the door. She looked through the peek hole, but whoever was on the other side had the audacity to put their hand over the glass.

"Who is it?" she snapped. Somebody had some nerve.

"It's David."

She yanked open the door, mouth wide open. "David? What are you doing here?" Self-consciously she quickly ran her slender fingers through her hair. "How did you find out where I live?"

He chuckled as if he knew a deep secret. "This is Columbia. Everyone knows where everyone lives."

David did have a point. Of Columbia's population of seventy-five thousand, only about twenty-five percent were black. Everyone either worked together, were college students or were related in one way or another.

He was lounged casually against the door frame still dressed in his suit and tie. His cocky grin sparked her anger.

"Well, what is it you want?" Her tone was not as polite or as composed as was his.

"Aren't you going to invite me in?"

"I was trying to take a nap," she stated firmly, hoping he would just go away.

"I can tell," he commented as he ruffled her hair. Not giving her a chance to retort, he moved past her into the house. "Very nice," he mumbled as he looked around the room.

"Why the arrogant son-of-a...," she muttered under her breath. Who did he think he was walking into her house? She had half a mind, to demand that he leave right now. However, as much as she wanted to give him a piece of her mind, she reminded herself of his offer to help her find her mother. She forced back a retort that was on the verge of spilling from the tip of her tongue. "I'm not in the mood for company tonight." Calaine wrinkled her nose and shook her head. She'd had no idea that when she had agreed to his help it meant he would come to her house. It was much too personal.

Hoping to see some sign of the reason for her mood, David studied her face. Unspoken pain was alive and glowing in her eyes. He gave her a soft relaxed smile, hoping to cheer her up. "You need to shake off your gloomy mood," he suggested as he moved to her couch and took a seat.

She ran a frustrated hand through her hair as she stepped further into the living room. "You've got a lot of nerve! You have no idea what I've been going through or what I'm going through now."

No, he didn't, but he did know that she was hurting. If only she would let him in. There was a prolonged silence before David replied in an apologetic tone, "You're right, I don't know, but nevertheless I want to help."

"Why?" she asked suspiciously.

"Because I want to," he replied. "Now come and have a seat."

"But I don't want your help," she mumbled. How could she tell him that she didn't want anyone's help? What if what she found out was something so embarrassing that she would never be able to hold her head up in their town again?

"Please, sit down," he tried again. At her hesitation he continued, "I spoke to my mother tonight and asked her about the photo."

Calaine's eyes widened. "You did?" Immediately she moved and took a seat on the loveseat across from him. "Does she know who my mother is?" She knew it was too much to hope for but she had to ask, and wasn't at all surprised when he shook his head. "Well, what did she say?"

David leaned back comfortably and draped his arm across the cushions. "She said she vaguely remembered the other women. She would have to see the photo to be sure. She did however identify one of the women. Let me see the photo."

Eyes wide with anticipation, Calaine scrambled to the dining room, grabbed her purse, dug out the snapshot and handed it to him. This time without even realizing it, she dropped down beside him on the couch.

David glanced down at the photograph again and started to chuckle. "Yep, that's her."

"That's who?"

"My Aunt Wanda."

She looked down at the woman he was pointing to. "That's your aunt?" This was getting weirder by the minute.

He turned to look at her. "She isn't really my aunt, we just call her that. She's more like my godmother. I've known her all my life."

Calaine looked down at the nut-brown colored woman with long curly hair whose arm was draped across his mother's shoulder. Could she be her mother?

David read her mind. "I don't think so. Wanda never had children. Not because she couldn't, she just never wanted any. She worked as a nurse for the military and always had a thing for soldiers. She enjoyed traveling and the excitement of living in different countries. Children would have altered her lifestyle. Don't get me wrong. She loves children. She just never wanted any of her own. You would enjoy talking to her."

She nodded absently. Her mind was twirling with different possibilities. She wasn't about to scratch Aunt Wanda off her list just yet.

"My mother said if she could get a closer look at the photo she could probably remember who the other four are."

She looked at him, uncertain if she was ready to part with the photo although she could run to Kinko's and make a copy.

"I'm flying down for my sister's graduation next Friday. I'd like you to come with me."

Calaine shook her head as the warning bells went off in her mind. There was no way she was going to travel with him to San Antonio—alone. "I don't think so. I'll just make a copy of the photo."

David shrugged. "Suit yourself. My aunt will be attending. We will be having a dinner at my parents' afterwards." He paused, noting the indecisiveness that had crept into her expression. "I'll just talk to them myself." With that, he reached for the remote control and flipped to the news.

Calaine frowned. She didn't want him talking to his mother about her. She wanted to talk to his mother herself. How would

David know what questions to ask?

"I'll think about it," she mumbled.

Expecting as much, David smirked triumphantly. "Good decision." At the prospect of them spending more time together, he felt a tightness in his loins. He shifted uncomfortably on the couch.

David hadn't expected the hard tug of desire when Calaine opened the door with the soft glow of sleep on her beautiful face and her tussled hair. She wore a t-shirt with no bra, leaving the outline of her nipples clearly visible through the delicate fabric. He tried to stay focused, keeping his gaze at eye level, only it was beginning to become impossible.

"Once we have their names, we can look them up on the Internet."

Calaine frowned. "I'm not very computer literate. So, I would definitely appreciate all the help I can get in that area."

"KeKe, I would be happy to."

Her heart fluttered at the sound of her name sliding off his tongue. She turned and tried to concentrate on the news.

At a commercial break, David finally spoke, breaking the silence. "I wonder if any of the women are currently working at the University? If I knew their names I could look them up in the personnel system."

Calaine nodded. "I've already thought about that. My uncle is looking into it for me." She took a few moments to explain to him Thaddeus's connection to the group of women. "If they're not still around, I'm hoping that maybe one of his colleagues at the nursing school might remember them."

David shifted sideways on the couch. "Have you thought about visiting the nursing school to see what you could find?"

She nodded. "I thought about that today but where would I begin?"

He snapped his fingers. "I bet they have old yearbooks we could look at."

"That's a wonderful idea!" In her excitement, she threw her arms around him and kissed him on the cheek before she realized what she had done. Hastily, she dropped her arms and slid away, pretending to watch television.

It took David several seconds to pull himself together. "Did you get a chance to speak to your sales staff?" he asked, trying to ease the sudden tension.

She grinned, relieved that he hadn't made more of the kiss than it really was. "Yes, and they're as excited as I am."

"Good." He was glad he was able to give her something positive to consider. He tried to avoid thinking about how the way her breasts had felt as they rubbed up against him during the brief contact, but he couldn't. "Have I told you how good you look?"

Oh brother. "Don't even go there with me, okay? I'm a wreck and it shows."

"Beauty starts in here." Leaning forward, he tapped her lightly on the chest. The innocent contact, to her annoyance, caused her nipples to harden. She hoped David hadn't noticed.

He'd noticed.

Placing a hand to her knee, he commented, "We used to be close. I want that back."

That was before we got drunk and shared a kiss.

David must have been thinking about the same thing because he looked at her at that particular moment and their eyes locked.

Despite herself, she liked looking at him. For just a heartbeat, she found that she hungered to have him touch her, bring his mouth to hers, feel his body moving against hers. She was irritated that David could evoke such foolishness. *You enjoyed it before!* The thought made her blush. She hastily dropped her eyes and removed his hand.

"I've spoken to Donna."

Now why the hell did she have to bring her up? David scowled. "How's she doing?"

"She'll be down at the end of the month for a visit. She just broke up with her fiancé so she's single again." She was fumbling nervously with her words. "I told her you were back in town and she's looking forward to seeing you."

"I'd like to see her again." He smiled absently. *Wait a minute.* She couldn't possibly think he was still interested in Donna. It wasn't until he had run into Calaine last week that he had for the first time in years thought about Donna. They had never been anything more than friends, not that he hadn't tried. However, once he had realized intimacy was out of the question, he had settled for a platonic relationship.

Calaine saw the dazed look on his face and decided he was probably reminiscing on his and Donna's failed relationship. Maybe this time David might have a better shot.

Clearing her throat, Calaine rose from the couch. "Would you like something to drink?" she offered.

"Yes, that would be great."

Nodding, she moved awkwardly towards the kitchen, completely aware David's eyes were following her. "Coke, iced tea or water?" she called over her shoulder.

"Iced tea," he answered.

She released a sigh of relief when she rounded the corner entering the kitchen. His scent had attacked her senses. What had she been thinking, throwing herself against him like that? Stroking David's ego was the last thing on her mind. The man attracted women as easily as flowers drew bees.

Shaking her head, she opened the refrigerator and removed a

pitcher of iced tea. She tried to concentrate on finding a glass. Her heart was pounding and her thoughts were scattered. Feeling slightly off balance, she blamed it on her not eating earlier. "Would you like some Chinese food?" she called into the living room. "I've got plenty left."

"That would be wonderful."

Spinning around she collided into his hard chest, spilling iced tea on his shirt, down her arm and onto her slippers. She slowly lifted her gaze to his. She hadn't heard him move from the couch. Dang, why did he have to be so handsome? He was so close she found it hard to draw a normal breath. David was too close, his scent much too powerful.

"Look at what you made me do!" she snapped, trying to mask her attraction.

"Here, let me take that from you."

He was standing so close she could feel his sweet breath on her chin, causing her to shiver. His large fingers brushed her as he reached for the glass. She stepped away as if she had been burned by the contact. Quickly, she swung around and opened the refrigerator, then removed several cartons of food and placed them on the counter.

Calaine was confused by her reaction. It had been almost a decade and yet she still responded to him. In fact, her response had intensified. Her heart was pounding heavily in her chest and her throat was dry. She had never acted like this before. Maybe it was because she had been without a man in her bed for so long. Well, whatever it was, she needed to get herself in check, quick!

"Have a seat," she ordered. The words came out sharper than she had intended. Having him invading her space was driving her crazy. She moved over to the cabinet and removed two plates. Reaching into a drawer, she grabbed serving spoons and eating utensils.

David watched her rush around the small yet quaint kitchen. He knew the electricity from their contact had unnerved her. He knew because he had felt it too. It was the same feeling he'd had the time that they had kissed. He'd known then something about her was special. Now he knew it for sure.

She pointed to the counter. "Fix your plate so I can pop it in the microwave for you," she instructed, breaking into his thoughts.

She loaded her own plate, then moved to put it inside the microwave.

David moved towards the counter. "Mmm, you have all of my favorites." He glanced over at Calaine with an irresistible smile as he spooned orange chicken and fried rice onto his plate.

She tried to steady her heartbeat. She didn't want to feel an attraction to him. David could only be her downfall. He would break her heart again. Besides, Donna was looking forward to seeing him again. If she kept reminding herself of that, then there was no chance of her getting involved.

"My staff is very excited about subcontracting. I think it will work out for everyone. A lot of our temporary employees have been seeking employment at the university for years." She was rambling. She knew it but what could she do?

"I think this will be a great opportunity for everyone," he said as she removed her plate. He brushed past her to put his in the microwave. The contact caused the hairs on her arms to stand.

"So do I." She tried to deny the contact and was pulling her t-shirt from inside her sweatpants when she realized her hardened nipples were evident. Why hadn't she left her bra on? She scowled and crossed her arms over her chest. "I'll be right back."

She retreated to the bedroom where she slipped a sweatshirt over her t-shirt and dragged a brush through her hair. When she returned, David had already taken his plate out of the microwave and was seated at the table.

"I was feeling a little chilly," she lied. Dropping her eyes, Calaine took a seat across from him. Before she could bring the fork to her mouth, David stopped her and reached for her hand. She looked down at his large, well-shaped hands and hesitated, unsure as to what he wanted with her hand. When she saw him close his eyes and bow his head, she felt embarrassed by her assumption. He was only trying to bless their food. His large hand engulfed hers and she tried to ignore the sensation as she lowered her head and listened to David say a prayer in a way that sounded as natural as saying, "Good morning."

Religion had never been a major part of her upbringing. She had attended services with her aunt and uncle on numerous occasions but there had never been any consistency. As an adult, she had visited several churches in the neighborhood, hoping to find a place where she felt right at home, but so far, she had come up empty.

They were silent as they ate. David watched her carefully out of the corner of his eyes. Calaine was trying so hard to be in control as she stared out the window behind his head. He was well aware that her past was bothering her. He knew he was also a cause for her uneasiness. She would fight the attraction. Deny it to the end. He couldn't blame her. He had also considered doing the same.

David looked around her small kitchen. It was just what he would expect of a woman whose job was her life but not what he'd expect of a woman raised as Calaine had in an upper class environment. A small microwave cart in the corner was stocked with rows of ramen noodles, popcorn and teas. He'd bet her freezer was full of TV dinners and other ready-made meals. Next to a blender were several instant breakfast packets.

Her curtains could be found at Wal-Mart as well as the wooden table and chairs they were using. He'd felt that same way in her living room. If he had not known she had been raised in a wealthy family, he would have never guessed it.

"Your house is…" Eyes traveling around the room, he allowed his voice to trail off for added emphasis.

"Not at all what you expected," she said as if she read his thoughts.

He looked across at her and smiled. "No, not at all. I'm curious about why you haven't moved into your parents' house."

She frowned as she chewed. "It never felt like home. Besides, it reminds me too much of my mom and dad." Now that she knew Katherine wasn't her mother, it felt weird referring to her as such. "As soon as I'm ready, I'm going to put it on the market."

David nodded. Watching the expression on her face, he knew he had touched on a delicate subject. "I just bought my first home."

She looked up, startled.

"Why do you look so surprised?" he asked.

"Because I never imagined you doing something as settling as buying a house."

"There are a lot of things about me that you haven't realized."

His statement was met by another pregnant silence.

"Are you still a big Lakers fan?" she blurted. Her words sounded forced.

He smirked at her attempt to relieve some of the tension. "Of course. Are you still following the Bulls?"

She frowned. "Not since Jordan left." She spooned food into her mouth and swallowed. "While he was still with the Wizards, I followed his game but the Lakers have been my favorite for the past three seasons."

"A woman after my own heart."

She choked on a grain of rice. Reaching for her napkin, she

covered her mouth and coughed.

David leaned over and patted her lightly on the back." I'm sorry. I'm not trying to make you uncomfortable."

"Then quit saying things that embarrass me," she retorted as she returned the napkin to her lap.

"What would you like for me to say?" A challenging glint lit his eyes.

She sat silently staring at his silly smirk for several seconds, then resumed eating. She wasn't even going to go there. Not today. He was trying to get the better of her.

"I want us to be able to talk without feeling like we have to watch what we say. You are a beautiful woman. I have always enjoyed being around you. That has not changed. You used to be one of my favorite people."

Calaine gaped. "I couldn't stand you."

"Quit fooling yourself. I never believed you disliked me. We had what is considered a love/hate, sister/brother type of relationship."

She snorted rudely. "I thought you were a dog." Then with a shrug she added, "You're a Q, so you can't help yourself." In her opinion, all Omega men were dogs.

He let out a shout of laughter. "Is that what you thought of me?"

"Don't act surprised. I told you that on several occasions. Why do you think I was so dead set against hooking you up with Donna?"

He tilted his head slightly to study her. "I thought maybe you wanted me for yourself."

"What! You must be mad!" Despite her protest, she could do nothing about the flush of heat to her face.

"Then why did you kiss me that night?" he challenged.

Her blood warmed with intimate memories. "We both had too much to drink. Donna had just dumped you and Joseph had decided he was ready for something I obviously was not. We were both on the rebound and feeling a little lonely." She tilted her chin stubbornly. "Besides, as I remember, it was *you* who had kissed me."

"Then why were you on top when Donna knocked on the door?"

He was right. She had been on top. After completing a pitcher of Jungle Juice, the two played a few hands of UNO. Before they realized what they were doing, their bodies were entwined on the floor between her and Donna's beds. She wasn't sure how far it would have gone if Donna hadn't knocked on the door when she had. Calaine remembered opening her eyes and staring down at David.

Her cheeks warmed. She wasn't sure if she'd ever been so aggressive before that night. That night she had initiated the kiss, and being the horny teenager that he was, David had responded to her advances.

Calaine simply shrugged. "I was caught up in the moment."

"So was I. I also enjoyed our kiss very much."

She was annoyed that her pulse was reacting to him in a wild uncontrollable manner. Sure, she'd had a crush on him but that was long before he started sleeping with every woman on campus. Anyway, when he had started dating Donna, she'd tucked that crush away. Well, at least she'd thought she had.

Calaine had been too afraid to tell Donna and even more terrified of her finding out. As a result, whenever she saw David she'd run in the other direction.

"Isn't there someone else you could be bothering this evening?" she dryly replied.

He stared at her, wondering where this conversation was heading. Calaine was looking for any excuse to keep him at a distance. She didn't trust him and he couldn't blame her. He had gone through a string of women, all of them in the interest of a good time. However, that was then and this was now.

"If you are trying to find out if I am seeing anyone, the answer is no."

Calaine didn't know why but his answer gave her an annoying sense of relief, which agitated her further. The longer she was around David, the more she starved for his company. There was no way she was going to get used to him being around.

Anxious to end the evening, Calaine rose from the table to scrape her plate, then turned on the faucet and began filling the sink with dishwater.

David rose from the table and brought his plate to the sink. While reaching around her, he pressed his body against hers as he placed the dish in the warm sudsy water.

"We are two consenting adults. There's nothing for either of us to be ashamed of." His breath was warm against the back of her neck causing a stir at the pit of her stomach.

The arrogant bastard had never known when to quit. Calaine realized she was playing with fire.

Carrying the dishrag, she ducked under his arm and moved back to clear off the table. David moved to help. They worked together quietly while Calaine tried to get her emotions under control. She left the dishes to soak in the sink and ordered him to follow her back into the living room.

An uneasy feeling swept through her. "Thank you so much for your help but I have an early day tomorrow."

He nodded knowingly. "I see you're still running from your feelings."

"Not at all. I just have more important things to worry about right now. The only thing I plan to focus my energy on is finding my mother. Everything else will have to come second." Calaine hoped she had made her intentions clear.

David paused to look at her. "We're going to find your mother." He reached for his suit jacket and moved to the door with her close behind. When they reached it, he turned to face her. One long arm shot out and pulled her snugly against his hard frame.

"I enjoyed spending time with you this evening. Thanks for dinner." With that, he lowered his head and kissed her.

He crushed her to him, claiming her mouth, and when her lips parted in surprise, he took swift advantage. Calaine tried to protest but found she could not. Her hands rose to his chest to push him away but she couldn't. There was no way she could fight the fury inside her because her heart wasn't in it. Instead, her stiff body began to relax.

His lips moved with gentle pressure at first. Then the kiss deepened. The taste and scent of him enveloped her and the firmness of his mouth sent a quiver through her. When had David slipped a mint in his mouth? The result was clean tasting, yet demanding attention and shooting fire through her veins. She found herself succumbing to the passion. He moved his hand to hold the back of her head as a wave of intense pleasure swept deeply within her.

Under the skillful stroke of his tongue, Calaine felt as if she were drowning, drowning in the desire that surged through her veins. A sigh escaped her parted lips and she felt herself leaning into him, giving in to temptation as she met his strokes eagerly. She welcomed the possession of his lips. She liked the pressure of her breasts pressed against his chest. She felt as if she had been waiting for this all her life. Heat surged through her and spread fast through her body. Her world was spinning like a top and all that mattered was being right here, right now with David. Her arms snaked around his torso and she clung tightly, afraid that if she let go, she would discover it had all been just a dream. She heard David groan and then his hold on her tightened, drawing her closer to his hard male body.

The need for air finally pulled them apart. They stared at each other, hearts thumping and breathing heavily.

David's eyes had darkened. "I knew the passion was still there."

"You shouldn't have done that," Calaine replied in a shaky whisper.

"You could have stopped me at any point, but you didn't. You felt it just as I did."

She pushed him away. "I have no idea what you're talking about."

He pulled her back into his arms. "Don't you feel that? Listen to what your heart is telling you," he commanded in a husky whisper.

She could not deny the strong beats of their hearts. David's was beating just a rapidly as her own.

"That's lust, nothing more," she lied.

"So, what's wrong with lust?"

"Everything." She pushed away again, needing to put some space between them fast.

"Good night, Calaine," David said as he opened the front door. "Sweet dreams."

All Calaine could do was nod, then watch him walk through the door. She knew her dreams were going to be far from sweet.

She moved to turn the lock on the door, then collapsed against it and slid onto the floor.

The kiss that they had shared in college now seemed tame in

comparison. With maturity, his kiss was now more confident and skillful. He had given her a glimpse of his erotic skills and had stirred her desire. She had always known his kisses would fill her with more intensity than those from any other man. What she hadn't expected was the magnetic pull that came along with them. She was drawn to him like a bear to honey.

Calaine had truly underestimated David's power over her. He had touched her deeply. His touch had aroused an almost frantic ache deep within her. Nothing else would ever compare. Absolutely nothing.

She closed her eyes as she realized she was in trouble.

David pulled out of the driveway in his BMW. It was after eight, so he turned on the radio and tuned into FM 89 Quiet Storm hosted by Lincoln University.

While listening to Alicia Keys' *Fallin'*, he had to nod his head. He was definitely falling for Calaine Hart.

He found his mind wandering to the many nights he had spent sitting out on his deck long after everyone else was asleep with only the occasional sounds of the leaves ruffling in the wind. It was somehow comforting to David. Peace and quiet, alone with his own thoughts. It was so odd that he would feel that way. For years he had craved excitement, partying to the wee hours, always in the company of a woman, rarely spending a night alone. And now what? Of all things, he yearned for one person with whom to share his life, with whom to start a family. It was strange that such an emotion would assail him. He had sworn himself a confirmed bachelor, practicing precautions because he didn't want any baby's momma drama. He had stayed away from women who sought commitment. He'd run away from emotional attachments. He'd sought women who challenged him and when the conquest was over, he'd moved on. He'd liked knowing that however he left his house in the morning, it would be in the same condition when he got home.

However, for the past several months, long before he had even considered returning home, his heart and his soul had seemed to yearn for something unfamiliar to him, something he had run away from for years. Love. He had to ask himself if he really wanted to give up his freedom and move through the trenches they called a relationship. The only thing he was sure of was that bachelorhood was going to put up one hell of a fight.

CHAPTER SIX

Calaine woke up the next morning feeling more tired than she had before she went to bed. *Damn you, David.* After a night of tossing and turning with memories of their attraction pure and clear, she arrived at the office an hour later than usual.

She entered through the side so she would not waltz through the maze of applicants normally in the lobby at this time of the day. Mornings were a busy time for them. Her interviewer scheduled most of the interviews and typing tests early, allowing her plenty of time in the afternoon to conduct reference checks.

As she moved down the hallway, the sound of her pumps was muffled against the thick plush mauve carpet. She stepped into the large office on the left to find each of her staff on the telephone.

On the floor were her staffing supervisor, Sherrie Sneed, and two staffing specialists, Tracy Parks and Amber Boswell. They were responsible for taking job orders, screening candidates and filling positions with the best person possible. Her sales team consisted of her manager Debbie and two sales associates, Jean and Sandra. All three were already out in the field making sales calls. In the front office were her payroll specialist, Allison Simmons, interviewer, Tyla Gavin, and her longest employee, receptionist and part-time mother hen, Norma Brown.

Calaine moved near the cubicle to the left just as Sherrie completed a call. "What kind of morning are we having?" she asked.

The very petite coffee-colored woman swiveled around in her chair with a deeply embedded frown at the center of her forehead. "We're having a bad morning. Five call-ins, three no-shows and Aisha showed up at work yesterday with a newly pierced tongue ring."

"She what!" Calaine gasped. "What's wrong with that girl?" Calaine grumbled as she lowered her briefcase to the floor. "Where is she working?"

When Sherrie hesitated, Calaine's eyes widened with realization. "Pleeease don't tell me she has already started in the finance department."

The supervisor gave her a pained nod. "I'm afraid she started last Friday. Georgia is livid."

Damn! Georgia Jefferson was manager of the city's finance department and a hard woman to please. She seemed to have one problem or another with over half the temporaries they had ever sent her way. Aisha would be their third replacement in a month.

Before the city stepped in and began monitoring staffing expenditures, Georgia had had the liberty of using any service of her choice. In the ten years that she had been in charge of the finance department, Georgia had built a relationship with the manager of Staffing Unlimited. When the city had decided to cut employment costs, temporary agencies were forced to bid on yearly contracts with the city. Kelly Services had won the contract and Office Remedies was used to subcontract the large demand.

Georgia had argued both of the agencies were incompetent to provide qualified candidates. Even though she had lost the battle, she made certain the two agencies knew they were second rate every chance she got.

Feeling a headache coming on, Calaine dropped down in the chair beside Sherrie and faced her. "What does Georgia want, besides my head on a platter?" Her bark of laughter lacked humor.

Sherrie leaned forward, resting her chin in the palm of her hand. "She wants someone to come over this morning and ask Aisha to either remove the ring or leave."

Calaine glanced down at her watch. It was almost nine o'clock. "Why didn't she call yesterday and complain? At least then we could have called Aisha at home and asked her not to wear the ring again."

"That's what I told her, but she said her supervisor had just brought it to her attention this morning." Unable to sit still, Sherrie leaned back in her chair with her thin fingers tensed in her lap.

Calaine threw her hands up in the air and mumbled under her breath that it was going to be one hell of a great day. She could feel it already. Damn you, David! She scowled inwardly. Her bad morning wasn't really his fault, although he was the reason she hadn't gotten much sleep. Not that she had been getting much sleep lately. Nevertheless, she had to blame someone and he was the only person who came to mind.

"Have you tried to call Aisha at home?" she asked.

Tracy, who had been quiet up to this point, twirled around in her chair and replied, "I did. Her phone is disconnected."

"Great," Calaine mumbled. She tapped her fingernails lightly on top of the desk as she pondered a solution, then settled back, disappointed. What could have possessed Aisha Winters to do something so stupid as to pierce her tongue? Calaine sighed. She had done everything she could to help Aisha, who had very limited skills. Calaine had advised her interviewer to train Aisha on Word and Excel, two very demanding software packages. Calaine had even gone a step further. When Aisha informed her that she didn't have proper clothing, Calaine had started a clothing pantry so people in similar situations would not have to feel ashamed. She and her staff spent a Saturday afternoon converting a large room in the rear of the suite they weren't using to store the clothing. She had since received donations from organizations all around the city.

Office Remedies had been partnering with the Welfare to Work Program for almost two years. Their program had a high success rate. Several participants of the program had gone on to full-time positions, allowing them to finally get off public assistance.

Aisha was one of several participants who had been sent her way. Barely twenty-one and already with two children, she had come to them eager to find a full-time position. Sherrie had been hesitant about sending her out to do anything other than short-term assignments. However, because she had received high marks while on three other assignments, Calaine had ignored the warning bells and insisted that Aisha be given a temp-to-hire position. Now she wasn't so sure.

"I'll go," she finally said.

Sherrie looked surprise. "Calaine, you don't have to."

"Yes I do." She rose from the chair. "I'm the one who wanted to give her a chance." She sighed. Sherrie had over ten years experience in the industry and was good at what she did, but under the circumstances, she was ill equipped to undertake the task of Georgia Jefferson. Calaine wouldn't have forced that kind of stress on her worst enemy. It was like sending Daniel into the lion's den. However, somebody had to do it and that person was she.

Reaching down, she picked up her briefcase and headed towards the break room. "I hope there's some coffee ready, because I'm going to need it."

Calaine pulled her car into a thirty-minute parking space in front of the municipal building just before ten. Staring out at the building, she thought about how old the gothic structure was. Her grandmother had once told her the building had been around long before she was a child.

Climbing out of the car, she reached into her purse and fished out two quarters, then fed them into the meter. When a breeze ruffled her hair, Calaine scowled. It was too beautiful a morning to have to deal with personnel issues. However, it wasn't the first time and definitely wasn't going to be the last.

On an average of three times a month, Office Remedies was asked to replace an employee. Lately their replacement rate had been at an all time low, which was proof they were taking the extra time to fill the position with the most qualified individual, as opposed to just filling it with anyone just to get the job done. Recently, however, personalities had begun to play a major part in the screening process. Companies were not only wanting qualifications but also an individual whose personality was a perfect match for their organization.

This appeared to be one of those situations.

Calaine pushed through the revolving door, then moved across the marble lobby with purposeful strides. She smoothed down the front of the long white skirt that molded her hips and thighs and straightened the blue linen jacket with short sleeves. The sound of her navy blue pumps echoed in the hallway as she strolled into the last office on the left.

She entered the administration office where Georgia's receptionist was on the phone. Delaney acknowledged Calaine with a smile and pointed a pink fingernail toward the right of the office, signaling it was okay to go back.

Georgia was sitting behind her desk just finishing up a call when Calaine strolled in. She was an average looking, fifty-plus woman with an olive complexion, silver gray hair and a rotund body. As she hung up the phone, she returned Calaine's smile with one that didn't quite reach her blue eyes.

"I'm so glad you're here. We have a problem."

She signaled her to sit. Calaine took the seat across from her desk, dropping her purse strap from her shoulder. Reading Georgia's strained expression, Calaine nodded knowingly. "Sherrie told me. I want to apologize. I will ask Aisha to remove the ring at once."

Georgia was still. Her gaze intent, she replied, "I would like you to ask A-Asia not to return."

Calaine frowned at the way she'd purposely mispronounced the name. Vertical lines appeared around her eyes. "But why?"

Georgia looked surprised that she would have even asked such a question. "I think that part should be quite obvious. Asia, well, she just isn't right for this department. I don't think she has the maturity this position requires and the tongue ring proves that."

Pursing her lips, Calaine tried to keep her tone light. "*Aisha* works in the mailroom. How much daily interaction with the public does the job require?"

Georgia met her direct stare. "Well, none. However, that's not the point."

Calaine's frustration was growing. "Then what is the point?" she asked around a tight smile.

"This department requires a very well-rounded individual with not only skills but maturity."

Though her temperature flared, Calaine reminded herself that the customer was always right. "Very well. We will begin screening for someone else as soon as I return to the office." She rose, slipped the strap of her purse back over her shoulder, then forced a polite smile. "Where may I find Aisha?"

Georgia pointed. "The mailroom is down the stairs, first room on the left."

Calaine nodded and spun around, heading towards the door.

"Calaine, um, just a moment," Georgia called behind her.

She turned and looked at Georgia.

The older woman cleared her throat, then leaned forward with her fingers steepled. "I'm willing to wait as long as it takes until we find just the right person."

"I understand," Calaine replied with a nod. "Since this will be our third replacement we will take that into consideration."

Georgia cleared her throat. "I would like for you to also consider the individual's ethnic background."

Calaine's brow rose in surprise. "Excuse me?" She stood there shocked. There was no way she had heard her right.

Georgia smiled, trying to lighten the mood. "I think it is only fair you take into consideration the feelings of the individual as well. My staff is predominately white. I believe Aisha may feel a little uncomfortable."

Calaine dropped her arm, the strap falling from her shoulder again. "Are you sure it isn't *you* who feels uncomfortable?" she asked bluntly.

"Oh no, no, no, not at all," Georgia stuttered. "I just feel that if you could find a mature Caucasian woman it would be to everyone's best interest."

Calaine shifted to one hip, no longer able to hide her mounting anger. "As you know, Georgia, screening according to race, creed or color is against the law."

"All I'm asking is that you take it into consideration," Georgia quickly corrected.

"And I'm telling you I won't do it," Calaine retorted. "That's not that way I do business. I can screen for the best fit and that's where I draw the line. Color will not now or ever play a role in my company's screening process. I hope I've made myself clear." With that, she spun on her heel and departed the room. She didn't care if Georgia ever used her services again. Discrimination was one thing she would not tolerate.

Looking straight ahead, she walked through the office. Calaine wanted to grab Aisha and depart the building as quickly as she possibly could. She hated dismissing employees; however, this was one time when she felt she was doing an employee a favor. As long as she was in business, none of her employees, black or white, would ever be subjected to that type of racial behavior.

Last year, a Baptist church had called requesting a secretary. After sending them almost a dozen employees to interview, the director had called and made it clear that they were a black church and were only interested in interviewing black women. Calaine had made it clear in no uncertain terms that she did not conduct that type of business. Anyone that lived in Columbia, black or white, was fully aware Rolling Meadows Baptist Church had a predominately black congregation. If anyone other than a black woman was interested in seeking employment at their church, then who were they to judge?

She had expected a lot more out of a church and it had disappointed her greatly to know they condoned that sort of unethical behavior. She had since scratched the church off her list of possible churches for fellowship.

Returning to the problem at hand, Calaine descended the stairs and followed the signs that led her to the mailroom. She nibbled on the inside of her jaw, hating to break the news to Aisha even though she knew it was her responsibility to do so.

Aisha had come into the office only last week to thank her staff for providing her with steady employment and had even gone on to say how great it felt to have a purpose to wake up every morning. Now she had to burst her bubble.

As she entered the mailroom, the floor supervisor, a fat bald man, met her at the door. Seeing the grin on his face when she introduced herself, she could almost bet he was the one who had called Georgia and complained.

He directed her to a cubicle at the back of the room. She moved through the maze and found Aisha in front of a sorter, humming while she tossed mail into several bins. Aisha turned when she saw her coming. She looked surprised, then delighted Calaine had come to see her.

"Hi, Calaine."

She returned the smile. Aisha's glowing youthful face had finally emerged. She remembered the sorrow that used to weigh her down. Her self-esteem issues had slowly vanished. The lines around her eyes had since softened. She seemed more relaxed and happy about life, which made the task at hand even harder to perform.

"Hello, Aisha."

"Are you checking up on me?" she teased. When she smiled, Calaine noticed the gold stud protruding from the center of her tongue and remembered it was the original reason for her visit.

"Can I speak to you privately for a moment?"

Aisha saw the sober expression on her boss's face and she stilled. "Is something wrong?"

Calaine nodded. "I'm afraid so. I need you to grab your things and follow me."

When Aisha lifted her eyes, Calaine saw pain flicker there.

"D-did I do something wrong?" she asked.

Noting her sad expression, Calaine shook her head and gave her a tender smile. "No, you didn't, but we'll talk about it when we get outside."

Quietly Aisha put the mail down and moved to grab a beat-up leather purse and a brown sack that looked to contain her lunch. Together they walked past the others. The floor supervisor stood to the side, still grinning, as they departed. Calaine ignored him as she signaled Aisha to walk beside her. She shuffled her feet as they moved out of the room.

"Are you sure you got everything?" she asked when they reached the lobby.

Aisha nodded.

"If not, call me and I'll pick it up. You are not to return to the mailroom for anything," she informed her as they traveled through the revolving door.

As soon as they reached the sidewalk Aisha swung around and faced her. "Will you please tell me what's going on? I mean just last Friday they was tellin' me I was doin' a good job."

Calaine could see that she was hurting and it tugged at her insides. Shifting her weight to her other leg, she looked at Aisha. "They didn't feel as if you were a good match. The position requires someone with several years' experience. They are also considering reclassifying the position to include a year of data entry experience."

"Oh," was all she could say. "You sure it wasn't 'cause I'm black? I see how all dem white folks be lookin' at me."

Calaine noted the dejected look on her face. She knew she had lied but she and Aisha both knew that other than in-house training, she had no real hands-on computer training. She hoped Aisha accepted her explanation because there was no way she could ever mention color. All she needed was for the local NAACP chapter to come knocking on her door. In a small city like theirs, discrimination would cause quite a stir.

"No, not at all. However, that piece of jewelry you stuck in your tongue didn't help matters at all. It is very unprofessional. That's like showing up at work dressed like a hoochie."

Aisha smirked at Calaine's choice of words. "My cousin dared me to do it."

"Well, it looks tacky. Stick out your tongue," she ordered.

Like an obedient child, Aisha obeyed. After a quick examination, Calaine could tell the piercing had been done rather recently. The base of her tongue was red and swollen.

Calaine sighed with frustration. "Aisha, I can't help you if you do stuff like this." She didn't normally talk to an employee on such a personal level, but she had known Aisha long enough to know what it would take to talk some sense into her.

Aisha nibbled on her lower lip like a scolded child. "I'm sorry. I promise not to wear it to work no mo'. Does dis mean I'm fired?"

"No, not at all." Calaine noticed her shoulders relax and was glad that some of the tension had dissipated. "It's not your fault. The finance department is a tough department to please. You are their third replacement in a month." She watched Aisha smile, pleased she wasn't the only one they had let go. "They require a certain caliber of person that I don't think we can provide them." She thought about the conversation she'd had with Georgia in regard to *caliber*. "Call the office tomorrow and I'll have Sherrie find you another assignment."

"Thanks, Calaine."

She smiled. "You're welcome."

Glancing around, Aisha hesitated before asking, "You think you can give me a ride home?"

"Sure, come on." She signaled for her to follow her to the car.

By the time Calaine had returned to the office, Sherrie was waiting for her in the hallway. "How did it go?"

"As well as could be expected. Aisha was hurt but she's a big girl. She'll get over it. I told her to give you a call in the morning so you can find her another assignment," she said over her shoulder as she stepped into her private office with Sherrie right behind her. "Be careful where you send her. Her tongue is pretty swollen so it will be a while before she can remove that ring." Calaine dropped her purse and keys on the desk. "I guess you need to start finding a replacement for the mailroom."

There was a pregnant pause before Sherrie spoke. "Georgia called just before you arrived."

With an irritated sigh, Calaine moved behind her desk. "What does she want now?" The woman was definitely a pain in the behind.

"She decided to let Kelly Services refill the position."

Calaine mumbled several four-letter words before deciding it was probably for the best. "I think that is probably a wise decision."

"Did something happen I need to know about?" Sherrie asked curiously.

"Nothing that I can't handle." To her, Georgia was already water under the bridge.

Calaine sat down then smiled up at Sherrie. "How are we doing screening for the customer service positions for Verizon?" Sherrie beamed with pride. "We've already filled ten."

"Good. That means we still have ten more to go."

When Sherrie returned to the floor, Calaine removed her shoes and leaned back in the chair. With her palm to her cheek, she sighed. It was going to be a long week.

She spent the rest of the morning returning phone calls and signing bills that her secretary had prepared. The bonus checks looked quite well this billing cycle. Her staff was going to be pleased.

The phone rang and she reached for the receiver by the second ring. "Office Remedies, this is Calaine."

She heard a faint voice on the other line. "Yes, I would like to request fifteen telemarketers for tomorrow."

"Excuse me?" Someone was out of their cotton pickin' mind.

She heard chuckles. Someone was playing with her. "Who is this?" she insisted.

The laughter grew deeper until she realized it was David.

"I'm sorry, Calaine, I couldn't resist."

"Still the jokester, I see."

"Life's too short. We're supposed to have fun."

"If you say so," she murmured, unconvinced. "What do you want?"

If David had registered the ice in her voice, he totally ignored it. "Can I come by? I have something I think you'll want to see."

"What is it?" She could not camouflage the curiosity in her voice.

"If you want to find out you'll have to invite me over." After a prolonged pause he said, "It's the only way. I have a lead for you."

"Did you visit the school of nursing?" she asked, hoping he would at least give her a hint. She hated surprises.

"Yep," he finally said. "But I'm not telling you anything more. Can I come over or not?" he repeated.

Calaine let out a sigh of pure frustration. David was nerve-racking and wasn't going to give her a moment's peace until her mother was found. The corner of her lips curled upward at his determination. She needed him more than she had realized. Just thinking about it caused her brow to curve.

Finally, she gave into her curiosity. "Why don't you drop by the house this evening."

"Sounds like a plan."

"I'll see you at seven," she replied.

"I'll bring dinner." David then hung up before she could protest.

CHAPTER SEVEN

All the way home Calaine's mind raced with possibilities. After the incident with Aisha, she had been so busy she'd hardly had time to think, though she took a few minutes between phone calls to weigh her options and decided to accompany David to San Antonio. She had also made the decision to call her mother's sister and try again for answers. There had to be a reason why Aunt Greta hadn't told her the truth and she was determined to find out what that was.

Turning onto her street, she sighed with content. She lived in a comfortable family neighborhood a short distance from work. She waved at her neighbors, an elderly couple who had lived on the block longer than she had been in existence. Together they were outside tending to their yard.

Calaine hurried into the house. She dropped her mail on the table without looking at it and rushed to her bedroom to take a quick shower. After toweling off, she rubbed down in her favorite peach-scented lotion, then slipped into a pair of jeans and a white cotton shirt. She fingered mousse through her hair, vowing that tomorrow she would call her beautician. Looking in the mirror, she found herself reaching for her makeup bag before she stopped herself. What was she doing? It was only David. Yet, she had bathed, brushed her teeth, rubbed on her favorite lotion and was now considering lipstick and eyeliner. What was the point? She tried to convince herself she wasn't interested in him as her fingers curled around her mascara brush. She was doing it for herself. *Just a little mascara nothing more.*

By seven, she had washed a load of laundry and was folding clothes on the dining room table when she finally heard a knock at the door. Even though she had been listening for the purr of his expensive car, her heart went off in a tailspin. She took a deep breath to maintain her composure and after a brief moment, moved through the foyer to greet him.

Calaine opened the door. Suddenly breathless, she blinked at the man in her doorway. David's smile curved his lips, deepening the dimples on either side of his face. She took in the shirt he was wearing that revealed strong dark forearms. His jeans, faded with wear, fit his hips snugly. This was the first time she had seem him in jeans since college and he still looked just as good as he had then. And the magnetism… There was no escaping his magnetism. David was the most masculine man she'd ever laid eyes on.

"Hi beautiful." His voice was low, soft and intentionally seductive.

Her gaze went back to his face and froze. No man should look that good, Calaine thought. Over the years, nothing had changed. Sexy, irresistible, sensual, those words didn't begin to describe him. It went a lot deeper than that. And it bothered her. It bothered her that she had noticed and her traitorous body had chosen to respond.

"Are you going to let me in?" David asked with a glint of humor in his eyes.

She moved aside so he could enter. She had been so busy eyeing his handsome physique, the bags in his arms had gone unnoticed.

"What do you have?" she asked.

He waved a large bag in front of her nose. "Tony's pizza and gyros."

"Yummy." The Greek style pizza was the best in town.

She followed him into the kitchen as if it were his house. While he sat the bags on the table, she went to the pantry to find paper plates and napkins, then placed them on the table next to a large Greek salad.

Moving towards the refrigerator, she called over her shoulder, "Iced tea or lemonade?"

"Iced tea would be great," he answered as he finished emptying the bags.

She removed a cold pitcher of freshly brewed sun tea from the top shelf, then looked in the dishwasher and removed two glasses.

While filling each glass with ice, she glanced out the corner of her eye as David unwrapped one of the gyros. The smell of lamb and onions drifted under her nose. Watching his large hands, she imagined their touch against her and her traitorous body immediately responded. She jerked. What was she thinking? She had to pull herself together quickly.

David must have sensed her watching him for he paused from what he was doing and smiled over at her, a smile so charming the warning bells went off. Calaine took a deep breath. Why had she made the mistake of inviting him to her house again?

She carried both glasses over and sat them on the table, making certain not to brush against David. When he lifted the lid of the pizza box, her mouth dropped open. "Ham and pineapple! How'd you remember it was my favorite?"

Standing very close yet not touching her, he glanced down with a smile as intimate as a kiss. "Some things you never forget."

Her skin tingled at the double meaning of his words and all she could think about was how wonderful his lips had felt. She remembered clearly how her heart had leaped against her chest, how every cell in her body had urged her to respond to his kiss. Never had she felt anything remotely close to the fierce hunger that had ripped through her body as he held her in his arms. However, her intense response right now came close. Calaine shook her head and as swiftly as the memory had arisen, she shifted it.

"So what is the big surprise?" she asked.

"I'll show you after we eat," David said as he lowered into a chair and reached for a slice of pizza.

Calaine nodded, although the last thing she really wanted was to feel as if the two of them were spending quality time together. Dropping by with information was one thing; coming over to share a meal was another thing all together. She had been waiting since this afternoon for the information she was certain David had gathered about her past.

"What if I don't want to wait?" she challenged.

He took a thirsty sip, then glanced up at her towering over him. "Too bad. I can bet you haven't eaten anything all day."

He was right, she hadn't.

"If this is the only way I can get you to eat, then so be it. Now eat," he ordered.

Without any further protest, Calaine flopped down in a seat opposite him. This time, when he reached for her hand, she was prepared to bow her head.

As they ate in silence, David couldn't resist watching her eat. He was mesmerized by her full succulent lips as she took each bite, the fall of her chest with every breath. Even though she was wearing a bra tonight, the shirt outlined the curves of her full breasts. With a conscious effort he had to force his hands to behave when all he wanted to do was drop his gyro, stroke her cheekbones, then travel down to the base of her neck and beyond. What was it about Calaine he found so intriguing?

David wiped his mouth with a napkin. He was ashamed of

himself. Here he was trying to undress Calaine when it was obviously the furthest thing from her mind.

She glanced up, straight into his eyes. Finding him watching her, she rolled hers, then looked past his shoulders and out into the backyard.

Her mind was a million miles away and he was certain he knew why. A look of tired sadness passed over her features. He had every intention of erasing that expression.

"Have you made a decision yet about San Antonio?"

When Calaine glanced at him, her expression had softened. "Yes, I'll go with you."

"Good," he replied, trying not to show his excitement at her decision. "How about we leave next Friday and return on Monday?"

She nodded, then reached for her glass. "How long a drive is that?" Twelve, fifteen hours? She couldn't imagine being in the car with him for that many hours. It would be completely unnerving.

David chuckled openly. "Too many to count. We're going to fly."

She sighed with relief, then raised another slice of pizza to her lips. "Fine, just let me know what time so I can book my flight."

"I've already taken care of it," David mumbled with his mouth full.

She stopped chewing to glare at him. "If you had already taken care of the arrangements then why did you even bother to ask me if I would go, much less be ready to leave on Friday?"

David shrugged a broad shoulder. "Out of courtesy."

"Courtesy!" she barked. He had a lot of balls and was still as arrogant as ever. "What if I had said no?"

"Did you?" he challenged.

Heat flared at her cheeks. "No, but that's beside the point."

"No, I think that is the point. I knew you were so anxious to find your mother that nothing was going to stand in the way of this opportunity."

She chewed her pizza in silence, wishing she had a quick retort for his arrogance. Instead, she met the challenging glint in his eyes and said nothing.

David noticed her tightly compressed lips; she was angry with him again. He studied her a few seconds longer before he heard himself say, "Would you like me to apologize?"

Calaine made a sound halfway between a snort and a chuckle. "Would you even know what you'd be apologizing for?"

"No, not really," he admitted honestly.

"Then don't bother." She took one last bite of her pizza, then rose from the table.

He scowled. Apparently his aggressive manner bothered her. He'd assumed she would appreciate the considerate gesture. *You assume too much.* That was the problem with him. He had always taken it for granted that any woman would feel honored to have the great David Soul taking control of the situation. Well, this was one time he had been sadly mistaken.

After wiping his mouth again with a napkin, he reached into a small bag on the table. "Here, I brought you something," he said.

Calaine swung around and noticed the dark bound book in his hand. Her breath caught in her throat and she paused noticeably before asking, "What is it?"

"It's a yearbook."

Calaine didn't even have to ask to know the book was from the school of nursing. She took it from his outstretched hand. Holding it like a newborn baby, she slowly moved into the living room and sat onto the couch.

Her fingers froze as a multitude of emotions vibrated through her body. She felt as if the wind had been knocked from her lungs.

"Are you okay?" David asked.

She hadn't even heard him follow her into the room, nor had she realized he was caressing her cheek. She began to shake. She was scared. Fear of what she might discover in the pages of the book made her blood cold in her veins.

Worried about her reaction, David reached over and draped a comforting arm around her shoulders. Even though he was aware of the burning sensation from the contact, he ignored it. "KeKe, are you sure you're okay?"

She glanced up at him and could see that he was genuinely concerned about her. The look in those gold-green eyes was compassionate. His tenderness brought tears to her eyes. Resting her cheek against his chest, she squeezed her eyes shut and took several seconds to feed off his strength. She was going to get through this. As hard as it might seem, she was going to manage, no matter what she found out.

After a long silent moment, Calaine finally raised her head and nodded. "Yeah, I'll be fine."

Sitting back, David draped his arm across the cushions of the couch, just brushing her shoulders. She flipped through the black and white photos until she came across the faces that had become familiar to her.

Calaine saw David's mom and godmother in several shots together before she found a group photo of the freshman class. It was easy to identify the six women since they were the only African-Americans in the group.

Girl number three, Ursula Winters, had long brown hair pulled up in a loose ponytail, had dark mahogany skin, enormous brown eyes and a generous smile. The woman identified as Dorlinda Meyers was tall, with a raisin-brown complexion, a wide nose and short hair. In the center was Coletta Ross, who was light-skinned, with tight, oriental-looking eyes. On the third row was the final woman, Eunice Roberts, who had allegedly committed suicide. Of medium height and build with a cinnamon complexion and large round topaz eyes, she wore her shoulder length hair in a traditional seventies flip.

Calaine could not pull her gaze away from the photo as she tried to catalog every feature from their hair to their lips.

"One of these women is my mother," she finally whispered. "I just know it."

When David glanced over at her, his heart wrenched at the sight of her misty eyes. He squeezed her hand. "We've got our work cut out," he said, breaking into her thoughts.

Calaine had forgotten he was there. She pulled back to look at him. "We?"

As he leaned closer, the fragrance of his body lingered in her nostrils. "We're in this together."

Closing the book, she shifted from under his arm. Her head came up slowly and she found David watching, waiting for her to speak. "Why are you helping me?"

Eyes fused he replied, "Do you have to ask?"

She swallowed. "Yes."

"Because I want to. I like being around you." He still couldn't explain it but he had a deep, inexplicable desire to do whatever he could for her even though he knew that was the only reason she allowed him around her. What was this really about? Helping an old friend or the challenge of melting her icy heart? He just hadn't quite figured it out yet.

She stared wordlessly at him for several seconds and suddenly felt self-conscious under his watchful eyes. Calaine smoothed down her hair and frowned. "Isn't there some woman you could be spending your time with?"

"This is the second time you have tried in a roundabout way to find out if I'm seeing someone," he replied with dangerous softness.

Her voice was hesitant. "No. I just think there has to be something else you could be doing besides hanging out with me."

"You're right. There is something else I could be doing." David's eyes were fixed on her mouth. He heard the sharp intake of her breath as he scooped Calaine up in his arms and positioned her across his lap.

Her heart galloped, making mincemeat of her willpower. Was he about to kiss her again? She didn't want David to get the impression that he could kiss her whenever he felt the urge. However, despite her best effort, her lips yearned to feel his again. Ever so slowly, she tilted her head and parted her lips.

It occurred to Calaine that she might have lost her mind, but she didn't say one single word to stop David from settling his mouth against hers. After all, she had pretty much given him the green flag. Slanting her mouth, she met his lips eagerly. His soft mustache caused tingles of excitement to race through her like a raging river. This was what she had been wanting all day, no matter how much she had tried to deny it. His kisses were sweet, hot and gentle. As he pulled her snuggly against him, Calaine wrapped her arms around his neck and the kiss deepened.

It had been too long since she had been held by a man. When David traced her lips, she opened for him without a second thought. The feel of his tongue gently sliding into her mouth sent heat soaring through her veins as David explored her with his tongue, she lost control, giving into the need. Her tongue met his every sensual stroke as he tasted and teased. Her toes curled and an empty ache pooled deep inside her. A feverous moan escaped her lips. Only David was capable of kissing her with such mind-shattering tenderness and mastery.

Somehow, his hand slipped under her blouse. He pushed her lacy bra aside to cup the fullness of her breasts. It wasn't until she felt his fingers caress her rock hard nipple that her brain zapped back to reality.

"Don't," she commanded, suddenly anxious to put some distance between them. She tried to scramble off his lap but David held on firmly to her waist, refusing to let go.

"Why?" he asked in a thick breathy voice.

"Because I'm not looking for that," she snapped, annoyed at herself for letting things go as far as they had.

His lean, dark fingers came up to caress her cheek. "Then what are you looking for?"

Seeing the smoldering desire in the depths of his hazel eyes, her heart pumped rapidly. She paused a moment longer, then admitted softly, "I-I'm not sure."

When he motioned her head to his chest, Calaine did not resist.

"Give it time. You'll soon figure out what it is you want from me." He buried his face in her hair and took deep breaths, inhaling her sweet scent. "You're as attracted to me as I am to you. Next time I ask you that question, you'll know the answer."

Lying against his hard chest, Calaine closed her eyes, confused about what she was doing. This was not what she wanted, she told herself. There was nothing going on between them besides a friend providing comfort when she needed it most.

David reached over for the remote and clicked on the television. While they listened to the sounds of Ashanti on BET, she closed her eyes again. In the comfort of his arms, she soon felt drowsy. Her lips curled into a smile as she allowed herself to dream that things were different in her life.

David took a deep breath and tried to keep his emotions under control as he felt her breasts crushed against his chest. Her nipples had hardened. He could feel them. He had to grit his teeth in order to stay in control.

This was what he wanted in his life. This wonderful feeling of holding someone who was special close to him. In a few short days, Calaine had become a part of his life he wanted to explore. Her style and grace were what he needed. Her vulnerability was what he wanted. *What am I saying?* He wanted to be there to see her face when she discovered who her mother was, nothing more…or so he tried to convince himself.

He could not deny that Calaine felt good in his arms. Holding her, he savored the ripe curve of her hips. He could have held her that way all night and never have grown tired but he knew he needed to get away fast if he wanted to hold onto his sanity. He was fighting the need to lower her onto the couch, part her legs and bury himself deep inside of her. Calaine made him feel a sense of deep longing he wasn't yet sure he wanted to feel.

David brushed back several strands of her hair, enjoying the feeling of her velvety smooth skin against his fingertips. "Sweetheart?"

"Uh?"

She snuggled her body closer to him. David took a deep breath as the heat of her body burned through his clothes, causing his loins to go hot and hard.

"Are you falling asleep?"

"No," she denied.

Leaning down, he noticed her lowered lashes were long and curly. "Then what would you call it?"

Her lips dipped into a smile. "I guess I am a little tired." Her voice had a dreamy sound to it.

David dropped a kiss to her forehead, then to the side of her face then traveled down near her ear. With a soft sigh, she threw her head back, giving him access to her neck. He moved to taste the hollow of her throat and realized that again it was growing almost impossible to control himself. "I'm going to go home and let you get some sleep. If I stay any longer I might not be responsible for my actions."

She looked up at him, eyelids heavy, and saw the open emotion smoldering in the depths of his eyes. She made a noise that sounded like a moan, then closed her eyes again, snuggling closer.

David's jaw dropped. He had suddenly realized that Calaine was the most sensuous woman he'd ever met. She had every nerve in his body quivering. He was totally aroused but he wasn't going to take advantage of a vulnerable situation. Instead, he would wait until Calaine was ready. For now, he'd better get away from her fast while he still could.

Standing with her in his arms, he carried her to the front door, where he lowered her gently to her feet. Holding her close he whispered in her hair, "I borrowed that book from the alumni office."

She locked her arms around his waist and tilted her head up to meet his heated gaze. "I promise to take care of it."

"Good." With a groan, his hands came up to caress her face. He captured her lips in another passionate kiss, tasting the sweetness there for a long sensuous minute before he moved to her chin and then her throat. Finally, reluctantly, he broke it off. "Lock up. I'll call you tomorrow."

With a sleepy yawn, she nodded and closed the door behind him.

Calaine strolled to her bedroom. Quickly, she pulled off her clothes and climbed under the covers. It was almost midnight before her mind settled and her eyelids shut only to dream of David.

She missed him already.

CHAPTER EIGHT

That Saturday, David pulled into the long driveway. As he shifted the truck into park, he couldn't stop smiling.

He was finally home.

Through the driver's side window, he stared out at the large, federal style house. It faced the fairway and the view was through mature trees to open, rolling land beyond. Just the other day, he'd sat out on the wide rear deck. Looking out through the veil of leaves had felt like being in a tree house. The privacy and beauty of the setting extended to the community itself.

The house was situated on two acres in Castle Rock Estates, a private lane of ten luxurious custom built homes that climbed into the woods. The surrounding undeveloped land and woods enhanced the feeling of seclusion. The special features of the house included a gourmet kitchen, hardwood floors, high ceilings, arched openings and exquisite exterior stonework.

"Man, are you going to keep gawking at your house all day or are we going to get this truck unloaded before nightfall?"

David grinned over at Kietel Thomas, his frat brother, who was sitting on the passenger side, swallowing the last of several cheeseburgers they had grabbed at a fast food restaurant.

"I'm just doing like you do when you spend hours primping in the mirror," he joked.

Kietel flashed him a quick smile. "Hey, if you looked as good as I do you'd be standing in front of the mirror too." Crumpling up the wrapper, he tossed it in a bag.

"I ain't heard no complaints," David boasted as he climbed out the truck.

"That's 'cause you don't have a woman to complain," Kietel replied as he opened the passenger side door and climbed out.

"Hey, I'm just waiting for that one special lady to come into my life," David returned.

Kietel rumbled with abrupt laughter. "You can't be serious?"

David's expression changed, becoming sober. "I'm definitely serious."

Arms crossed beneath his chest, Kietel stared numbly at his friend with complete surprise freezing his features. "What's gotten into you?"

David shrugged as he reached up to unlock the rear door of the truck. "Maturity, man. I think it's about time I thought about settling down."

"Man, you're trippin'!" Kietel threw his head back and roared again with laughter.

David frowned. He knew better than to expect his homey to believe him. He might as well have held his hands to his ears. The brotha wasn't hearing it!

David glanced over his shoulder, to find Caress and her husband coming up the driveway in a Ford pickup. The back was loaded with stuff that had been stored in her basement for years. After living in a condominium before he returned, David owned barely enough furniture to fill one room.

Caress stepped out of the truck wearing shorts and a skimpy t-shirt. With a tight abdomen and toned legs, she didn't look like a thirty-six-year-old woman with three children.

"Hi, Kie." Her eyes crinkled in a warm smile as she extended her arms and wrapped them around his neck.

Cradling her to his hard torso, Kietel leaned down and planted a kiss on her forehead. "Hey, baby doll." Kietel had been using the nickname for years. From the first time he'd laid eyes on her, he'd believed she was as pretty as a porcelain doll.

Pulling apart, Caress paused to admire David's companion. She'd known him since their college days when the two were getting into trouble. Thirty-year-old Kietel Thomas was a handsome man. He looked like a body builder dipped in rich mocha ice cream. He had a generous mouth and a crooked nose because of his football days. If she'd been five years younger and not already been in love with Leroy, who had been her fiancé at the time, she might have acknowledged his teenage crush. Instead, Kietel had become another little brother to her.

"I haven't run into you lately. Where've you been hiding?"

"Just working," he replied. Glancing over her shoulder, he acknowledged Caress's husband with a warm nod of the head and a friendly, "Whatzup."

While the men began unloading the truck, Caress went into the kitchen to prepare something for lunch.

After two hours of hauling furniture into the house, David went to find something to eat. He moved into the large kitchen. He didn't know why he needed a house with such a large kitchen he would rarely use. It had numerous cherry cabinets, an enormous angled island with a pot rack hanging overhead, beige tile, and a five-burner gas cook top.

David found Caress removing several items from paper grocery bags.

"You didn't have to shop for me," he said although grateful for the gesture.

Caress smiled as she moved over to the refrigerator to put a

109

gallon of milk on the top shelf. "Yes I did. Otherwise you'd be eating out every night." Caress shut the door and turned, holding out a beer.

"What makes you think I still won't be eating out?" he smirked.

She gave him a knowing look as she handed him the can and moved to the island to uncover a pan.

"What's that?" he asked.

"The reason why you won't be eating out." She lifted the foil.

David smiled down at the deep-dish lasagna. His sister's recipe was the best he'd ever tasted. Caress layered it heavily with mountains of different cheeses and her secret meat sauce.

Caress moved over to the stove and stuck the pan in the oven.

"Thanks, sis," he said as he popped the top on the can and took a sip.

"Don't mention it." Caress leaned over and gave him an affectionate kiss on the cheek. A look of motherly concern creased her face. "Now if you'll hurry up and find a woman, I won't have to cook for you."

He pretended panic. "Oh, no!"

Leroy walked into the kitchen with a broad smile. "What's my wife fussing about now?" He kissed her forehead as she reached into the refrigerator and handed him a chilled can of beer.

She shrugged. "I'm not fussing. I just think it's time my brother finds a good woman and settles down."

Leroy looked at David over the top of her head and mouthed, "She's your sister."

Caress knew her husband well and caught him in the act. David chuckled when she swatted him in the arm. With a playful roll of her eyes, she reached for a large tossed salad she had prepared earlier and carried it to the small card table.

Kietel entered, his deep powerful voice carrying easily in the room. "Did someone decide we were taking a break and didn't bother to tell me?"

David jabbed him playfully in the forearm. "I guess that's what happens when you have your own business. You get stuck doing all the work."

Five years ago Kietel had started a local moving company that had since expanded to most of central Missouri. Even though he had a large crew, occasionally he still took on small jobs by himself.

"Remember, this one's a freebie since you were too cheap to hire any help." He glanced around the kitchen. "Although looking at the size of this house, I can see why you couldn't afford my services. Maybe I should have thrown the extra muscle in as a housewarming gift," he joked, since David didn't have enough furniture to fill even half of the moving truck.

The bulk of the load was an old leather living room set, and a dining room table and six chairs that used to belong to his grandparents. The items that Caress had brought were definitely needed.

"I have lasagna warming in the oven and there's salad and breadsticks on the table," Caress said.

"Alrighty." Kietel rubbed his palms together and moved toward the table. Caress stopped him in mid-stride and pointed towards the sink. "Wash your hands first," she ordered.

"Yes, ma'am," he mocked while moving over to the sink. "Anything for lasagna."

"My wife makes the best lasagna in the state." Leroy had just finished washing his hands and was drying them with a paper towel. He then pulled his wife flush against his lean hard body and landed a trail of kisses on her face.

Caress smiled up at her husband with affection, then instructed him to take a seat at the table.

"When was the last time you had a home cooked meal?" she asked Kietel as he took the seat across from Leroy.

"Not since I visited my momma for Christmas," he admitted sheepishly.

Caress tunneled her fingers through her thick shiny curls as she shook her head. "I don't know what the problem is with y'all men. I was just telling my brother that he needs a woman in his life. This place needs a woman's touch."

David leaned against the island and hesitated, knowing where the conversation was heading. "Why can't this just be a bachelor's pad?"

She frowned as she sat down beside her husband. "It's too big for that."

"She does have a point," Kietel instigated.

David was the only one left standing. He gave them both a long penetrating look before responding, "Maybe I just like a lot of space."

Caress's eyes grew wide and confused. "What about the conversation we had the other day? I thought you were ready to settle down? What happened to your interest in Calaine?"

David glanced over at Kietel's curious expression before returning his gaze to Caress. "What happened to brother/sister confidentiality?"

"Who's Calaine?" Kietel asked as he moved to the refrigerator for the bottled water he had stuck in the freezer earlier.

"You remember Calaine, she used to date Mike." Kietel shook his head. "She was skinny with glasses and long hair. She was also roommates with that Delta I used to date, Donna Davidson."

Kietel gave him a skeptical glance. "You've got to be kidding."

"What's wrong with Calaine?" Caress asked with a defensive

expression.

"Not Calaine, Donna," Kietel chuckled. "We used to call her the Virgin Mary. My frat had a bet going. Whoever could score with Donna won the pot."

David rubbed his chin. "Yeah, and no one won. We had collected so much money that by the end of the year we held a big party." He chuckled with fond memories.

Kietel took a thirsty drink before adding, "She wasn't putting out for all the tea in China." Shaking his head, he sat back in his chair. "That girl was definitely a knockout."

"Well, now Calaine's the knockout," David blurted, then realized what he had said.

His friend saw the look in his eye and quirked his eyebrow. "You struck out with one roommate and now you've moved on to the other. I ain't mad atcha."

Caress fingered him lightly on the shoulder. "And what's your problem, Kietel? When are you going to find someone and settle down?"

David snorted rudely. "I think we have a much better chance of hell freezing over."

"True that," Leroy chimed in. He was familiar with both of their track records. Seated next to his wife, he helped himself to the salad.

When Caress leaned back in the chair and let out a long exasperated sigh, David groaned. The debate was on.

David shook his head. His sister was fighting a losing battle. Kietel had a lust for women like the next man, only he sought dinner and occasional sex, not love and marriage. He didn't have time for a serious relationship. All his time and energy were poured into his business. Everything else came second, including women, and he preferred to keep it that way.

Before his sister could begin her big spiel on love and the sacred institution of marriage, David excused himself and moved to the powder room across the hall to wash his hands. While lathering them with soap, he stared out the window over a large Jacuzzi tub at the pond. There was a half mile trail that went around the entire circumference of the man-made structure. He couldn't wait for Calaine to see it. He didn't know why but what she thought of his house was important. He wanted to see the expression on her face as they pulled into his driveway and her smile when she saw the geese swimming in the water.

Drying his hands, David realized he had a serious problem on his hands. He'd found himself thinking about her all day. He couldn't get her off of his mind. He barely remembered loading up the truck or dropping by Furniture World to pick up his new bedroom set. All he'd been able to think about was Calaine and the kiss they had shared. All he wanted to do was hold her in his arms again, feel her slim, lush body pressed against his. He couldn't get that image of her sleeping snuggly in his arms out of his thoughts for anything in the world.

He tucked his hands in the front pockets of his jeans and moved out into the hallway. What was going on? He wished that he could blame it on the fact that he had been without a woman for awhile, but he had gone without one before and he hadn't felt the same burning need. He wanted to hear Calaine's voice, to see her smiling face. It didn't even matter if she was annoyed with him, all that mattered was being with her.

He strolled into a small room at the back of the house that his realtor told him had once been a playroom. He wasn't sure what he was going to do with it. Maybe a playroom for his nieces and nephew wouldn't be a bad idea.

Part of him was still rebelling against the fact that his thinking had become more family-oriented. A little voice was telling him to pull out his little black book and let his fingers do the walking. Kietel had even invited him to a night out on the town. But none of it appealed to him. He would rather spend the evening with Calaine. If not with her, then thinking about her. Even thinking about how he could help her find her mother.

David chuckled with disbelief. It was no wonder Kietel had laughed at him. It wasn't like him to allow a woman to consume his every thought or get under his skin as Calaine had. Now he was hoping to be settled in as quickly as possible so he could give her a call and see how her weekend had gone. He just hoped she hadn't returned to her depressed state. It was amazing how quickly he had grown to care about her.

He did not want her to feel like she was in this alone. As soon as he got his office set up downstairs, he was going to begin researching the names on the Internet.

Staring at his home and its surroundings, he suddenly knew for sure that he had bought the house with every intention of filling it with a family.

The possibility of marriage for him had crossed both his mother's and sister's minds quite often, and of course neither had ever hesitated to express her view. For many years, his mother had been after him to find a nice woman and settle down, but she had never been particularly happy with the types of women she'd seen him with. In retrospect he had to admit that most of them had been spoiled and drop-dead gorgeous. The majority had turned out to be gold diggers. It had been a relief to his mother that he had never taken any of them seriously. Calaine's background and sense of independence made her completely different from the other women who had slipped in and out of his life. He couldn't wait for his mother to meet Calaine. The realization hit him full force and shook him.

His stomach growled, reminding him there was lasagna waiting for him in the kitchen. David moved down the hall and entered just as Kietel roared with laughter.

"Man, check this out! Your sister is trying to hook me up with one of her friends again."

As he moved around the table to his seat, David chuckled. "Caress, don't even go there. The last girl you hooked my boy up with was crazy!"

She graced her brother with an innocent look. "No she wasn't. Mya was just socially challenged."

Shared laughter echoed around the room. While Kietel and Caress started another friendly debate, David fixed his plate, wearing a wide grin.

He was glad to be home.

Calaine spent her Saturday at her parents' house rummaging through their things. By the time the sun had begun to set, she was frustrated. She had found nothing at all pointing to her birth or her mother's identity. Feeling discouraged, on Sunday she decided to pay her uncle a visit.

It was a thirty-minute drive from her driveway to theirs. Thaddeus and his wife Alaina lived near the state capitol in Jefferson City.

Shortly before five o'clock, she pulled in front of the cozy, two-story red brick home. Beautifully maintained, it was in an older established neighborhood where most of the residents were retired.

The front garden had a large oak tree and the petunias on the side of the house had blossomed since her last visit. She saw her aunt among them.

Hearing the car door slam, Alaina looked up. She was a round, petite woman who wore a short, tapered cut for her salt and pepper hair. The effect was dramatic with her round face and pug nose. When Alaina realized it was Calaine, she raised from her kneeling position on the ground. "Hello, dear." Removing her gloves, she moved to Calaine and gave her a warm embrace. "How are you holding up?" she asked as they pulled apart. Her coal black eyes studied her.

Calaine smiled at her lovely aunt. "I'm managing."

Alaina's expression grew sober and concerned. "If you need any help with the house, please let me know."

"I promise." Her eyes misted. Her aunt had always managed to make her feel loved and welcomed.

Hand in hand, they moved into the house, where they found her uncle sitting in the sunroom sipping iced tea and reading the newspaper.

Thaddeus smiled when she entered the room. "There's my KeKe. Come sit down and keep me company." He folded the paper and lowered it to the table.

Calaine leaned slightly over and planted a kiss to her uncle's cheek. "I didn't mean to disturb you. I won't be staying long," she said as she lowered into the seat beside him.

He shook his head, dismissing the idea. "Nonsense, you're always welcomed here. Please stay for dinner."

She glanced from her uncle to her aunt. "Oh no, I don't want to impose. I can eat when I get back home."

Alaina quickly shook her head. "There's no imposition. I made a meal big enough for a football team."

Calaine giggled knowingly. Alaina liked to cook extra and

freeze servings for future meals. "Well in that case, dinner sounds wonderful."

Thaddeus patted her hand. "Good. You could use a little fattening up. You don't look like you've been eating much lately."

Calaine understood their concern. She hadn't realized how much weight she had lost until she climbed on the scale the previous night. It was a shock to discover she had lost almost ten pounds. At one hundred and twenty-two pounds and five-foot seven-inches, she had always been a slim woman, so ten pounds was quite a bit.

"I promise to clean my plate." Though she was teasing, her aunt and uncle both looked pleased.

Alaina left and returned with another glass and a pitcher of iced tea, then retreated to the kitchen to finish preparing dinner.

"What have you been doing?" Thaddeus asked, his eyes sparkling with interest.

Calaine sighed. "I'm still trying to find my mother."

Thaddeus gave her a nervous smile. "Something will turn up eventually."

"Actually, I've been doing quite well. I ran into an old friend of mine and discovered that one of the women in the photograph is his mother." Calaine then explained to him how David had discovered the photo in her office.

He studied her. "You're one determined young lady."

"I've learned from the best." She grinned. With her elbow on the table, she rested her chin in the palm of her hand. "I know it's going to take time but I am certain she's still out there."

"KeKe, I—"

"Please Uncle Thaddeus, don't say it. My mind is already set. I have to find out the truth."

Thaddeus took a sip of his tea, then stared at her for the longest time before saying, "I hate to see you get hurt. Sometimes people just don't want to be found."

Calaine disagreed. "And sometimes they do. I won't be able to rest until I know for sure."

Seeing the stubborn set of her jaws, he simply nodded. "I've passed the word around at the hospital. Hopefully someone will remember something. Columbia's small. I'm sure someone is bound to know how to get in touch with at least one of them."

"I hope so." She poured herself a glass of tea. "David borrowed a copy of their yearbook from the nursing school, so I now have the names of each of the women. He's going to San Antonio on Friday to attend his sister's graduation, and I've agreed to go with him so I can speak to his mother and Wanda."

Thaddeus ran a hand over his face as he sighed. "Then that leaves four women."

Ursula, Coletta, Dorlinda and Eunice, Calaine thought.

She took a long drink before saying, "David is going to search on the Internet and see what he can come up with."

Thaddeus studied her quietly for several seconds before asking, "How do you feel about spending the weekend with this man?"

Calaine sat down her glass and deliberately looked out at the rose garden behind them. "What do you mean?"

"I mean, is there something going on between the two of you?"

"N-no, nothing at all. He's j-just helping me," she stuttered.

Thaddeus raised a brow at her rapid response. He also knew she only stuttered when she was nervous. "You're not fooling yourself, are you?" he asked watching for her reaction.

"Absolutely not. I don't have time for a relationship right now."

He shook his head at her protest. "That's not what I'm saying. I just think you're fooling yourself. I saw the way your face lit up when you spoke of him."

Thaddeus captured Calaine's hand. "You have every right to

get on with your life. No one will blame you if you do. You're a young beautiful woman with her entire life ahead of her. I don't want you to become so consumed with finding your mother that you put everything else on hold."

"How can I ever have a relationship with a man without knowing who I really am?"

"You're Calaine Hart. What else is there to know?"

Her expression narrowed. "Uncle Thaddeus, you know what I mean. I need to know where I came from. What if I want to start a family?"

"I wish you would. Alaina and I aren't getting any younger. We're depending on you to make us grandparents," he replied with a lopsided grin.

She smiled.

As he released her hand, his expression sobered again. "KeKe, I want to see you happy."

"Happy or happily married?" she teased.

"Both would be nice," he admitted with a sheepish grin.

Tapping a fingernail lightly on the table, she said, "I would like to talk to Aunt Greta and see if she can shed a little light on my past."

Thaddeus frowned. He had never cared for the woman. "When was the last time you talked to her?"

"It's been awhile. She hasn't taken my mother's death well. I thought about driving to Kansas City to see her."

A troubled expression crossed his face.

At that moment Alaina called for them to come and eat. The two left the sun porch and moved to the dining room where Calaine found her aunt had fixed her favorites: pot roast and mashed potatoes with homegrown string beans and her special made-from-scratch biscuits. After eating fast food and microwave meals all week, she looked forward to a home-cooked meal for a change.

She turned to her aunt with her brown eyes wide with surprise. "How did you know I was coming?"

"Call it an auntie's instincts." Alaina leaned over and draped an arm around her waist. "We haven't seen you in a while. I figured you'd start feeling guilty and come by sooner or later. I was hoping it was today. If not, we would have had to eat all this pot roast by ourselves."

Calaine's eyes became misty at the love she received in this house. How could she have ever felt as if she were alone in the world? If she never found her mother, it was good to know that there were at least two people in her life that adored her.

Calaine stayed long enough for dessert and a game of chess with her uncle before she kissed them both goodbye and promised to call before she left on Friday.

Calaine pulled her car into her garage, then lowered the electric door. When she turned off the car, she was met with a wave of silence, the same sound she would hear when she moved inside the house. She sighed, then reached across the seat to retrieve her purse before getting out. Entering through the side door, she put her keys and purse on the table and moved to check her messages, only to find there were none. Who were you expecting to call? she asked herself. David? She didn't bother to answer; instead, she climbed the stairs to her room and slid her feet out of her tennis shoes and into a pair of pink slippers.

Now what? she wondered. Was she going to spend the rest of the evening staring at the photograph or spend another solitary night in front of the television eagerly searching for something to occupy her mind? Or would her mind be occupied with someone?

"This is ridiculous," she mumbled under her breath and rose. She refused to waste another minute thinking about David.

He wasn't the type of man any woman in her right mind would trust with her heart. So why couldn't she get him out of her head?

She scowled. It was because of that kiss, or kisses, for that matter. She had made the mistake not once but twice.

Angry with herself, she went into the kitchen and looked inside the refrigerator for her last tropical wine cooler. She hoped it would help her sleep. She had no time to waste thinking about David. She already had enough on her mind.

Besides, he was only supposed to help her find her mother, she reminded herself. Nothing more. Yet she found herself yearning for something she didn't have. A lover, a husband, a friend, someone to love her unconditionally, someone to comfort her in her time of need. *Like now.* It just disturbed her that the only possibility she could think of was David.

David told himself the logical thing to do was to close his eyes and go to sleep, but lying in a brand new king size bed alone was not easy.

Several hours later, he was still wide-awake. He eventually got up and went to take a shower. However, standing under a spray of cold water did nothing to stop his brain from jumping from one scenario to the next, with images of a naked Calaine so vivid he almost believed they were real. He imagined her lying beneath him, her legs wrapped around his waist, calling out his name. Rock hard and frustrated, he climbed out of the shower and toweled off. He slipped into a pair of boxers and went out onto the deck. Rearing back in the chair, he stared up at the stars twinkling in the sky. The moon was full. Other than his uneven breathing, the only sound was the crickets below.

Always having had his pick of women, David found himself puzzled. He was more drawn to Calaine than to any other woman he had ever dated. Something had swept over him, had quietly snuck up on him and refused to leave. It was such an unfamiliar feeling that his first reaction was to take his bachelorhood and run with his tail tucked between his legs. However, another part of him wanted to see it through to the end, whatever "it" was. Besides, he couldn't bail out now even if he wanted to. He had made a promise to help Calaine find her mother.

And a promise was a promise.

CHAPTER NINE

"IDX experience seems to be the most important qualification," Calaine informed her staff as her gaze swept around the table. They had spent the better part of the morning going over the proposed contract with the university. After addressing every issue with a fine tooth comb, they could identify that the teaching hospital's largest demand was for qualified receptionists for the over two dozen clinics.

Sherrie sat back in her seat and relaxed. "Yeah, but finding people with IDX is going to be difficult because anybody who already has hands-on experience scheduling appointments is definitely not unemployed." Her professionally-waxed eyebrows shifted slightly when she saw doubt register on her co-workers' faces. "Calaine said so herself. SOS can't keep those employees. By the time the clinics have spent hours training them to use their system they have already made the decision to keep them."

"So how about partnering with the hospital's training and development department? We could ask them to train our temporaries to use IDX," Amber suggested with the usual twinkle in her blue eyes.

Sherrie quickly agreed. "It isn't a bad idea. SOS sends their employees for training. I don't see why they won't let us send ours. After all, the computer training is to benefit the hospital."

"I like that idea, but I'll have to run it by Human Resources."

Calaine had been making notes of all their suggestions on a legal pad. All changes and additions would be drafted tomorrow and sent by carrier on Friday. "Okay, anything else?" she asked, looking around the table. When they each shook their heads no, she nodded. "Good, then let's move on. What else do we need to talk about?"

Sherrie looked down at her notes. "We've nominated Janet Jones as our employee of the month."

Calaine's gaze widened with approval. "Wonderful choice." Janet was a long time employee who had been assigned to the courthouse for almost six months.

Dropping her pen, she reached for her coffee cup. The employee of the month program had been implemented a year ago and had thus far proven to be quite successful. Employees were given an engraved plaque and dinner for two. In addition, their picture was included in the monthly newsletter. "What kind of gift certificate are we giving out this month?" she asked as she took a sip.

"How about Olive Garden?" Amber suggested.

Tracy's lips thinned noticeably. "We did that last time. We haven't used Red Lobster in a while."

When the others agreed, Sherrie nodded. "Sounds good."

Calaine leaned back in her chair and listened to Debbie as she went over the prospective businesses she had solicited the prior week and the type of employees used in each department.

"Calaine," Norma intruded over the intercom. "You have a call on line three. He says it's important."

Calaine lowered the cup to the saucer, then moved to answer the telephone sitting on a table in the corner. "Calaine Hart speaking."

"Hi, beautiful."

"Hello." She blushed despite her best intentions not to. She wanted to be mad that he was calling her when she was in the middle of a meeting but she was in such a good mood today that not even David Soul could ruin it.

"Sorry I told your receptionist that little white lie, but I have something I know you'll want to see. Are you free for lunch?"

She closed her eyes briefly, pleased at his offer. The weekend had been a long one with David constantly on her mind. Even though she would never admit it, she had missed him.

Glancing down at the slender gold watch on her arm, Calaine smiled. It was barely eleven o'clock. She still had plenty of time to go over rates for the next fiscal year and make any changes long before the day was over. "Lunch would be fabulous. I should be ready around one."

"I'll see you then."

As he said goodbye, the deep sensual tone of his voice caused her to tingle. When she turned to face her staff, there was no way to mask the effect his call had had on her. Her staff definitely noticed. The table had grown quiet and all eyes were on her.

"There's only one thing that can cause that kind of glow and that's a man," Sherrie joked.

Calaine blushed openly but remained quiet. She wasn't in the habit of sharing her personal life with her coworkers. She did, however, grin and say, "Let's resume our meeting because I have a date."

David pulled in front of the building at one o'clock sharp to find Calaine already standing outside. As she moved towards his car, he felt a tightness in his chest. He studied her slender body. Her exquisite figure was nicely outlined in a beige rayon pants suit, which was accessorized with brown pumps and a matching clutch purse. He forced his eyes away and jumped out of the car so he could open the door.

Calaine greeted him with a wide, genuine smile that made his heart flip-flop. "Hey."

"Hey yourself." Latching onto her waist, he brushed a light, gentle kiss across her cheek, then reluctantly released her to open the passenger side door. He placed a hand to her elbow and guided her as she slid into the car. Once she reached for her seatbelt, David shut the door and moved around to the other side. Climbing in, he started the car.

"Where are we going?" Calaine asked once he pulled away from the curb.

Giving her a sidelong glance, he suggested G&D Steakhouse.

"Good choice." Nothing beats the taste of their charbroiled steaks, melt-in-your-mouth baked potatoes with lots of butter and sour cream, and their fabulous Texas toast.

Calaine turned her head and stared out the side window. David had the air conditioner on and the scent of his cologne was prominent. She closed her eyes briefly and inhaled. The smell was so male, so David.

When they reached a red light, David reached into the back seat for a manila folder and handed it to her.

She glanced down at it briefly, then over at him, her brow drawn in a puzzled look. "What's this?"

The light turned green. David accelerated then pulled his eyes away from the road long enough to say, "I have a graduate student working in my department who's a computer guru. He took each of the four women's names and ran a search on the Internet. I don't know how he did it but he came up with several possible matches."

If she hadn't already been seated her legs would have certainly collapsed. Calaine's hands trembled as she opened the folder and tried to focus on the papers in her lap. Lost in her thoughts it took her a moment before she spoke again in a soft far off voice, "I've got my work cut out."

Pulling up to another traffic light, David took her hand, drawing her attention to his compelling eyes. He grimaced as he read the faint traces of pain lingering in hers. "*We* have our work cut out."

Calaine was quiet as he continued to gaze at her with such intensity it astounded her.

"I told you we were in this together and I meant it," he assured her.

Calaine hesitated then nodded. When he squeezed her hand, she had to blink back the tears that clouded her vision. David's simple words touched her deeply. It pleased her more than she would have ever imagined that he was willing to hang in there until the very end. *Then what will happen?* she asked herself.

Just watching him from the corner of her eyes, caused her hormones to kick into gear. His hand on hers had sent a thrill so intense that she would have believed his fingers were magical. It was as if he had cast a spell over her. Had he felt it too? She thought she'd seen in his eyes a reflection of what she was feeling.

She glanced down at his big strong hand that made her feel safe, marveled at its gentleness as he continued to caress her skin. She didn't pull her hand back. Instead, her fingers tightened around his, enjoying the feel of his calloused palm as they pulled into the K-mart shopping center parking lot.

David dropped her hand only long enough to climb out of the car and open the door for her. As soon as the door shut behind her, he reached out and caught her fingers in his, tugging her in tightly against him. He then draped his arm around her waist and steered her towards the restaurant.

They both ordered KC strip steaks medium well, baked potatoes and an extra slice of Texas toast. Trays in hand, David gave her
the honor of leading them to a booth in the corner. Once they settled in their seats, Calaine opened the folder again. She stared down
at the list of women from all areas of the country.

"Maybe we need to narrow our list down to just the three
women and investigate Eunice at a later date," she suggested.

David sat back against the cushioned seat and crossed his feet
underneath the table. "I think we still need to investigate her. Just
because she's dead doesn't mean she wasn't your mother."

Glancing up from the pages, Calaine ran her fingers nervously
through her hair. "How would we research someone who is dead?"

David shrugged matter-of-factly. "It's public record. For a min-
imal fee, we can get the information off the computer. There's also
the possibility that we might locate a family member."

Calaine nodded, unable to speak, so full of emotion at his act
of kindness. To her relief a server arrived with their plates.

After he returned carrying a bottle of A-1 sauce and left again,
David reached for her hand. "Hey, everything is going to be all
right, just wait and see. We are going to find your mother." His gaze
was full of promises.

She smiled across the table at him, then carved into her steak
and found it as tender and mouthwatering as ever.

Sitting across from her, David caught a whiff of her perfume.
While Calaine ate her food, he discreetly studied how beautiful she
was. His eyes lingered on the length of her lashes, the curve of her
cheekbones, the delicate bones of her jaw. He wanted to pull her
into his arms again.

David bit into his toast, not liking how out of control he was.
He forced his attention away from her face and down to the food on
his plate. However, it was only a matter of seconds before he was

watching her eat again. Calaine caught him staring, flushed and looked down at her plate again. Regarding her over his glass, he asked, "Have you started packing?"

She shook her head. "Not yet."

"Mom says it has been pretty hot lately so dress comfortably."

"I'll keep that in mind," she replied quietly between bites.

Calaine tried to ignore his well-built body but it was virtually impossible. His jacket he had removed and had left it lying across the back seat of his car. A cream button-down shirt outlined his broad shoulders and forearms. She didn't dare look at him for long. His lean, muscled body made her tingle and remember how it had felt to be held against every inch of his fabulous frame.

She was grateful for everything David had done for her. But was it only gratitude she was feeling? Something about him instilled total trust. *Unbelievable.* David Soul was the last person she would have predicted a woman could trust. He had changed. She could feel it.

Calaine tried to tell herself that she would probably feel just as attracted to any handsome man. After all, she hadn't been sexually involved for almost a year. It just happened to be David she had been around a lot lately, so it was only natural to be affected by him. Only she was beginning to think that her emotions ran deeper than that.

Glancing up again, Calaine found his eyes still fixed intently on her face. It was so hard to concentrate on anything except him when he was sitting so close. His every movement, his every breath was a distraction.

She raised an eyebrow and swallowed a mouthful of potatoes. "What are you looking at?"

"Nothing." His eyes danced and she could see mischievous humor playing in their depths.

She set her fork down and folded her arms across her chest. "Are you going to tell me or not?"

"The real question is, do you really want to know?" A seductive, teasing smile set her nerve endings to tingling.

"I wouldn't be asking if I didn't."

David leaned back and folded his hands behind his head. The muscles of his arms bunched under the fabric of his shirt. "You are so pretty."

The smile that overtook his features made Calaine's insides tremble, but she tried to laugh it off. The compliment was more intoxicating than fine wine. She peered up at him from lowered lashes. "Pretty? What happened to beautiful?" She grinned playfully at him.

David laughed aloud.

For the next half hour, Calaine put her worries aside and allowed herself to relax and enjoy her time with David. He was so handsome, and when she was near him like this, she felt herself drawn to the intense pull of his energy, his security. He didn't have to do or say anything special. That frightened her the most.

On the drive back, she was quiet as they listened to Jill Scott. A warm pleasant feeling passed through her and she exhaled a deep breath. When they pulled up in front of her building, she said nothing for a long moment. "So where do I begin?" Calaine finally said.

David reached for the folder, removed several pages, then handed the folder back to her. "How about we split the list in half?"

Her eyes misted and she blinked rapidly as she agreed. "Okay."

David climbed out of the car and came around to open the door for her. Calaine rose and their eyes fused. When she saw his eyes move to her lips, she froze. David stepped forward and they were standing so close their shoes were touching. He was so close she could feel the heat of his body, smell his spicy scent.

David drew her nearer and kissed her with a ferocity that made her feel she was drowning. Her right hand rose and rested lightly on his chest. Parting her lips, she allowed herself to react. Fire swept though her, commanding her to erase her apprehensions and succumb to the attraction. She tilted her head back further, giving him total access to her mouth. Somehow her arms wound around his neck, urging him to deepen the kiss. David's tongue slipped inside. A groan rumbled in his throat and she kissed him back, answering his longing. Calaine savored the sweet sensuous taste as their tongues merged in a passionate dance. However, remembering they were outside in a public parking lot, Calaine ended the kiss as quickly as it had begun. She pulled back from him breathing heavily and met the dazed look in his eyes. A look so intense she suddenly felt weak in her knees.

"Thanks again." That was the only thing she could think to say.

David pulled her close again and buried his face in her hair. "You don't have to keep thanking me," he whispered.

"Yes I do," she insisted.

Loosening his hold, he looked down into her face. "All right then, how about doing me a favor?" he asked, pinning her with a gaze so sharp it made her head spin.

She smiled easily. "Sure, anything."

He was still staring deeply into her eyes when he replied, "See a movie with me tomorrow night."

"A movie," Calaine laughed. She had thought he was going to ask her to go home with him so he could make wild passionate love to her. *Stop it!* She couldn't believe she was even considering such a thing.

David pulled her closer. "Yes. When was the last time you saw a movie?"

She took a moment to think, then shook her head. "It's been a long time."

"Then it's settled." He released her. "I'll pick you up at eight."

She giggled. "You haven't even given me a chance to say yes."

His lips met hers, warm and persuasive, receiving her unspoken answer. "You need to start finding time for yourself and I am just the man to make sure that happens." His tone left little room for argument. He winked, climbed back in his car then drove off.

The next morning Calaine walked out of the salon into warm May sunshine, feeling like a new woman. She felt vibrant and more alive than she'd felt in…how long? Weeks? Months? Nevertheless, it was a good feeling. If this was what happened after spending a few hours with David, then she was going to enjoy it and accept their relationship for whatever it was. She smiled and closed her eyes. His patience and words of encouragement had lifted her spirits and had made her feel like a woman.

Stopping at the St. Louis Bread Factory, she lingered over her lunch, enjoying her broccoli cheese soup while thinking about him. When David was around, she somehow forgot about her problems and thought only about what was happening between them. Maybe her uncle was right. Maybe it was time for her to live her own life. One thing was for certain: she was attracted to David, no matter how much she tried to deny it.

David arrived promptly at eight, dressed comfortably in another pair of blue jeans that framed his muscular legs. This time, however, he was wearing running shoes. She had also decided on a pair of jeans and tennis shoes that she matched with a white blouse. Knowing that the theatre temperature had a tendency to be a little brisk, she slipped a blue button-down sweater over it.

They drove south of town to the Hollywood Theatre where they decided to see a new action movie. David loaded down their arms with popcorn, sodas and candy. During the movie, he held her hand and she did not object to the contact; in fact, she embraced it.

When the movie was over, they drove to the Outback Steakhouse. After gorging on popcorn and candy neither of them had much of an appetite so they ordered frozen drinks and a dozen Buffalo wings. The two talked about everything from life after college to where they planned to be in five years.

"Church's Chicken?" She gaped with the drinking straw between her lips. "I can't believe you want to buy a chicken franchise."

David nodded and reached for another wing. "Why not? We have just about every other restaurant in Columbia. Why not another chicken house? Kentucky Fried Chicken would be the only other competition." He swallowed down a bite with a glass of water.

Calaine reached for her napkin. "Why not Popeye's?"

He shook his head. "Don't you remember? We already had one and it didn't last, although I strongly believe the location was the problem."

"Church's wings look as if they've been injected with steroids," she said, sipping her drink.

David chuckled and nodded his head. "That's true, but they are definitely tasty."

Calaine pushed her plate aside and crossed her arms on top of the table as she watched him devour another wing. "I can tell you love chicken."

They shared a laugh. David wanted to lean across the table and kiss her. To resist temptation he leaned back and stirred his drink with his straw. "I love chicken but not as much as I love looking at you."

Calaine peered at him through narrow eyes. His compliment made her insides quiver. "Always the charmer."

"That's me. Charming, sexy and a wonderful lover. How about we go back to your house and prove it?"

Calaine launched a chicken bone at David and he ducked just in time.

"Hey, you can't blame a brother for trying," he chuckled.

They would have sat there all night if their server hadn't pointed to her watch, indicating closing time.

David was in no rush to end the evening. He suggested they take a stroll and Calaine agreed. Holding hands, they walked across campus while she talked about life since her parents' deaths and the void she had felt ever since.

They walked through the Francis Quadrangle, the symbolic center of Mizzou campus. It was located behind Jesse Hall, a large administrative building constructed of red brick. Its dome was one of the most recognizable landmarks in Missouri. Deciding to take a moment to rest, they took a seat on a bench near a set of six tall columns, the most prominent feature of the quadrangle. There was also an art and archeology museum, which had been her mother's favorite.

"I guess if my life had been different I wouldn't be so interested in finding my biological mother. Sometimes I feel so guilty as if I'm betraying my parents."

Still holding her hand, David caressed the back of her fingers with his thumb. "It's only natural to be curious. If it were me, I would do the same. Besides, your mother wouldn't have told you if she hadn't wanted you to find out the truth."

Calaine simply nodded.

They were silent as they stared up at the star-studded sky, both lost in their own thoughts. David moved closer and draped an arm around her, and Calaine rested her head against him. To her amazement, David began to sing Debarge's "Time Will Reveal." As the words to the song poured out with rich clarity, she raised her head in amazement. She had forgotten about his beautiful tenor voice. Now she remembered that David had once sung at a talent show in college and had every woman in attendance dropping to her knees.

Calaine gaped and tried to ignore the effect the sound had on her insides. "Oh, my God! I used to love that song."

"I know. I remember when you used to play it over and over again on your stereo."

She shook her head, still in awe. "You still have such an amazing voice."

"Thank you." David leaned forward and kissed her forehead. His gaze lingered, taking in the shape of her eyes and the curve of her face. His fingers spread and grazed the silky flesh of her cheek. She was ready when their lips met. The kiss was brief but just long enough to cause her pulse to race.

"I want to show you something," David whispered against her nose.

Calaine nodded.

They walked back to his car with his arm around her waist and hers around his. Then they made the 15-minute drive to his house.

"It's beautiful," she cooed as they climbed out of the car.

As he led her through the house, Calaine took the time to appreciate the elegance of the rooms. She moved through a large two-story foyer to the living room on the right, which led into a formal dining room. Though most of the house was empty, the parts that weren't reflected his taste — rich dark woods, dark greens and burgundies. David led her to the family room, which featured a fireplace and a 19-foot ceiling. Columns framed the wide entryway. The room was warm and inviting as well as dramatic. To her right french doors opened to the kitchen and breakfast area.

He then led her upstairs to the master suite. It had the ambience of a luxurious hotel suite—very large and private—with a sitting room and a large bathroom with a separate shower as well as his and her sinks. The large Jacuzzi tub was big enough to bathe a baby elephant.

However, it was where he slept that had all her attention. The king size bed had a massive mahogany headboard. An image of David stretched out on the bed wrapped in nothing but a silk sheet made her mouth grow dry and her palms sweaty.

Calaine wasn't sure how long she stared at the bed before David came up behind her and wrapped his arms around her middle. Fingers gentle but firm tugged her around until she faced him. His hands circled the back of her neck; his thumb stroked the delicate lines of her face. The light caresses sent tingling waves clear down to her toes. Gazing up at him, she saw the fire burning in the depths of his eyes.

"You're the most intriguing woman I have ever met," he murmured.

Calaine was speechless. She didn't offer any resistance when David pulled her to him and covered her mouth with his.

The kiss was gentle yet powerful, his lips warm and inviting. Abandoning herself to the whirl of sensations, she followed his lips mindlessly. Her arms snaked around his neck, her fingers gliding in between the locs of his hair. From a long ways off, she heard David moan as he pulled her snugly against him. She felt the tightening muscles of his chest under the crisp fabric of his shirt and registered his maleness throbbing against her thighs.

She parted her lips and his tongue slid into her mouth. Calaine found herself lost to overwhelming passion, meeting each of his thrusts with a stroke of her own.

Somewhere during the drugging kisses, they made their way over to his bed and Calaine found her body stretched out beneath his. She could feel him in every cell of her body and his hardness pressed against her inner thigh. She had no desire for him to move. Her body was burning with fire as David's mouth moved from her lips, searing a path down to the sensitive place at her throat. Hearing the moans escape her lips, he loosened the buttons of her blouse, exposing her breasts. His fingers slipped beneath her satin bra to caress them. Calaine was shocked by her own eager response to him as she arched her body up to meet his touch. He stroked her nipples until he brought them to throbbing fullness.

Just when the world was spiraling away out of control the telephone rang. Holding her tightly, David buried his face at her neck and breathed a kiss, making no effort to answer the phone.

Calaine, weak and lightheaded, clung to him. "Aren't you going to answer it?" she asked with deep uneven breaths.

"They'll have to leave a message. I'm busy," he murmured as his lips traveled to her neck.

The answering machine finally picked up and Calaine listened to David instruct his callers to leave a message. At the sound of the beep, she heard a woman's voice. "David, this is Lorene. Give me a call when you get in tonight."

Calaine stiffened as she suddenly realized where she was and what she was doing.

David sensed the change in her. "What's wrong?" he asked as he stared down at her.

"Nothing," she squirmed. "Can I please get up?"

David rose, not sure what had just happened except that his realtor had left a message on his machine. Could she be jealous? "That was my real estate agent you just heard."

Calaine sat up and commenced to re-button her blouse. "You don't have to explain. It's really none of my business."

He stood over her, annoyed by her behavior. "Then what is the problem?"

"I just think things were getting a little out of hand," she murmured, unable to look at him.

David took her hand, pulled her up from his bed, then placed a hand under her chin, forcing her to look at him. "I'm sorry you feel that way. I quite enjoyed myself."

Calaine pursed her lips.

David gave a ragged sigh and lowered his hand. "I would never do anything to you unless it was mutual. No pressures, no demands, nothing."

Calaine simply said, "I know."

On the ride back she was quiet and David couldn't figure out for the life of him what he had done except want her with a hunger that had exceeded any he had ever experienced. He didn't want to pressure her but there was only so much a man could take.

When he pulled in front of her house, he helped her out of the car and escorted her to the door. He leaned down and kissed her gently on the lips, then replied, "I'm officially putting the ball in your court." Without waiting for her response, he turned and walked away.

CHAPTER TEN

The following evening, Calaine left work at five-thirty and steered her car onto I-70 towards Kansas City. Aunt Greta had finally contacted her. Instead of calling Calaine at home, she had left a message on her voice mail at work, saying she needed Calaine to drop by her house around seven. Her tone had been so emotionless it had sent a chill down Calaine's spine. *What does she want to talk about?* The question tore at her insides. Maybe, just maybe, she was finally ready to talk to about the past.

She caught herself driving well over the speed limit. She couldn't help herself. Her mind was a crazy mixture of fright and anticipation. She was confident her aunt knew something that she did not, yet she was afraid of what she was about to reveal.

At exactly seven o'clock, Calaine pulled into the driveway that curved in a semicircle in front of the house... well, baby mansion would be a better description. The large French style house was fabulous; the grounds were country club impeccable.

Besides inheriting money from her father, Greta had married a computer genius who had designed a financial database that was being used by corporations all around the country. Her dearly departed husband had believed his wife deserved only the finest things in life and had had a massive stroke at fifty trying to give them to her. Greta never remarried; instead, she had spent the last ten years keeping her husband's memory alive.

Calaine shut the car door and climbed the steps to a pair of huge mahogany doors. Before she raised her hand to ring the bell, the right side door swung open. A round ebony woman with gentle brown eyes greeted her with a smile.

"Hi, Augustine." Calaine returned the smile, then wrapped her arms around the housekeeper's waist.

"Calaine, dear, it's so good to see you again," she said as they parted.

"Thank you. How's my aunt doing?"

Her expression turned solemn. "She's been having a hard time since your mother's death. How have you been getting along?"

"I'm taking it one day at a time."

Augustine nodded, understanding. She had lost her husband of thirty years almost two years ago. "She's in the parlor waiting for you."

Augustine moved aside and Calaine stepped into the white marble foyer. She glanced at the twenty-foot ceiling and the antiques prominently displayed along both sides of the long hall-way.

She hated the house, as much if not more than the home she had grown up in. She remembered that when she was a child, her aunt had made it clear that her house was not meant for nosey little people. Being the curious person that she was, Calaine had always been fascinated by the array of artifacts. As a result, she remembered having her hands spanked on several occasions.

Calaine moved towards a closed door at the far right of the foyer. She paused and took a deep breath before she pushed the door open.

The room was like a large library with oak paneled walls and shelf after shelf of books she had never been allowed to touch. Her uncle had been a collector of rare edition books. Just two hardbound copies would have covered Office Remedies' payroll for a month.

The furniture was all drab shades of brown. A large picture window was the only thing that brightened up the room, providing a view of the colorful garden beyond. To the far left a birch fireplace held a carefully-arranged stack of logs. Above it hung a large portrait of Aunt Greta and Uncle Bernard on their wedding day.

Stepping further into the room, she found her aunt sitting in the corner sipping a cup of tea.

"Well, don't just stand there! Come on in," Greta fussed.

Calaine moved across the gleaming wood floor to the Queen Anne chair where her aunt was sitting. Greta offered a wrinkled cheek and Calaine kissed her lightly. Then her aunt signaled her to take a seat across from her.

Greta was a short, plump woman with silver gray hair, dark skin and round amber eyes. She had high cheekbones and a wide nose. She wasn't a beautiful woman, and her well-bred qualities were her greatest assets. As usual, she was dressed tastefully in an outdated but nevertheless expensive black suit. A long string of pearls hung from her neck and gems graced each of her fingers. She smiled at her niece, but her smile was a trifle thin.

"Aunt Greta, how have you been?" Calaine asked pleasantly.

"I've been better. I just wish my dear Bernard was still here. My arthritis has been acting up something terrible. He always knew how to make things better."

Calaine nodded. That explained the strong scent of Ben Gay. "Have you talked to your doctor about it?"

"What do they know?" she said, frowning. "They're just a bunch of quacks trying to take rich folks' money."

Calaine watched thoughtfully as Greta's chin set in a stubborn line. Her aunt believed that other than her arthritis, she had never been sick a day in her life because she had stayed away from doctors. Bernard had been the only person able to convince her to see one when her arthritis had begun.

"Aunt Greta, I've been wanting to talk with you," she said, hoping to get right to the point and make her visit as short as possible.

Her aunt raised a hand signaling her to remain quiet as a man stepped into the room. Calaine swung around as he moved towards them carrying a briefcase.

Greta lowered her cup to a silver-serving tray. "Anthony, thank you for coming." She gave him a genuine smile. "This is Calaine."

He turned to her and put her at ease with a friendly smile. Olive-skinned with brown eyes, he had dark ebony hair graying at his temples. "A pleasure to meet you, Ms. Hart, " he said holding out his hand. "I'm Anthony Conley, your family lawyer."

"Nice to meet you." Calaine shook his hand and forced a smile until he released her hand. Then she looked to her aunt for an explanation. "What is this all about? I met with my parents' lawyer months ago."

"Please, Anthony, take a seat," Greta said before turning to gaze at her niece. "Anthony has been representing the Graves family for years. This involves *my* family's money, not your father's."

Calaine sat quietly with her hands in her lap, waiting for her aunt to enlighten her.

"As you know, I've been mourning my sister's death for several months, but I know some things can't be put off any longer." She looked to Anthony and nodded, giving him permission to speak.

Clearing his throat, Anthony reached into his briefcase before he finally spoke. "I'm here to read your mother's last will and testament."

Calaine sat there, blank, surprised and very shaken. How... why hadn't her aunt prepared her for such a visit?

As if she could read her mind, Greta replied, "Dear, I know this comes as a shock, but there is no way to put this off any longer."

She was too surprised to do more than nod and in a daze listen to the lawyer read her mother's will.

It seemed like something out of a nightmare. Her mother had been richer than she had ever known. Calaine had known the Graves family had money but never the fortune that the lawyer disclosed. A summer home in Jamaica, land on the East Coast, a winter home on the West Coast, stocks, bonds, and cash, all totaling over five million dollars. It was too much to absorb.

With a jerk she came back to the present, to her aunt asking crossly, "Calaine, are you listening?"

"I'm sorry." Flabbergasted, the words lodged in her throat.

Mr. Conley lowered the papers and gave her a sympathetic smile. "I'm sure it's a lot to adjust to in one day. I'm aware you knew nothing about your mother's wealth."

Calaine nodded, meeting his kind gaze. "You're right, I didn't."

Aunt Greta rudely cleared her throat. "Very well. Now that we've gotten that out of the way, we need to discuss another matter."

The lawyer looked uncomfortable. "Would you like me to leave the two of you alone?"

"No, you need to hear this too," Greta drawled.

As she spoke, Greta leaned over and poured herself another cup of tea. "You asked me months ago about your mother and at the time my mind was in a turmoil. I couldn't bear to speak ill of my sister, not while her grave was still warm. Unfortunately, now I have no choice." Meeting the fear in Calaine's eyes, a shadow of annoyance crossed her face. "You indeed are not my sister's child. Your father forced her to either take you in or shame the family with a scandal. She had no choice but to become your mother."

Calaine flinched at her sharp words. Watching her spoon sugar into her cup, she asked, "Did she tell you who my mother was?"

Greta looked appalled. "Of course not. She tried to pretend you were her own child, that what your father had done never really happened."

Calaine was stunned by the harsh reality. Her aunt's stare was brutal and unfriendly.

Greta took several sips of her tea before setting the cup back on the saucer. "I have asked Anthony here today because I think we need to do what my sister never had a chance to do."

Calaine turned to Mr. Conley. Sympathy mingled in his glance. "And what is that?" she asked.

Aunt Greta intervened. "Relinquish her estate to the family."

Her aunt's tone aroused and infuriated her. "You mean to you."

"I have to admit that I'm the last of our generation. However, I have three children and several grandchildren who are entitled to Katherine's estate."

Just thinking about her three spoiled cousins, who'd never had to lift a finger in their lives and who could never do any wrong, caused Calaine to raise her chin defensively. "She was still my mother."

"Not by blood," Greta said with unwelcome frankness. "And that's what we are talking about today. Our family line has been pure for generations and it's my duty to continue that. My sister would have wanted it that way."

"Then why did she leave everything to me?" Calaine challenged.

She gave a dismissive wave. "She wasn't thinking straight at the time. However, she told me she had every intention of leaving everything to the family estate."

Calaine looked to Mr. Conley for answers but he stared down

at the papers in his hand and said nothing.

"I had Anthony draw up papers that would relinquish all your rights to the Graves fortune. All that is required is your signature. I think it's the honorable thing to do. Your mother would have wanted it that way," Aunt Greta added with a twist of her thin, raspberry lips.

"I don't agree." Calaine glanced to her right. "May I have a copy of my mother's will, please?"

"That won't be necessary," Greta replied sharply. "I believe it's time for you to break the ties and move on with your life. For your honorable gesture, I'm willing to give you a sizable amount." She mentioned an amount that wasn't even a fourth of her mother's total worth. Her shock yielded quickly to fury. "I think I need to get my own lawyer."

"What!" Greta sputtered as she fell back in her chair.

Calaine rose, ignoring her aunt's distraught face. She bid Anthony a goodbye and walked out the room, ignoring her aunt's cries for her to come back that instant.

She climbed into her car, feeling a mixture of anger and sorrow. To make matters worse, it started to rain just as she pulled onto the interstate. She didn't know which was streaming harder, her tears or the rain beating down on her windshield. How could her aunt have been so cruel? It just wasn't fair. In her own stuffy way, Aunt Greta had always been pleasant. Now, because of money, she had shown her true colors.

Calaine wasn't sure how she had made the long drive back to town. When she pulled off the highway, she considered going to her uncle and crying on his shoulder, but she could not. She couldn't bear for him to know how her aunt had treated her. Not now, maybe not ever. She knew he had never cared for Greta and would probably commit murder. Nonetheless, this was not the time to think about Greta, not after the way she had treated her.

Instead, she headed south and went to the only person she knew would understand. The only other person who had shown her he cared.

David.

Calaine was surprised she even remembered where he lived. After all, she had only been to his house once. She turned into the driveway barely able to see as the rain increased. As she parked the car, Calaine hesitated, not sure if she had made the right move. *What if he already has company?* When the tears began to fall again, she decided to take her chance. She turned off the car and ran out into the pouring rain. In her blind state, she tripped over a garden statue and fell flat on her face. Slowly she scraped herself off the ground and after fishing her left shoe out of the mud, she climbed up the stairs and rang the doorbell.

David was eating a bowl of his sister's homemade chili when he heard the bell ring. Wiping his mouth, he rose from the chair, then moved through the foyer towards the door. He opened it to find a soaking wet version of Calaine.

"KeKe, what…?" His voice trailed off as he noticed her sad, desperate eyes. She was wet, dirty and held a muddy shoe in her hand. "Come in."

He stepped aside so Calaine could enter but instead she dropped the shoe, fell into his arms and burst into tears. "Oh, David!" she wailed.

Not caring about getting wet in the process, David scooped her into his arms, kicked the door shut and carried her up to his room where he sat her gently on the end of his bed. Calaine's head was bowed, her body slumped with despair. She was crying and sneezing at the same time, her feelings too raw to discuss. Her suit was plastered to her body and she was covered in mud.

David moved beside her and tenderly caressed her cheek. "You're soaking wet. We need to get you out of these clothes before you catch pneumonia," he commented softly.

Looking up, she met his gaze, then lowered her lids and nodded. Calaine didn't object when David reached down and removed her other shoe. He then peeled her jacket from her shoulders and discarded it. After he instructed Calaine to stand, he unzipped her skirt, which dropped in a heap around her feet.

He bit back a groan. She was beautiful but also soaked and in desperate need of a hot bath. He helped her slide off her pantyhose, ignoring her toned calves and thighs. When she was down to her bra and panties, he took a deep breath and swallowed. He had never seen a more beautiful woman. The lacy pink set looked as if it had been made just for her. *Snap out of it, Romeo! She needs your help.* Quickly, David reached for a blanket and wrapped it around her. Then taking her hand, he moved over to one of the side chairs and settled Calaine onto his lap.

She was shivering and he clutched her tightly to his chest. Although her crying had quieted, the tears continued to stream down her cheeks, spilling onto his shirt. David didn't ask any questions. Instead, he held her in his arms and rocked her back and forth until she quieted. She felt so good in his arms. He held her, not wanting to ever let her go.

David closed his eyes and lowered his chin to rest on top of her head. His heart hurt to see her in such a state. He squeezed her close. All he could think about was that she needed him. Of all the places or people she could have gone to, she had chosen him. The feeling caused his heart to swell with pleasure.

Even with his eyelids shut, David was well aware of the woman he was holding in his arms. Her head fit perfectly in the hollow groove of his neck and shoulder and her hair was damp against his cheek. He breathed in her enticing feminine scent and listened to the strong beat of her heart.

David's arms were wrapped protectively around her. His tender hold and the light strokes of his fingers were caring. Even when her sobs slowed to jerky breaths, David continued to stroke the center of her back. She pressed her nose into his shoulder, feeding on his strength. She didn't want to appear vulnerable or weak but the blow she'd received had rocked her to the core.

In less than six months she had lost both of her parents, found out her mother wasn't really her mother and one of the last connections she had to her roots had knocked her to the ground and then had spit in her face. Closing her eyes, Calaine told herself that it couldn't possibly get any worse. Only she wasn't so sure. No matter how she looked at it, all she had left was hope and Uncle Thaddeus.

When her breathing returned to normal, David leaned down and kissed her lightly on the forehead. "Let me run you a bath." Chilled, Calaine nodded. David slid out from underneath her and trotted into the master bathroom to run her a hot bath. When he returned to his room, he found Calaine curled up in the chair.

David kneeled down beside her and reached for her hand. "Baby, are you going to tell me what happened?"

Calaine took a deep breath before her sad eyes came down to rest on him. The look in his own told her he was genuinely worried about her. "I don't know where to begin."

He leaned forward and kissed her lips. "Take all the time you need."

Tears swelled within her eyes again at his patience and understanding. Her arms came up and wrapped arms around his neck. "Please hold me," she replied quietly. David sat and pulled her down into his lap as she began to weep again.

"Baby, it's going to be all right," he cooed as he attempted to comfort her. With one hand he made circular motions on her back. "I'm here for you." Closing his eyes, he tightened his hold and allowed her to surrender to the protectiveness of his embrace. He felt her pain as if it were his own. Ever since they'd begun spending time together, he'd found himself drawn to her vulnerability, her sorrows and feelings of rejection. When they were apart, he often found himself worried, sensing that she needed him. He had felt that way only an hour before she had appeared on his doorstep. He'd felt compelled to dash to the phone to call Calaine, only to find that she wasn't home. Now she was here with him.

For several minutes, she yielded to the compulsive sobs that racked her body and David continued to rock her in his arms. He whispered words of reassurance in her ears.

Calaine swallowed hard, fighting back tears. "She was so mean to me. What did I ever do to be treated that way?" With her eyes closed and her cheek resting at the crook of his shoulder, she felt safe and protected. Eventually she got her sobs under enough control to pull away. She slid from his lap onto the floor beside him, then took a deep breath and glanced up at him. The expression on his face told her David was willing to give her as much time as she needed to collect her thoughts.

A light coming from the bathroom cast shadows on his face and emphasized his strong nose, his wide firm mouth and somber eyes. Deep concern was written all over his face.

Looking away, her cheeks burned in remembrance. Calaine wanted to avoid relating the entire humiliating incident with her aunt to him, but somehow she believed that if she talked about her problems she would feel better. David had seemed to be so understanding thus far. Maybe he could help her sort things out. Her throat ached with grief. Calaine crossed one leg over the other and told him everything that had happened.

David listened without comment as she told him what had transpired earlier that evening. It was as if a dam had burst. She expressed her feelings and emotions past and present, only stopping long enough for him to turn off the bath water.

Afterwards he pushed his fingers through her damp wavy hair and held her tightly in his arms again. He fought the rage that devoured him over the way she had been treated. His need to protect her consumed him. She clung to him desperately, needing his understanding, his strength. It had become his job to look after her. Terrible regret assailed him that he had not been there to do so earlier.

When she finished, he was silent for a long moment, waiting for his anger to cool off. Biological niece or not, how could Greta have treated Calaine that way? He shook his head, then pulled back so he could look down into Calaine's face. "Don't let her greediness kill your spirit. It would be exactly what she wants. And don't give her the benefit of the doubt." David's tone was firm and deep.

"I-I can't help it." Calaine felt her throat tighten with emotion again, making it hard to continue. Then she began to sneeze uncontrollably.

David lifted her shivering body effortlessly in his arms and carried her into the bathroom. After he tested the temperature, he placed her into the tub of water with her still wearing her undergarments. Then he kneeled on the rug beside the tub and planted a kiss to her cheek. "I'm going to make you a drink. Try to relax until I get back."

David went down to his study and reached behind the bar for a brand new bottle of vodka. An apple martini was in order.

As he filled the glass, he tried to understand how he managed to hold her lush body in his arms without ravishing her. Her half-naked body was more beautiful than he had envisioned it to be. Just thinking about it caused the blood to stir at his loins. As an afterthought, David decided that maybe it wouldn't be a bad idea to also make a drink for himself. He could definitely use one.

Once she was alone, Calaine climbed slowly out the tub and removed her undergarments. Catching a glimpse of herself in the mirror, hair plastered to her head and dirt smeared across her cheeks, she gasped. She climbed back into the tub and commenced to lather her washcloth.

After scrubbing her body a second time, she leaned back in the tub and groaned. She had made a total fool of herself. Not only had she come crying to David, but she had fallen into a puddle of mud and almost lost her shoe. She groaned. If she hadn't felt so pathetic, she might have found humor in the situation. She had run from one humiliating scene to another. Aunt Greta had made it clear she was no longer considered family. It hurt. It hurt like hell.

Calaine shook her head as if to clear her jumbled thoughts. Maybe Aunt Greta was right. Maybe she should relinquish her rights to the inheritance. After all, the Graves family wasn't really hers to claim.

Calaine heard a light knock at the door. She reached for a large bath towel and draped it over her body before telling David it was okay to come in.

David walked in carrying two martinis. He took a seat on the edge of the tub and handed one to her.

"Thanks," she said, feeling only slightly embarrassed.

Glancing down, David noticed her underwear on the floor and

had to swallow. She was naked behind that towel.

He cleared his throat and tried not to look below her neck. "How are you feeling?" he asked.

"Much better. I...um...thanks." Self-consciously she pulled the towel up higher.

"I've told you, you don't have to keep thanking me." He bent over and kissed her on her forehead.

Calaine closed her eyes, savoring the sweet scent of apple on his breath. Right now David was one of a few comforting things in her life.

"KeKe," she heard him call, breaking into her thoughts.

"Yes?"

As he looked at her, he tried to ignore the fact that she was naked in his tub, a tub that was meant for two. "What can I do to make it all better?"

Tears she couldn't control spilled from her eyes at his question. "Just allowing me to be here with you is more than enough."

"Please don't cry," he pleaded. He wasn't sure how much more he could handle. *"Mi casa es su casa."*

Wiping her eyes with the back of her hand, Calaine nodded.

"You hungry?" he asked.

She nodded. "Maybe a little."

"How's a ham sandwich sound?" he offered.

She managed a smile through her mask of despair. "Sounds wonderful."

David rose and looked down at her. "Take as long as you want. I'm going to lay a t-shirt and a pair of boxers on the bed. Just come downstairs when you are ready." With that, he reclaimed her lips, then departed.

Calaine found herself smiling long after he was gone.

By the time Calaine emerged, the clock at the end of the hallway read midnight. She found David in the family room asleep in an overstuffed chair. Soft music was playing from the stereo and candles lit the room. She gasped. It was so romantic.

"Come in, KeKe," he said, startling her.

"I thought you might be asleep."

"Nope. Just waiting for you." He was mesmerized by how gorgeous she looked in his shirt even though it hung down way below her thighs. His thick socks covered her shapely legs all the way to her knees. He could tell she hadn't bothered with the boxers. They had probably been too big. Seeing her wearing his clothes, David felt tender feelings of possessiveness towards her.

Throwing caution to the wind, Calaine sashayed over to him. On a napkin on the TV tray beside him was her sandwich. "Thanks." She reached eagerly for the sandwich at the same time David reached out for her waist and lowered her onto his lap.

Calaine felt every nerve in her body quiver as David pressed her to him. The heat from his body seeped into her and she shivered noticeably.

He pulled her closer and tried not to think about the fact that there was nothing on beneath the shirt. "Are you cold?"

"No, just hungry."

David rested one hand at her waist, with the other took the sandwich from her hands and brought it to her lips.

Calaine never had a man feed her before. Overwhelmed, she opened her mouth, taking bites until it was gone. She declined his offer to make another.

"Would you like another drink?" he asked as she lowered her head to his chest.

She shook her head, not wanting to lose the comfort of his lap. "How about I share yours?"

He handed her the glass and she took a sip. Some spilled from the glass and onto her hand.

"Look what I did."

David reached down and took her hand. Turning her palm upward, he kissed the smooth texture, looking straight into her eyes as he did so. Calaine found the gesture quite erotic and when his tongue slipped between her fingers, she moaned softly.

He lowered her hand to his heart. "Feel that?" he asked. "That is what you do to me, Calaine Hart."

She closed her eyes a moment, savoring the feelings. His nearness kindled fire and desire. There was a bond between them and they both felt it.

To the sounds of a piano melody pouring from the speakers, she relaxed in his arms. "I can't believe you like this type of music."

"There are a lot of things you don't know about me. If you'd just give me half a chance you just might find out."

Laughter burned in the depths of her eyes. "Just shut up and hold me."

He pulled her tightly in his arms and nuzzled her neck, causing her to giggle. As the laughter died, he planted light kisses across her cheek down to her chin and finally on her lips. Taking the glass from her hand, he set it down on the table next to him and captured her lips once again. When she shifted slightly, David once more tried not to think of what lay beneath the cotton material that separated her nakedness from him. "You feel any better?"

"Quite a bit."

"Let's go to bed."

He rose and carried her in his arms up the stairs to his room. Pulling back the covers, he laid her down on the bed and moved beside her. When he saw the hesitation in her eyes, he stopped. "I told you nothing is going to happen between us until you make it happen." He was ready to make love to her. He wanted her with a hunger that exceeded anything he had ever experienced but he would wait. "Now roll over so I can give you a massage."

"You don't have to."

"But I want to."

She obeyed and rolled over onto her stomach. David moved to the center of the bed and straddled her. He made sure he didn't sit on the back of her legs, not only because he knew he was heavy but he also didn't want her to feel his obvious hard-on.

David placed his hands lightly to her neck and began kneading the muscles between her neck and shoulders. Calaine closed her eyes and bit on her bottom lip. She had the taste of warm blood on her tongue and knew she had bitten harder than intended.

"How does that feel?"

His words seemed to come from far away. David's fingers seemed to strip away all of her tension from the past several weeks and the devastation of earlier in the evening. She felt his thumb digging into the muscles at the base of her neck, and though it was painful, a few seconds later the relief was so significant.

"You are so tense. I think I've already smoothed out three knots," he informed her.

"It feels wonderful," she moaned as she folded both arms beneath her head.

"Good, I aim to please."

Oh, he was doing a lot more than pleasing her. She inhaled deeply, trying to ignore the fact that her nipples pressed against the mattress were now hard as pebbles. She felt so relaxed, so very…sleepy.

As his fingers continued to knead the strong muscles surrounding Calaine's shoulder blades, David admired the curves of her small narrow waist. He made sure his erection did not touch her although he was now sitting lightly on her buttocks. Only a piece of thin material separated them.

As her breathing became easier, he slid down past her buttocks and began kneading the backs of her legs, loving the feel of her taunt muscles beneath his hands. For the next several minutes, he contemplated venturing further between her thighs but a sound made him stop.

Calaine was snoring.

Chuckling, David rolled to his side and lay beside her. He pulled a sheet over both of them and fifteen minutes later, he was also sound asleep.

CHAPTER ELEVEN

Calaine raced around the room trying to find her other black sandal. Mumbling under her breath, she peeked beneath the bed again and luckily found it in the corner underneath her comforter. Rising from the floor, she tossed it into the side pocket of her suitcase, along with the mate.

She had a bad habit of always waiting to the last minute to pack, no matter how many times she told herself to do otherwise. Unconsciously her brow furrowed. Once again she was paying for her procrastination.

While retrieving a bottle of cocoa butter from on the top of her chest of drawers, her eyes traveled to a small digital clock on the nightstand. A soft gasp escaped her lips. She had less than thirty minutes to get ready. Calaine raced into the bathroom and in two minutes she was under the stream of hot relaxing water.

Calaine gave a ragged sigh. Unfortunately, she hadn't been able to relax since the night at David's.

She had awakened the next morning to find it still pouring outside and David's body against hers. Without waking him, she had slipped out of the bed and out the door without making a sound. She had never felt so embarrassed in her life and couldn't bare to face him. At least they hadn't made love. Not that it had been easy. Lying next to someone as sexy as David had been almost impossible. He had held her through most of the night, his arousal evident against her thigh. With a long weekend ahead of them, she knew she had to pull herself together quickly, otherwise, she was going to be in trouble.

Ten minutes later, she was dressed in a pair of sweatpants and a t-shirt. She took a seat on the end of the bed and was slipping on a pair of white socks when the phone rang.

She glanced down at the caller ID before picking up the receiver.

"Hello, Uncle Thaddeus," she sang merrily.

"Hi, KeKe. Are you all packed?"

"Just about," she answered as she reached down and slipped on her Nike tennis shoes.

"Well, I just wanted to catch you before you left and let you know that a colleague of mine knows Coletta."

"Really!" she gasped. "Have you talked to her?"

"No, not yet. She used to work for Boone Hospital but retired last year. I'm hoping to get some more information on Monday."

"That's wonderful! Thanks, Uncle Thaddeus."

After a moment he said, "You know there isn't anything I wouldn't do for you."

"I know, and I love you for it," she replied, filled with emotion.

"KeKe, I...we —"

"Don't worry. Everything is going to be just fine." She had heard the worry in his voice. "I better go. David will be here any minute."

"Good luck in San Antonio. I hope you find some answers."

"Thanks. I love you, Uncle Thaddeus."

"I love you too."

As she hung up the phone, Calaine's heart sang with delight. Her uncle's discovery brought her that much closer to finding her mother. What if her mother had been right under her nose all this time? Her pulse jumped with anticipation and Calaine had to take a deep breath. She was getting ahead of herself and maybe setting herself up for disappointment in the process. Then... maybe not. She pondered the possibility. Now all she had to do was find the other three. Hopefully, David's mother or godmother Wanda had answers.

The doorbell rang, startling her. Quickly, Calaine gathered the last of her things that were spread all over her bed and dumped them in her suitcase. She knew it was only for three nights, but with uncertainty as to what to wear, she had overpacked.

By the time the bell rang a second time, Calaine had finally gotten her suitcase to close. She sighed with relief and was just about ready to scramble down the hallway when the phone rang again. Groaning, she stopped in the spare bedroom at the end of the hall and retrieved the cordless phone as she made her way towards the door.

"Hello?" she barked.

"Are you ready?"

She gasped. "David, why are you calling me? I-I thought you were at..." Her voice trailed off as she opened the door and found David standing on the porch with his cell phone to his ear. Calaine's puzzled expression changed to irritation. "Very funny." Pursing her lips, she clicked the phone off and turned away from the door.

"I thought maybe you were trying to bail out on me," he chuckled as he followed her into the room.

She swirled around and snapped. "That's what you get for thinking."

When David stared at her, her anger suddenly flared into desire, hot and consuming.

"I knew we had a lot in common but I never thought it would include clothes," he replied with a smile.

Calaine's eyes traveled over his attire. He was wearing Mizzou

Tiger clothing. Black and gold jersey, black sweats with tiger paws on the right leg, and a gold fitted hat with black lettering. He wore them well.

She raised a hand to her forehead and shook her head. They were going to look like a couple. Not only was she wearing a black t-shirt with gold lettering, but she had matched it with gold sweatpants with black letters and black tiger paws across her backside.

"Great, just great," she mumbled under her breath. David threw back his head with abrupt laughter. Annoyed at him, she rolled her eyes.

While David made himself at home, Calaine went back to her room to retrieve her suitcase. As soon as she walked through the door, she tossed the phone on the bed and took a deep breath. She had to pull herself together. David looked so good she wanted to fall into his arms and have him smother her with his mouthwatering kisses. She raised her hand to her racing heart. She had to pull herself together, quickly.

David strolled into the kitchen and grabbed a glass from the cabinet above the sink, then moved to the refrigerator and found a pitcher of lemonade. He hadn't heard from Calaine; not once since she left his house two days ago. His pride had prevented him from calling her to find out why she had left.

Tilting the glass, he took a thirsty swallow. He'd thought Friday would never come. The prolonged anticipation had been almost unbearable. As soon as they boarded the plane, he would have Calaine all to himself for seventy-two hours. His loins stirred at all the possibilities.

When he returned to the living room, Calaine was coming down the stairs lugging a large suitcase. His brow rose. Where in the world was she going?

"Don't you think that's a little much for a weekend?"

She pouted her lips and shrugged. "I was undecided and it is always better to be safe than sorry."

David reached out and took her suitcase. It seemed to weigh a ton. He made a joke of pretending the bag was so heavy he couldn't stand up straight. Calaine couldn't help laughing despite her best intentions. After she locked up, they started on their hour drive to the airport.

Calaine's heart was beating a mile a minute and she wasn't sure how she was going to be able to survive the journey with the scent of his cologne penetrating her senses. She was ashamed to even look at him after the other night and knew that was the reason for her ill temper. David probably thought she had one leg inside the looney bin.

However, it was easier than she'd expected. David as usual made her feel at ease. He told her he had sent postcards to each of the women on his list who might be Dorlinda Meyers. Every time his gaze met hers, her heart turned in response. Calaine remembered her discussion with her uncle and relayed the information to David.

Happiness filled her as they talked. She relaxed in her seat as the situation switched from her heritage to David's. He told her stories about his family while he was growing up and claimed his parents still behaved as if they were still newlyweds.

"You wouldn't believe those two," he was saying as they pulled into the airport parking lot. "They are always slobbering and touching one another. I've gotten used to it but as a kid it used to be quite embarrassing."

She smiled, not missing the deep affection in his voice. "It sounds like you grew up in a very loving household." David simply nodded.

Staring out the window, Calaine couldn't help thinking about her own life. It was nice to know there were still couples out there that truly loved one another and were not ashamed to show it. Her parents had never been that way. Calaine had faith that she had enough love in her heart that she would someday have the same kind of marriage as the Souls'. As David searched for a parking spot, she found her imagination running wild as she envisioned spending that kind of life with David.

The next couple of hours went by quickly and it was almost six o'clock when their plane landed in San Antonio. Calaine was so exhausted that she had slept most of the trip in the air. Once they boarded the hotel shuttle, she settled back on the seat next to David.

David draped an arm around her shoulders and pulled her closer to him. "How are you feeling?"

"Rested." Tilting her chin, she smiled up at him sheepishly. "I can't believe I slept the entire trip."

"I can. You've had a long exhausting week," he replied. Lowering his head, David pressed a light kiss to her temple.

"You're right," she nodded as she settled comfortably against his chest, enjoying the feel of his arm around her. She closed her eyes and refused to think of anything except David and the way he made her feel. She didn't open them again until they pulled in front of the hotel.

She loved the Embassy Suites. She tried to stay at one every time she traveled. Even though they were all structured the same, each hotel had its own unique style. This one had a red, Spanish style roof and a terra cotta ceramic floor that started outside and traveled into the hotel lobby.

David retrieved both of their bags and Calaine followed him to the registration desk. She was amazed and a tad bit disappointed to find he had reserved separate rooms for them. When David had told her the next move would have to be hers, he'd obviously meant it.

Keys in hands, they took the glass elevator to the fourth floor and found that their rooms were right next to each other.

David walked Calaine to her room, then opened the door and handed over the key. "Are you hungry?" he asked.

Nodding, she took her suitcase from his outstretched hand. "A little but I'd like to settle in my room and freshen up a bit first."

David agreed. "How about I meet you near the bar in an hour?"

Her full lips softened with a smile. "Sounds good."

Lowering his head, he kissed her waiting lips. As he moved away, their eyes met and they found their passion mirrored. After one final glance, Calaine moved into her room and closed the door.

David entered his own room and dropped his bag on the floor near the king size bed. Faintly he heard water running and groaned, dropping down on the bed. Calaine was taking a shower. He envisioned her lush, naked body prancing around her room. After holding her in his arms for one night, he had discovered once was not enough. He needed her to be in his bed and in his life on a permanent basis. He needed Calaine to be his friend, his wife, his lover and the mother of his children.

Lying back on the bed, he rested his head in the palms of his hands. He had memorized every curve in his mind during the massage he had given her, however he had yet to touch the area he craved most.

Calaine was right next door. He smiled, thinking that a door was the only thing separating them for the next three nights. The mere thought was delightful.

Keeping his promise was going to be difficult but he was riding on the hope that it would be just as difficult for her. Sitting beside her on the plane the sweet scent of her skin had traveled to his nose and instead of reading a book, he had spent the majority of the ride watching her sleep.

David rose from the bed and headed towards the bathroom. Pulling his shirt over his head, he frowned. He hoped something happened soon because he wasn't sure how many more cold showers he could handle.

Calaine was at a small table near the bar when she saw David coming off the elevator. Her mouth went dry as her glance slid rapidly from a white cotton t-shirt to a pair of comfortably fitted navy walking shorts. She had forgotten how gorgeous his legs were. David had never played football but his calves and thighs were as large and defined as those of a running back.

She waved him over in her direction and he greeted her with a pearly white smile that set her pulse racing.

"Have you ordered yet?" he asked.

Calaine shook her head and answered in a low sultry voice, "I was waiting for you."

David liked the way the sound of her words caused a stir in his loins. He couldn't pull his eyes away from her. A simple pink sundress flattered her coloring while hugging the swell of her breasts. Her hair was damp and wavy around her face. He had to force his eyes away to look at the menu. "What are you having?"

Calaine hadn't missed the hungry look in his eyes before David dropped his head. Fighting urges of her own, she also reached for a menu and studied it. There were several precious seconds of silence before she replied, "I'm not sure." She couldn't think straight. How could she with David's clean masculine scent traveling over to her side of the small intimate table.

"I think I'll have salmon and rice with a spinach cream sauce," he announced as he dropped the menu and gave another heart-stopping smile.

Calaine felt her menu slip from between her fingers. Nodding her head, she looked down and replied, "I think I'll have the same."

David leaned forward and rested his chin in his palm. "How about a bottle of wine to celebrate?"

"What are we celebrating?" She was surprised by his suggestion.

"Finding your mother."

She was touched by his confidence that they would uncover the truth. She just wished she could feel so sure. With that in mind, she was able to put her relationship with David into perspective. As long as she didn't have a clue about her past, her future would forever be uncertain. That included anything past a physical relationship.

Forcing a weak smile, she agreed to a bottle of Chardonnay and was relatively quiet until their waiter returned.

Calaine found her eyes traveling out through a pair of double doors to the garden where a pool was visible. The blue green water gleamed beneath the sun that had begun to set on the horizon.

David was the first to break the silence. "I called my mom after I got out the shower. The graduation ceremony begins tomorrow around two. That should give us plenty of time to get up, have brunch and meet the rest of my family."

"That will be great."

Their food arrived, and while she dived into her meal David observed her. Her expression had changed and he could tell she was deep in thought. He wondered if it was about meeting his mother tomorrow.

"We can go and visit with my mother this evening, if you'd like."

Her fork froze in midair as she looked up at him. How was he able to read her mind like that? The thought was tempting but she decided against it. She still needed time to pull her questions together. Part of her was anxious to find out the truth but the other half was still scared to death. She shook her head and returned to her food. "No. Tomorrow will be soon enough."

He nodded, then attended to his plate. Tomorrow family and friends would surround them. He frowned and hoped she wouldn't feel overwhelmed by the clan. They could be overpowering. He could guarantee his sisters would be busy trying to matchmake.

"What's wrong?" Calaine asked after noticing the change in his expression.

"Nothing. I was just thinking about something at work," he lied smoothly.

They were silent as they finished their food. Calaine hadn't realized that she was stirring her rice. Just thinking about lying in the room next to him was going to be difficult.

"What's on your mind?" he asked.

"Nothing," she lied.

""Yes it is. I know you."

"You don't know me," she argued.

"Yes I do. I always have," he replied as he reached for his wine glass. "The problem is I never bothered to notice until recently. Now I can't seem to get enough of you."

His words caused a stir down low between her thighs, causing Calaine to shift slightly in her chair. The weekend was going to be quite a challenge. How she was going to make it through Monday was beyond her.

"I spoke to Donna, she should be in Columbia the end of next week," she replied, trying to keep their relationship in perspective.

David smiled. "I can't wait to see her. Maybe the three of us can have dinner."

Calaine stirred her glass. "Donna was thinking maybe just the two of you. I wouldn't want to impose."

"No imposition." He reached across the table and cupped her hand with his. "Besides, I don't want to spend time with Donna. I want to spend my time with you."

Calaine averted her gaze and tried to ignore the twinge she had at his response. She scolded herself for having had more than a few sips of wine. Now she felt her resistance was low.

After another hour of conversation and three glasses of wine, David finally asked for the check. As they rose from the table, he placed a large hand around her waist and drew her near him.

When they boarded the elevator, Calaine could feel the full effects of the alcohol. She felt loose and very relaxed and had to fight the temptation to lean over and kiss his smooth cheek.

The doors closed and the car rose. The quick jerk sent Calaine stumbling into David's arms. Her breasts brushed against his chest. David's fingers slipped up her arms, bringing her closer to him. Then one hand rose to trace her cheekbone to her hairline, then captured her chin and lifted her gaze to meet his. "You're something else, you know that?" His warm uneven breath against her cheek washed away any hope of resisting him. Instead, he left her feeling vulnerable and exposed. There was no way she could pull back, not with his arm warm and heavy against her hips. There was no way to deny this magnificent man's lips. Not when his warm breath was only mere inches away.

She blamed her behavior on the effects of alcohol and she would scold herself later. Now was not the time. She raised her hand and placed it against his cotton shirt. Heat seeped through, warming the blood in her veins. The heat, tautness of muscles and bone, and the hard pounding of his heart made her lightheaded. Her common sense vanished and she was lost in the deep pools of his eyes. Her heart was beating so heavily against her ribcage that it further disoriented her and she found her head tilting upward and her lips parting. Trying once more to extricate herself, she pushed back slightly against his encircling arms and moaned, "David, please!"

"Please what?" he asked as he brushed against hers lips. "Please kiss you?" he chuckled. "I plan to do just that."

He found her mouth, shutting off any further protest. At his first touch, Calaine was done for. Her head was spinning and she wasn't sure any longer what she wanted or didn't want. All she could think about was the warmth of his mouth sealed to her own, seeking a response and demanding it. She welcomed the invasion of his tongue. Blind with need, she dug her fingers into his back, pulling him even closer and felt the hardness of his erection against her belly.

"KeKe." He groaned her name in between a storm of brief, fierce kisses.

Calaine was ready to pull off her clothes and allow David to take her right there in the elevator. And she probably would have if she hadn't heard childish giggles.

She felt David stiffen and together they turned to find the elevator doors opened and two teenage girls dressed in bathing suits standing there with their hands cupping their mouths.

Calaine apologized and shoved hard against his chest. She was certain she turned beet red as she moved out of the elevator and down the hall towards her room.

"KeKe, wait a minute," David called as he came around and stood in front of her, blocking her escape into her room. "Why don't I come in and we talk about this."

"Why don't we wait until tomorrow to talk? I'm a little tired and would like a little private time to sort out my thoughts."

His jaw hardened but at least she wasn't giving him the brush off this time. She just needed time to think. He probably needed to do the same. "All right. We'll talk in the morning." He leaned forward and pressed his lips to her once more, then stepped aside. She swiped her keycard and scrambled into her room.

Calaine fell back on the bed, eyes closed.

She had fallen in love with David. She was shocked and still reeling from it. Although she had known love would strike her like this, she hadn't expected it to strike her here and now with this man. A man who loved women and did not believe in the kind of love that had just dislodged her world from its stable foundation. There was no denying he felt a powerful attraction, one she felt too, but there was a subtle difference in what they felt. She had fallen in love with him. Heart and soul she wanted his tenderness, his love, his heart. There was something extra where he was concerned. That indefinable something that put what she felt beyond the scope of any attraction she had experienced before. That something was the magic ingredient that told her she was head over heels in love.

Unfortunately, love wasn't part of David's equation. As far as he was concerned, what he offered was a little harmless affair to pass the time. Had her heart not been engaged, she would have perhaps seen it in that light, too. Now that her heart was ruling her emotions, they were no longer playing the same game. There was a lot more at stake. To have a brief affair with a man you were physically attracted to was one thing. To have an affair with a man you had fallen in love with was a different story altogether.

Deciding what she was going to do had consequences she couldn't ignore, which was a cruel joke. What could she do about it? It wasn't as if she had multiple choices. There were in fact only two. To sleep with him or not to sleep with him. Common sense said it would be less painful in the long run to call it quits now but to do so required more strength and will-power than she possessed. How could she do that when he was what she had been searching for all her life? Maybe it hadn't turned out the way she'd expected. David didn't love her and never would, but that didn't change how she felt. She loved him and the painful truth was this type of love might never come again. Any time with him, no matter how short, was better than nothing at all.

CHAPTER TWELVE

Calaine didn't sleep well. Her mind was consumed by the fact that David was on the other side of the wall. Some time between one and two o'clock she found herself clicking the television on, hoping to drown out her erotic thoughts.

Tossing the pillow over her face to muffle the sound, she screamed with frustration. She was torturing herself when all she had to do was open the door and run to him. But she couldn't. She had too much pride for that. All David wanted was a brief affair and even though that was all she could offer, Calaine just wasn't strong enough to go down that road because she knew her heart would yearn for more.

Around nine her stomach began to growl and Calaine knew there was no way she could hide in her room any longer without dying from starvation. She contemplated calling room service but decided against it, remembering the fabulous buffet the hotel provided.

Boarding the elevator, uneasiness swept through her. How was she going to feel when she saw him again? If those teenagers hadn't arrived, there was no telling what she might have done.

Through the glass, she quickly scanned the dining area, hoping David had already eaten and returned to his room. Calaine sighed with relief when she didn't see him. However, upon exiting the elevator and rounding the corner, she found him sitting at a large table in the corner with his sister Caress and her children. Although her heart lurched at the sight of him, she was grateful for the small distraction.

She ignored the fluttering of her heart, plastered on a warm smile and moved to greet the group. "Good morning."

David lifted his head at the gentle tone of her voice. He had half expected her to spend the entire morning in her room. He was glad to see that she hadn't.

"Good morning," he returned warmly. "How did you sleep?" Their eyes met briefly, too briefly for him to read what she was thinking.

"Like a baby," she lied before moving to the end of the table.

As she bent over to give his sister a friendly hug, his loins stirred at the sight of her in a pair of white shorts that showed off the curves of her legs.

"I haven't seen you in quite a while," Caress said as they parted.

Calaine took a seat between her and her youngest Latasia. "I've been really busy since my parents' deaths."

"I'm so sorry for your loss," Caress said.

"Thanks," Calaine replied. Then her eyes traveled around the table. "Who are these adorable children?"

Caress beamed with pride as she introduced her children. "That's Kyree, Latasia and Lashawn."

They were all between the ages of four and eight with eyes identical to their mother. Each of them waved, then returned to their pancakes swimming in syrup.

Glancing at Caress, Calaine wasn't sure how she managed to look so young. Even after three children, she had managed to hold onto her naturally youthful glow. Her thin, toned body was draped in a flattering peach cotton dress.

While she engaged in conversation with Caress, Calaine felt

the heat of David's eyes. She wanted to ignore him, but despite her best intentions, the effort was growing harder by the minute.

"Excuse me," Calaine said as she rose from the table. "I'm going to get something to eat."

David watched her as she moved to the buffet, hips swaying, head moving with poised dignity. His jeans tightened just thinking about holding her in his arms.

"Your lip's hanging," he heard Caress say.

He blinked, then turned to her and tried to keep a straight face and couldn't.

"It's that obvious, huh?" he asked as he reached for his mug of coffee.

"It's quite obvious that you're stuck on her," she replied, chewing on a slice of bacon.

He stared at her a moment with pursed lips. "I guess you're right."

"Uncle David, can I have some more cantaloupe?"

He glanced down at Kyree's upturned face that was smeared and sticky with strawberry syrup. "Sure, let's go." Lowering his cup, he was relieved by the small diversion. His sister's questions would have to wait until later. Maybe by then he might have the answers to some questions of his own.

As soon as he rose, the other two decided to tag along. Taking his four-year-old nephew by the hand, they headed over to the fruit.

Calaine returned shortly after, carrying a plate of sausage, eggs, a cheese Danish and fresh fruit.

"Where'd everyone go?" Calaine asked as she sat.

Caress tilted her head to the left. "They're standing over there. David has a thing for homemade waffles."

Calaine nodded as she opened a package of sugar and poured it in her coffee. "I'll have to remember that."

"David is spoiled. If he had come alone, he would have stayed with our parents. Mom has been making him monstrous breakfasts for as long as I can remember, so David has grown to expect it. My kids have picked up that nasty habit. Now every Sunday morning I have to get up early and make a breakfast big enough for an army. My husband even looks forward to it."

"That sounds like a nice tradition," Calaine commented in between bites.

Caress curled her fingers around her mug. "Mom has always been a wonderful cook, and looks forward to doting on my children, but I knew she had enough to do with my sister's graduation party. She has plenty of room at her house for all of us but I thought we'd give her a little space today. The kids and I will stay with her tonight."

Calaine glanced over at the buffet. "Doesn't look like your kids are sulking over the lost meal."

Caress's eyes sparkled with amusement. "No, not at all. Whenever we travel, Latasia picks this hotel just so she can have the breakfast."

Calaine nodded. Staying in a hotel as a child had been a big thing for her also, because it had represented vacation. It was the only time they really spent time together as a family.

"Where's your husband?"

Caress smiled affectionately. "He couldn't make it. He has a major case on Monday and is still preparing his defense." She shrugged her left shoulder. "I could complain but his law firm gives me the luxury of staying home and being a housewife and mother."

Calaine could tell she was pleased with the choices that she had made. Chewing her eggs, she wondered if she would ever consider giving up her own career for the man she loved. Her stomach quivered as she looked over at David and his niece and nephews as they headed toward the table. They each had their plates layered high with food.

Caress leaned across the table and whispered, "See, what did I tell you?"

Calaine agreed with a nod.

"I hope my sister hasn't embarrassed you," David said as he returned to his seat.

Calaine locked eyes with Caress and they giggled. "No, not at all."

She dug into her eggs while Caress cut Kyree's cantaloupe into small pieces. The kids began to all talk at once, fighting for the spotlight and their uncle's attention. Calaine watched the way he patiently answered all their questions and felt her heart flutter at his tenderness. David would make a wonderful father someday.

Calaine tried again to ignore him but found herself watching the way he shoveled his food in his mouth between questions and the sexy way his right brow quirked when he smiled.

As she sipped her coffee, her hand absently rubbed her temple. The hardest part for her was knowing all she had to do was look up at him or walk around the table and whisper in his ear that she wanted him to make love to her. She knew it would be an experience she would never forget. That worst part would be never forgetting. The memories would probably be unbearable.

"Calaine," she heard Caress say. She glanced over at David who had one eyebrow lifted in silent query.

"I'm sorry, did you say something?" she asked, turning her attention to Caress.

Caress appeared amused by something or someone. "David was telling me that he was helping you find your mother."

"Yes," Calaine replied as she pushed her plate away. "I'm hoping your mother and godmother can shed some light on my past."

Caress snorted, then glanced over at her brother before continuing. "I wish you luck. My mother and Aunt Wanda have a tendency to start talking without knowing when to stop. I hope you can make heads or tails out of whatever they tell you."

Calaine grinned. "I hope so."

The children began to get restless. Caress excused herself and the four of them left, leaving Calaine and David alone.

Calaine stared off at the growing crowd as she sipped her coffee.

"Are you going to ignore me all day?"

She glanced across at him reluctantly and replied, "I'm not ignoring you. I'm drinking my coffee. As a matter of fact I'm finished," she declared as she sat down her mug and rose to her feet.

"Stay, keep me company," he insisted.

She tried to ignore his heart-pounding smile. It was so difficult to think, let alone speak, when he smiled at her that way. Nevertheless, she was determined to maintain her composure. "Can't. I need to call and let my uncle know we made it safely. Ring me when it's time to go." Before he could get a word in, she retreated towards the elevators. Once she was there, she turned and found herself disappointed that he had not followed her. *It is for the best.* If David had followed, there was no way she would have been able to resist again.

An hour later with a towel draped around her neck, Calaine headed down to the pool. A convention was in progress and the lobby was flooded with middle-aged men in suits. She was conscious of their appreciative glances as she sashayed confidently through the area.

Reaching the pool, she laid her towel on a lounge chair and slipped out of her shoes. The area was relatively quiet. There were a few senior citizens doing water aerobics at the other end but otherwise it was empty.

"The water must have been calling both of our names."

She turned to find David climbing out of the pool. She swallowed as her eyes followed a trail of water that had fallen from a loc of his hair and traveled down his chest. He was wearing navy blue trunks that emphasized his long, strong legs. Fine water slicked hairs covered his legs and arms while his chest was as smooth as a newborn baby's bottom.

Tearing her eyes away, she murmured, "I thought I'd try to burn off breakfast."

"So did I."

She tried to ignore the attraction as he stood beside her. She turned away, slipped out of her cover-up and moved to the edge of the pool. Bracing herself, she dove in, glad for the shock.

David stood there staring long after she had begun swimming to the other side. The black two-piece revealed more than it hid. Her stomach was firm and tight, as well as her rear and legs. Even though he had undressed her the other night, he had no idea she'd look so good in a swimsuit.

Calaine swam to the surface awkwardly, knowing David was watching her. However, when she surged out of the water, he was no longer standing where she had left him. Several seconds later, he emerged from the water and appeared before her. She froze, unable to move.

David wiped the water away from his eyes and smiled. "The water is wonderful."

She nodded, then swallowed, watching water trickle from his left nipple. She felt the overwhelming desire to dart out her tongue and capture it before it dripped back into the pool.

"What's wrong?" he asked, obviously noting the play of emotion on her face.

"N-nothing," she lied.

More water trickled down his chest. His body hair was slicked to his skin. Ignore him! That was easier said than done.

"Nothing?" He paused to laugh. "I don't believe you."

She lowered her eyes to the water but David moved in closer and cupped her chin, raising her eyes to meet his again.

"You feel it too, don't you?" he whispered against her face.

That wasn't all she felt pressed up close against his body. She shook her head trying to deny the attraction, but it was useless.

David moved even closer until their bodies were touching and reached down and brought her hand to his chest. "Go ahead…touch me."

She couldn't move her hand if she wanted to. With his fingers around her wrist, he circled her hand slowly along his chest and up to circle one nipple and then the other. She had to fight back a moan.

"Ever since you shared my bed, I've dreamed of your return." He looked down at her and regarded her with an intensity that made her pulse race.

"All you want is an affair," she said quietly.

His fingers grazed her cheeks. "I don't know what I want except that I want to be with you. Give us a chance and let's see what happens." Lowering her hand, he reached out and encircled her waist. "I'm not sure what's going on. All I know is that I never felt like this before." He had never been good at expressing himself but this was one time he was willing to put his pride aside. Placing his hand under her chin, he tilted her face so that she was forced to look directly into his eyes. "I want to explore this… this thing that is happening between us and see where it leads us." He planted small kisses from her cheek to her neck. "Will you do that for me?"

Looking up at him, her gaze was as intense. "Do what?" she

asked, stalling. She couldn't think straight when he was this close, looking that good. His gentle kisses were only making matters worse. Calaine collapsed weakly against him and her entire body shuddered in his arms.

"Give us a chance?" His lips brushed her ear in a whispery caress.

"Yes, I'll give us a chance," she answered with a long sigh.

He kissed her lips gently, parting them with his tongue with measured slowness. The slow flow of desire was intoxicating. Her tongue greeted him and as she tasted him, all restraints fled. He slid his arms tightly around her waist. With their bodies pressed together, she was aware of his manhood, thick, hard and aroused by her. Everything about him was so masculine, so tantalizing. His moans of desire set her heart into a spin.

Just as she reached around to his buttocks to pull him even closer to her, they heard giggling.

Calaine opened her eyes and found the teenagers again.

Shifting her head, she buried her face against his shoulder. "Oh, God, not again."

David turned and gave them a sheepish smile, then shrugged his shoulders apologetically.

"We're being a bad influence," Calaine groaned.

Pulling back, he smiled down at her. "You're right, let's go," he murmured as he escorted her from the water. They had reached for their towels and were heading through the lounge when he made a suggestion. "We can resume this in my room."

She stared wordlessly at him. The offer was tempting. "We have two hours before graduation. We need to get ready if we're going to get there on time."

"Are you running from us again?"

She moved away and tied the towel around her waist. "Not at

all. When I decide I'm ready for you to make love to me, two hours will be nowhere near enough time." With that, she sashayed towards the lobby, ignoring his stunned expression.

CHAPTER THIRTEEN

It was close to five when they pulled up in front of the Souls' Spanish style home, which was located in a quiet upscale neighborhood with tree-lined streets and old-world architectural charm. The neighborhood exuded privacy, invited sidewalk strolls, and promised the shortest commute to the city.

The number of cars in the driveway indicated that most of their family and friends had already arrived. Caress had rented a van for the weekend and it had been one of the first to arrive.

Calaine had fussed over what to wear but after David told her the weather was expected to be well over ninety degrees, she had decided on a pair of pink Capri pants and a cool white cotton blouse.

I'm nervous, Calaine thought as she stared out the windshield at their red tile roof. Her feelings were a mixture of uneasiness about speaking to his mother and anxiety about finding out about her own.

The graduation ceremony had been long but surprisingly interesting. The female guest speaker, who was from one of the state departments responsible for the tobacco lawsuit, was both interesting and delightful. Calaine had been grateful that the ceremony had been held in the convention center away from the scorching heat and humidity.

There were about two hundred in the graduating class. By the time they arrived, the room was already full and she and David were unsuccessful in locating the rest of the Soul family. As a result, David suggested they sit near the rear. They would see his parents later at their home.

David shut off the rented Jeep Cherokee and looked over at the passenger seat. "You ready?"

Calaine removed her sunglasses from her eyes, folded them and put them in her purse. "As ready as I'll ever be," she murmured as she reached for a small compact. While David came around to her side, she quickly buffed the shine from her nose and applied a fresh coat of lipstick.

David opened the door and helped her out of the air-conditioned SUV. Climbing out, it was hard to ignore the hot San Antonio breeze as it swept across her face. He laced their fingers together and led Calaine up the driveway and into the house.

They stepped into the foyer and her gaze traveled around as David toured her through one room after the next. Her lips curled into an unconscious smile as she found the house warm and inviting. Each room displayed proud photographs of several generations. There were also handmade crafts, crocheted afghans and an unlimited amount of personal comfort. It was the kind of house she dreamed of someday having for her own.

They moved into a spacious kitchen where a lovely young woman was tossing a salad.

"Lil' sis," David greeted.

His sister's startled gaze shifted in the direction of his voice. "Hey!" she shrieked with delight as she rushed around the island and threw her arms around his neck. "I was wondering when you'd get here." David twirled her around in his arms and kissed her playfully on the cheeks, lips and forehead. She giggled like a teenager until he lowered her to the ground.

Turning to his right he said, "Calaine, this is my annoying little sister Daphne."

"It's a pleasure to meet you."

"The same here." Daphne's voice was low and soft.

She was a feminine version of her brother. Her dark brown hair was pulled back and secured in a plait that hung to the center of her back. She had also inherited hazel eyes and a wide nose, which was striking against her tawny brown skin. She was short and heavy around the hips.

"When Mom told me you arrived last night I was planning to surprise you at the hotel." Her face brightened with animation. "That was before I found out that you had brought a friend along," she smirked as she glanced to his right. "I didn't want to intrude."

"We're just friends," Calaine blurted but the look on Daphne's face told her she didn't believe a word she had said.

Calaine shifted uncomfortably. She should have known his family would think they were an item.

"Where's everybody?" David asked after sensing her discomfort.

"Dad's out on the patio, Mom's upstairs changing into something more comfortable and everyone else is in the family room."

He tugged his sister's braid, then reached for Calaine's hand again.

"Let me introduce you to my dad." David led her out onto the deck where Robert Soul was in front of the grill with an apron tied around his round body.

"Dad."

The elder Mr. Soul swung around holding a pair of tongs in his hands. "Son, you've made it." He moved forward and embraced him.

When they moved apart, David motioned his head to his right.

"Dad, I'd like you to meet a friend of mine, Calaine Hart."

Robert lowered the tongs to the table and wiped the grime from his hands on his apron before he extended a friendly handshake. "It's a pleasure to have you."

His brown eyes crinkled and he presented her with an irresistible smile that was so much like David's. It was as if she were looking at David through a looking glass thirty years into the future. His salt and pepper hair was collar length and his mustache was full, covering his upper lip. "I'm pleased to be here, Mr. Soul."

"Please, call me Robert. We're all family here." He brought her hand to his lips and kissed her lightly on the knuckles before releasing it. "I don't remember my son ever bringing a woman home so you must be someone special."

David saw his father assessing Calaine and knew that at any minute the questions were going to become personal. He placed his hand lightly to her elbow. "Why don't we go find my mom?"

As if on cue, a beautiful woman stepped out onto the deck. Calaine knew immediately she was his mother. Not only because she resembled the woman in the photograph but because she and Caress looked so much alike. Her dark brown hair with its generous strands of gray was stylishly cut, complementing a smooth, wrinkle-free face.

She handed a platter of raw seasoned meat to her husband, then turned to observe the woman standing beside her son. Seeing David's possessive hand on her shoulder, she knew instantly she had to be someone special. "So this is the lady who's searching for her mother," she said with a warm smile.

Calaine nodded.

"Welcome, sweetheart." She greeted her with a hug and a kiss.

"Thanks," Calaine replied, feeling at ease.

"Come on, you two, it's too hot out here. David go on inside and introduce her to the rest of the gang."

Calaine followed David into the family room where the others had gathered. She smiled and shook hands as David introduced her to several friends of the family. It was a small intimate group of no more than twenty. Finding Caress smiling across the room at her, Calaine waved in greeting and hugged each of her children when they ran over to her to say hi.

David then led her over to the fireplace where a man was holding a little girl.

"Calaine, I'd like you to meet my brother, Carlos."

At the sound of David's voice, his brother swung around and lowered the little girl to the floor. He then turned to embrace his baby brother.

Calaine gasped. He was so breathtakingly handsome she had to force herself not to stare. David was the same height and build as his brother but that was where the similarity ended. Carlos had a smooth tawny complexion and long black hair secured by a rubber band at the nape of his neck. With her head tilted, she stared into chocolate-colored eyes that were surrounded by lashes long enough to make any woman envious.

"It's a pleasure to meet you." He greeted her with a warm smile that revealed dazzling white teeth.

"The same here," Calaine said as she accepted his proffered hand. "Your daughter is lovely."

He frowned while David chuckled heartily. "She's my little cousin." Carlos's eyes narrowed at his brother's laughter. "I don't have any kids or a wife, for that matter. I'm not the marrying type."

Calaine was surprised. "But you looked so natural."

"That's 'cause I had to take care of this big headed little brother of mine." He punched his brother lightly in the chest. Then the two passed several playful punches back and forth before Ruby told them to behave.

Calaine grinned, admiring the closeness between the two. She asked David for directions, then excused herself and moved to the powder room at the end of the hallway. The small room had hardwood floors, embroidered towels and a pedestal sink. After washing her hands, she took a moment to look in the mirror and straightened her hair before exiting the room. Moving down the hall, she found a woman standing near the living room watching her.

"You must be Calaine," she said.

She turned to look at a face that only took ten seconds to identify. "And you must be Aunt Wanda."

"In the flesh," she acknowledged with her hands clasped in a prayerful gesture.

Calaine stood admiring the nut brown woman with fine chestnut hair and realized that she wasn't the only one staring.

"You look so familiar," Wanda commented with a quizzical stare.

She nodded. "My uncle, Dr. Hart, was your instructor."

Wanda's brow rose with surprise. "You're related to Dr. Hart?"

Calaine nodded.

Wanda looked a little disturbed by the information, then quickly forced a smile just as David and his mother stepped into the hall.

She immediately called for their attention. "Ruby, did you know Calaine is Dr. Hart's niece?"

Ruby's eyes darted over to Calaine, wide with surprise. "Oh my! I used to have a huge crush on him. We all did." She moved into the living room and the three followed. "He was so handsome. I think I spent more time drooling over him than paying attention to his lectures," she chuckled.

Calaine smiled. She had heard countless stories of how handsome her uncle had been back in his day.

David moved beside her and placed a hand lightly to her waist. "Calaine, did you bring the photo?"

Glancing up at his handsome face, she was barely able to contain her excitement. "It's in my purse."

Ruby sat on a loveseat covered in rich gold fabric and crossed one leg over the other. "Why don't you go get it and we'll take a look at it."

Calaine went into a back bedroom where she had left her purse and within minutes returned with the photo.

Wanda had taken a seat beside Ruby and reached for the photo first. Shaking her head, she chuckled. "Weren't we something else back then?"

Ruby leaned over to get a closer look and smiled. "Yes, we were."

"I wrote the names of each woman on the back, if that helps," Calaine offered as she took a seat across from the two.

"Hmm, let's see. Ursula was the silly one. She always had a joke. I don't think she ever took anything serious. I remember our dorm mother used to be pretty angry with her." She gave Ruby a sidelong look. "Remember the time she played that joke on her?"

Ruby chuckled openly. "Oh yes, how could I forget."

Wanda related the time Ursula had put a diaphragm in the poor woman's denture cup. "She was too embarrassed to accuse any of us."

Ruby took the photo and studied it for several seconds before saying, "I don't remember much more about Ursula except she was smart as a whip and rarely needed to study." She paused to smile. "Coletta and I were very close. We lost contact over the years. These other two, I remember as being strange."

"How so?" David asked. He had moved and taken a seat beside Calaine.

Ruby looked up and saw the gleam of interest burning in her son's eyes. "Eunice used to act like she was Dorlinda's mother. I don't think the poor girl was ever able to make a decision on her own. They had come from some small southern town. I can't remember the name."

"How long were they there?" Calaine asked.

"Not long. Wanda and I were the only two to complete the program. Coletta went on to finish somewhere else. Ursula's mother got ill and she had to go home and run the family business. And the other two had left long before that."

"My uncle says that Eunice died a year later."

Wanda glanced over at Ruby with a puzzled expression that soon turned to amazement. "You're right. I think I remember hearing someone had committed suicide."

"Do you remember why?" Calaine asked, hoping for an answer.

Wanda frowned. "No, I don't."

"I don't remember hearing anything about that," Ruby added. "I never really got involved in campus gossip. I was already married with a two-year-old-son. As soon as my classes were done for the day, I had to hurry to pick up Carlos from the babysitter."

"Do you think any of them could have been my mother?"

Ruby leaned back against the cushion. "Anything is possible. Back in the seventies things like that were hush-hush."

Wanda stared at Calaine long and hard. Something in her eyes told Calaine that she wasn't going to like what she was about to hear.

Wanda shifted slightly, crossing, then uncrossing her leg before glancing across at the two on the couch again. "Calaine, you have to understand that things were hard for black women back then. We had to try even harder to compete with the other nurses. Even though it was the seventies, having a child out of wedlock was unacceptable for anybody, no matter what color you were. It wasn't like today when a teenager is allowed to finish high school with her stomach sticking way out here. Back then, no way, no how."

Waving a hand in the air, Ruby nodded. "Amen to that. People were quick to point the finger if you weren't wearing a ring."

Calaine nibbled slightly on her lower lip as she tried to understand what her mother had gone through. She must have been scared. "Do you think that's why my mother gave me away?"

Wanda was the first to speak. "Yes. We didn't have options like y'all have today. If she gave you up, then chances are she had reason to."

Calaine had the strangest feeling that Wanda was trying to convince her of something. She just wasn't sure yet what it was.

David reached for Calaine's hand and laced their fingers together. "Do you know how to find any of these women or know of anyone who would?"

Wanda frowned. "No, other than finding our dorm mom, Ms. Butler. She would probably be willing to tell you anything you wanted to hear. By now, she should be in her early seventies. If there had been a baby back then, she would have known. We couldn't get anything past her."

Ruby slapped her knee and chuckled. "Ain't that the truth. I used to wish I could stay in the dorm just so I wouldn't have to miss all the fun. The girls used to come to class with all kinds of stories. Wanda used to stay in trouble."

Wanda smiled. "Oh, yes. I was definitely a risk taker. I remember when I had a date with this medical student and tried to sneak in after curfew. Ms. Butler was standing behind the door waiting for me." She chuckled with fond memories. She and Ruby began to talk nonstop about the parties they had attended and how great a dancer Wanda had been.

Neither Calaine nor David could get a word in. Leaning over he whispered in her ear, "Caress warned you."

Eventually the two stopped talking about the dresses they had worn, as if they had suddenly remembered Calaine and David were still there.

"I'm sorry, we have a tendency to travel down memory lane. I really wish we could have been more helpful," Ruby said sympathetically.

Calaine shook her head. "No, in fact you have been quite helpful." She felt as if she now knew what her mother had been thinking.

The kids came running in from outside. They turned towards the door as Christie appeared wearing her cap and gown.

"There's my girl," Wanda said as she rose to embrace her. "I'm so proud of you."

She was grinning from ear to ear. "Thanks, Auntie Wanda."

As soon as they moved apart, David lifted Christie off her feet and kissed her soundly on the mouth.

"Hey big brother," she cooed as he released her. Christie turned to Calaine, her bottomless golden brown eyes sparkling with excitement. "You must be my brother's friend. It is so nice to meet you." Christie stepped forward and gave her a warm hug, then whispered near her ear, "He's never brought anyone home before so you must be special."

Taken completely off guard, all Calaine could do was smile.

Caress appeared at the door. "Now that our guest of honor is here, we should be eating shortly," she said with an affectionate smile.

"Do you need some help?" Calaine asked as she watched Ruby and Wanda retreat towards the kitchen.

Caress shook her head. "I think we've got everything under control but thanks for asking. I'm sure Dad could use David's help outside though."

"I guess that's my cue," David murmured. Looking down at Calaine, he planted a quick kiss to her cheek. "I'll be back."

"I saw that, big brother," Christie teased, causing Calaine to blush profusely.

"You just behave while I'm gone and don't fill Calaine's head with a bunch of lies," he warned his sister.

Christie pressed a palm to her chest and pretended to be innocent. "You couldn't possibly mean little ole me?"

Calaine giggled as she watched David ruffle his sister's spiral curls before he left the room.

Christie shrugged out of her gown and laid it on the couch, then signaled Calaine to follow her into the dining room. They cut through the kitchen where the countertops were covered with platters of side dishes, meats and desserts. Mr. Soul came in carrying a tray of smoked meats. Calaine could not ignore the mesquite aroma.

Christie reached down and scooped up a deviled egg. "You need me to do something?" she asked while she chewed.

Caress was pulling a pan of grilled corn from the oven when she said, "Yes, why don't you two help Daphne set the table."

Calaine followed Christie into the dining room where Daphne was removing the fine china from the cabinet and placing it on a large table. She glanced up in time to witness Calaine arch an eyebrow.

"I know what you are thinking, who uses good china for a barbecue?" She rolled her eyes heavenward and she reached up for the last plate. "My mother won't have it any other way. To her a special occasion means pulling out the china."

Christie groaned. "It also means that we can't use the dishwasher tonight."

Calaine moved around the table and retrieved the silverware from the drawer. "My mother was the same way." Only she didn't bother to say that her mother would have never dreamed of serving barbecue in her house in fear of sauce getting on her rugs.

"Well, at least you're the last Soul to graduate," Daphne groaned.

Calaine glanced over at Christie's smiling face. She had inherited her father's eyes and dimpled chin but that was as far as the physical resemblance went. Christie had dramatic high cheekbones, small bone structure and thick, sandy brown hair. The overall result had made her a shockingly beautiful woman.

"So how did you meet my brother?" she asked curiously.

Calaine took a moment to answer. She'd known the questions were coming, she just hadn't expected them quite so soon. "We went to college together."

Daphne looked up from folding linen napkins. "Do you live in Columbia?"

Calaine nodded. "All my life."

Christie frowned. "I was so young when we moved down to Texas that I don't remember ever living anywhere but here."

"Are you planning to teach in San Antonio?" Calaine asked, hoping to shift the focus away from her.

Smiling, Christie shook her head. "No, I'm going to be working in Dallas."

"Her boyfriend lives there," Daphne offered.

Christie flushed at the mention of her first and only love. "I can't wait. He had to work today, otherwise he would be here. Tavis is a wonderful man. He's building a home and we're going to live together until we decide we're ready for marriage. I'm in no rush. I want to take my time and make sure I'm doing this right."

Calaine nodded, impressed with her maturity at such a young age. "Sounds like you got a plan."

"Yeah, I don't ever want to get a divorce. I want to be like my parents and be married forever."

They spread out a lace tablecloth, then wiped each piece of china off with a cloth before setting the table.

Calaine was impressed by the closeness of their family. It was something she had always wanted. A father barbecuing on the deck and a mother cooking in the kitchen, not at all afraid of getting her hands dirty. Katherine had refused to boil water.

The family life of the Souls was more than she had ever thought possible and everything she would like to have some day. Calaine found herself relaxing around the two sisters and they chitchatted about life in general, joking and laughing as if they were lifelong friends.

When the table was completely set, they returned to the kitchen to retrieve covered dishes and take them to the table. Besides barbecue, there was corn on the cob, spaghetti, macaroni and cheese, baked beans, three different kinds of salads and a large variety of desserts.

Calaine stepped into the kitchen a third time to find David sitting in a chair talking to his father. As she passed, she found him watching her. Her breath caught in her throat as her body stirred all the way to her toes. A voice in her head shouted, "Look away!" But for the life of her she could not. She couldn't resist the smile that curled on her lips at the sight of his sensual smile.

Christie had seen the sparks flying between the two and as soon as they moved into the dining room again, she asked, "So what do you think of my brother?"

Calaine's mouth gaped as she tried to think of an answer.

Daphne clicked her tongue. "Don't embarrass her, Christie.

They're just friends."

"Friends, huh?" Christie dropped a hand to her slim waist and frowned. "You don't think my brother is handsome?"

Calaine didn't hesitate with her answer. "I think your brother is quite handsome. I also think he's quite arrogant."

Christie and Daphne laughed in agreement.

Calaine helped position the dishes on the table, trying to make room for more. "Your brother is helping me find my mother."

"Your mother?" Christie gasped.

Calaine explained the photograph and the questions she had about her past.

Daphne's eyes grew large as saucers. "Wow! I don't know what I would do if I found out I was adopted."

Christie shrugged. "It wouldn't matter to me. I have wonderful parents. Nothing could ever change that."

I wish I could say the same. If she had had a normal childhood then she probably wouldn't be looking so hard, but it was just the opposite.

Ruby announced it was time for dinner and shortly after the rest of the family joined them in the dining room. Everyone joined hands. David somehow ended up next to her. He covered her hand with his and they shared a tender smile before bowing for grace.

The younger kids moved into the kitchen while the rest sat around the table. Calaine listened to the sound of laughter as everyone tried to talk at once. They were an engaging bunch that made her yearn for what she had missed. She quickly found herself caught up in the family charm as they included her in several conversations.

However, each time she spoke, Calaine found Wanda watching her intensely. There was something about the woman that disturbed her. She wasn't sure what it was, but she had every intention of finding out.

CHAPTER FOURTEEN

It was close to midnight when they finally left to return to the hotel.

"Are you okay?"

Calaine exhaled, relaxing against the leather seat of the Jeep, then shifted her gaze to David, touched by the concern she saw. "I'm fine, why do you ask?"

He continued to study her. "Because you've been quiet since we've left my parent's house."

He was right. She had been quiet.

Turning away to stare out her window, she thought about her evening. She'd had a wonderful time with his family. They all had made her feel right at home. The only part of her evening that was puzzling was Aunt Wanda. Throughout the meal and even after they all moved to the family room to watch home movies, Calaine had had the strangest feeling that Wanda was watching her. Nibbling on her lower lip now, she couldn't put a finger on it. Was there something Wanda wasn't telling her? She sighed. Perhaps it was simply her uneasiness.

"Are you disappointed?" David asked.

At the sound of his deep voice interrupting her thoughts, Calaine gave him a sidelong glance. "What makes you think I'm disappointed?"

He shrugged. "Because you hoped my mother could shed some

light on who your birth mother was."

"No, I'm not at all disappointed. I learned quite a bit listening to your mother and Wanda reminiscing about the good ole days." In fact, some of her resentment had vanished. The pain of being abandoned had lessened. When she closed her eyes, she imagined herself young, pregnant and alone during a time when having a child out of wedlock was unacceptable. She would probably have done the same. What Calaine couldn't understand was why she had never thought to consider that maybe her mother had had no choice, that maybe society had played a part in her decision.

When David blew his horn at a car that was bold enough to jump out in front of him, Calaine snapped out of her trance of fact and fiction.

She reached out, linking her hand with his, needing to touch him. "I had a wonderful time today, thanks for inviting me."

"I thank you for coming." David said with a dimpled smile. She returned the smile and while David drove, she found herself watching him. She couldn't stop looking at him. He was the calm in a terrible storm. With him by her side, deep feelings of peace invaded her heart.

When David raised her hand to his lips and kissed her gently across the knuckles, an undeniable heat climbed its way up through her stomach. Fingers laced, he rested their hands on his knee.

Lowering her head onto his shoulder, she inhaled deeply before turning her gaze to the dark starry sky ahead. Closing her eyes, she tried to calm her thoughts. Everything about David added up to one thing.

She wanted him to make love to her.

She knew it was risky, that maybe she would regret it in the morning, but she couldn't think about the consequences. All she wanted to think about was right now.

David pulled into the parking lot on the east side of the hotel, then walked around to the other side and opened the door. Holding her hand firmly in his, he led her through the double doors. They boarded the elevator, then walked down the hall without an exchange of words. When they reached her room, Calaine stuck her keycard in the door, then turned the knob before facing David again. His arms came around her in a vice-like grip, cradling her close to his chest. He then pressed his lips to her forehead. The kiss though only a brush of the mouth, left both of them shocked by its electricity.

David's eyes traveled to her mouth, and then up to meet the haze of her brown eyes. A rush of heat swept her body, leaving her shaking with desire.

"Dream of me," he whispered.

Calaine surprised even herself when she pulled back and tilted her chin, coaxing him to kiss her. David lowered his mouth and they met in a powerful, passionate kiss, scorching in its intensity. His lips were like fire, licking and burning her tender skin. He kissed her ear, nipping the lobe. Then his tongue trailed across her jaw until he reached her mouth again. Her lips opened and he kissed her, wrapping his tongue around hers, licking the edge of her teeth.

"David," she moaned only seconds before her knees gave out.

Without breaking the kiss, David swept her up in his arms and made his way into her room. After kicking the door shut, he moved over to the king size bed, whipped back the covers and deposited her gently in the middle of the bedspread. Boldly, he followed her down and slid his hand to her buttocks, aligning her body firmly against his.

He darted his tongue inside her mouth and groaned with satisfaction when her strokes met his. His lips trailed away from her mouth and her head fell back, granting him greater access as he traveled down to her throat in a wet path.

David slid his hand along her spine and then across her side to her waist. Moving under her blouse, his hand cupped her breasts.

Calaine released small moaning sounds. Hungry for his touch, she arched towards him, pressing closer, and encouraged him to do more.

David found the zipper of her Capri pants, unzipped them and slipped his hand inside caressing her buttocks. Her skin was velvety smooth and warm. Just touching her made his loins throb.

Coaxing Calaine to lift her hips, he tugged off her pants, then her satin panties. At the sight of her, he took a sharp breath, feeding on her splendor.

"You're beautiful," he groaned. His hand caressed her smooth cheek and then slid down her neck before stopping at her blouse. Deftly, he released the top button of her blouse, followed with the second and third, until he finally released the last one. He swallowed when he parted her blouse and stared down at a dark green bra.

He released the front clasp and stared at the swell of her golden brown breasts.

"David," Calaine whispered. The sound was swallowed up by his mouth as his tongue delved deep, tangling with hers, drawing her into a hot fever of emotions and cries. His hands kneaded her breasts, his thumb making arousing circles over each nipple, drawing them into hard, pebbled peaks.

David released her to move off the bed and Calaine cried out at his sudden absence. Propping herself up on one elbow, she watched David remove his clothes. She was in awe. His body was beautiful. He reached into his pants pocket and removed a condom, as she watched him roll the latex over the length of his large, rigid flesh, her body began to tremble. He lowered on top of her, the weight of his torso resting between her legs, sending shivers of excitement through her limbs.

Sliding down, his lips closed over one aching nipple and his thumb grazed the other. Calaine gasped in sweet agony. His mouth was so warm, his hands strong, tender. Traveling even further, his fingers brushed through the apex of dark curls, seeking the hidden nub of pleasure within. She arched her back as he gently teased, her breathing now heavy and out of control.

"Yes," she moaned. Her chest rose and fell in shuddering gasps.

When David parted the moist folds that concealed her womanhood, he found her slick and ready, her need so strong that she arched into his hand. The urge to drive into her and let himself be swept away in a tide of pleasure was so great, he had to bite down on his lower lip to maintain a thin strand of composure.

"Oh David!"

"Tell me, baby." He stared down at her, watching as she whimpered and twisted beneath him. Her ragged breathing indicated she was losing control as quickly as he was. "Tell me what you want," he crooned.

She was ready to explode, desperately needing more of him than his touch. "I want you now!" If she had to wait any longer she was sure to come apart.

"Your wish is my command." Without any further hesitation, David positioned himself between her legs, his shaft pulsing at her opening. When he slid into her wet tunnel the joining of their bodies was explosive. He buried his face in her neck as passion pounded the blood through his veins.

"Am I hurting you?" he breathed against her lips as he searched her eyes in the dim moonlight spilling through the corners of the curtain.

Not yet, she thought inwardly. The real pain wouldn't start until long after the memory of their time together was over and the feeling of him deep inside of her had faded. She wouldn't fool herself. When they returned home they would both return to their separate lives. All she had time to worry about was what was happening now. To answer his question, she shook her head, then wrapped her legs tightly around his waist.

David began to move slowly at first giving her body time to adjust to his size, his invasion, until her nails dug into his back urging him to continue. He moved in and out of her moist body, increasing the rhythm, and together they found the tempo that bound their bodies together. He wanted to give her fulfillment, wanted her to come before he did, but as her cries increased, his control began to slip.

"I don't know how much more I can take," he said, groaning. He pushed harder and deeper into her moist heat.

Calaine wrapped her arms more tightly around his back and dug her nails harder into his skin. She met each of his strokes with equal intensity, moving further over the edge until she was ready to explode. "Now," she cried.

And that was all it took for David to grant her wish. He clutched an arm around her waist, burying himself deeper inside at the same time that he locked his mouth to hers. She arched off the pillow and her hips rose to meet his thrusts.

"Yes-s-s!" she screamed, loud with erotic ecstasy. Her cries of delight echoed off the walls as she felt his spasm of release. Shortly after, he held her in his arms as the two drifted off to sleep.

Calaine was the first to awaken and found her head on David's chest. Memories of the night before came flooding back. The last thing she remembered was David kissing her on the mouth, then pulling her snugly into his arms.

Swallowing, she glanced up at the face of the man who still had a protective arm draped across her waist. To be able to wake up beside such a considerate and patient man gave her a deep feeling of security.

As he slept, Calaine found herself in turmoil. The inevitable had finally happened. She had become one of David's conquests. She groaned inwardly. What had she been thinking last night when she finally gave in to her desires? The problem was, she hadn't been thinking. She'd fallen under his spell. And she was still under it. Nothing could please her more than to lie beside him, as she now was, and stare at his handsome face as he slept. He had mesmerized her, making it virtually impossible to think of anyone or anything other than him. Last night with David she had experienced something that she would never forget and for which she would be forever grateful.

Unable to resist, she skimmed her fingers down his arm as she wondered what would come next. Women were a challenge to David and now that he had succeeded in getting what he wanted, she wondered if he would toss her aside like an old shoe.

Closing her eyes, she tried to tell herself that maybe the sex had seemed so fabulous because it had been too long since she had been with a man, that it was only natural for her to have reacted the way she had. She couldn't allow herself to make more of what had happened than what it probably was: sex with no strings attached. So why did she feel a painful ache inside her chest?

"What are you thinking about?" David asked, startling her. She hadn't realized he was awake.

"I'm not thinking about anything. How did you even know I was awake?" she asked as she moved from his chest and onto her pillow.

David shifted slightly and propped his head up with one elbow.

"I could tell by your breathing. Now I'm going to ask you again, what's on your mind?"

He continued to stare at her with his gold-green eyes. Calaine could feel the caress of his gaze and tried to ignore the throbbing in her lower body.

"My parents," she lied. Actually for the first time they were the farthest thing from her mind. All she could think about was his right nipple that was only inches away from her mouth.

David raised his hand to stroke her hair. "You really miss them, don't you?"

She paused. "Yes, I miss them." Rolling onto her back, she shifted her thoughts from him, allowing the memories of her parents to resurface. "I don't know why I miss them so much. When they were around I rarely ever saw them. My dad and mom spent so much time trying to portray this perfect image. When he was mayor, I could understand, but once he served two terms and officially retired, I couldn't understand why they still acted that way." She paused, trying to pull her thoughts together before she continued. "Before they were killed they spent a lot of time traveling. My parents had just returned from a cruise. My dad called to tell me that they were back and before he said goodbye my mother asked to speak to me. She told me how wonderful Alaska had been. We chatted for a few more minutes and before she hung up, she actually told me she loved me. I had a strange feeling after that that something was going to happen and sure enough, two days later I received the phone call that they had been in a crash on the way back from dinner. The driver of the other car had just left a local bar where he'd had too much to drink. My father was killed instantly. My mother lived long enough to tell me I wasn't her daughter. I now think that she held on just long enough to talk to me."

David pulled her closer to him, sensing that she needed his

strength. "I'm sure they loved you in their own way."

"My uncle said the same thing."

She closed her eyes and found herself lost in the comfort of his arms. His arm was resting on the curve of her hip and her head was cradled against his shoulder.

Desire began to boil inside her. Awkwardly, she rolled away from him and rose. "We better get going if we're going to have breakfast."

Gently, David pulled her back down onto the mattress and rolled on top of her. She felt him grow hard again. Her body began to respond and she had no control over what she was feeling. Before she knew it, she was parting her thighs and had invited him back in.

"Don't try to fight it," David whispered against her cheek. "You want me as much as I want you, don't you?"

She moaned.

"Say it, Calaine!" he demanded. When she refused to answer, he stopped in mid stroke waiting for her response.

Calaine couldn't bear it and screamed. "Yes!"

"Yes, what?"

"Yes, I want this. I want you." He slid forward and moved slowly at first, then intensified his rhythm.

Calaine found herself helpless with desire. The second time was even better than the first.

After they had made love a third time in the shower, they dressed and headed to the River Walk in the heart of downtown. Lush green foliage and towering trees lined the banks. Holding hands, they strolled from one end to the other, enjoying the sights and sounds of the area. For lunch, they dropped into a restaurant and had what she believed had to be the best fajitas in the state of Texas. That afternoon they returned to his parents' house where they had dinner. To Calaine's relief, Wanda did not come. She found herself laughing and enjoying the evening. As sunset arrived, they stepped out onto the deck together. David moved up behind her and wrapped his arms around her waist as they enjoyed the serenity together. With a satisfied sigh, David turned her around. They stared at each other for the longest time before his mouth captured her. The kiss was demanding and passionate. Accepting the fact that she was in love was frightening and exciting. There was no escaping it. She had wanted to make love to him since college and when she saw him at the job fair she had wanted him all over again.

They left his parents a little earlier this time and returned to the hotel to his room where he spent the evening teaching her things in bed that she would have been ashamed to talk about. With David, however, they seemed to be natural things. He made her feel like the sexiest and most desirable woman on the planet. Their coming together was explosive and tender. Afterwards he held her in his arms while he drifted off to sleep.

Exhausted but unable to fall asleep, Calaine shut her eyes and tried to block out worry about what would happen when they returned home. If she hadn't known she was in love before she left for San Antonio, she definitely knew it now.

They rose the next morning in time for the buffet. An hour later, after a repeat performance in the shower, they checked out of the hotel.

Feeling like the lovers they were, the two dropped by one of his favorite spots on the way to the airport. It was a small mom and pop restaurant famous for its enchiladas. Their waitress had just returned with their food when a willowy, caramel-colored woman came up to stand beside their table. They both glanced up at her at the same time.

"David, I almost didn't recognize you," she replied, her gray eyes sparkling with excitement.

He gave her a polite smile. "Hello Chanel."

"Is that all you have to say? Why didn't you tell me you were coming to town? I've been trying to reach you ever since you moved back to that little college town," she pouted.

"I'm here for my little sister's graduation." He glanced across the table and made the introductions. "Chanel, I would like you to meet a good friend of mine, Calaine Hart."

Chanel looked as if she had just realized that he had not been sitting alone. "Hello." She gave a tight smile, then looked back at David. "Let's get together this evening. We can go to Maurice's for ole times' sakes."

He shook his head. "My flight leaves in three hours. I'll call you the next time I'm in town."

Calaine could tell the beauty wasn't used to being rejected. Chanel shrugged, then walked away. She didn't know why but the fact that he referred to her as a 'good friend' really bothered her.

When David excused himself and went to the men's room, she found herself thinking again about their relationship. Despite all that had happened between them, she feared that for David she might be nothing more than another conquest. Her mind was troubled as she stabbed her fork into her enchilada.

Calaine glanced over toward the restrooms and saw David standing outside the door talking to Chanel. His back was to the table but Calaine could tell they were standing very close. Then Chanel pulled his head down and kissed him, her long sculptured fingernails caressing his neck. For a split second, she was stunned. Then her heart began to race with disbelief. How well did they know each other? Her fingers tightened around the ice cold glass. She thought she'd known what jealousy was the day she had found McKinley with another woman but that was nothing compared to the pain she felt now. She felt as if she'd been stabbed directly in the heart.

Again, Calaine slept the entire trip. Once in his car, she closed her eyes again, thinking about Chanel. She also wondered if David were seeing someone in Columbia. It surprised her at how bothered by the idea she was. Then she reminded herself that David was free to see whomever he liked. After all, he had made no promises to her nor had he mentioned having any desire to continue their relationship when they returned home.

David broke into her thoughts to ask if she wanted to get something to eat.

She shook her head. "No, I'm anxious to get home. I have a few things to do before I get back to work tomorrow."

He wasn't ready to let her out of his sight. The last two nights had been unforgettable. Was she going to continue to act as nothing had changed between them? He had pondered that question all the way home. "Let's talk about the weekend."

Her defenses sprang to life. There was no way she was going to allow him to give her the brush off. "What's there to talk about? I hadn't been with a man in almost a year and was in desperate need for some sexual release. You just happened to be around at the right time."

"Is that all you think it was?" he asked, thunderstruck.

"That *is* all it was, a fling, David, nothing more. I'm not looking for emotional attachment and neither are you."

His brow quirked. "How do you know what I want?"

"Because I know you," she challenged. Turning on the seat, she looked him directly in the eyes.

David remained quiet. He had seen the questions in her eyes after Chanel stopped at their table and he could have told Calaine they had dated a long time ago, that their relationship had been a disaster from the start, but he'd held back. He still needed time to think, time to sort through his feelings for Calaine. Now, before he even had chance to put their relationship in perspective, Calaine had bluntly dismissed him and everything that had happened over the last couple of days. His fingers clinched tightly around the steering wheel. If that was the way she wanted it, then that's the way she would have it. *For now.*

They were silent for the duration of the drive. Once in her driveway, David carried her bags to her door, waited until she was safely inside, then drove away.

CHAPTER FIFTEEN

Calaine sat at her computer pondering the form letter. *How do I write a letter to someone asking if she's my mother?* Then what were the chances of the recipient even calling or writing her back? She sighed, releasing a lungful of explosive air. For all she knew, her uncle was right. Maybe her mother didn't want to be found.

She slumped back in the chair with despair. Maybe she just needed to leave well enough alone.

Tired of staring at the blank screen, she rose. Although she was frustrated, half ready to give up her search, she knew if she did the nagging ache of not knowing would never go away.

Moving into the kitchen, Calaine decided to make a cup of herbal tea. She removed a clean mug from the dishwasher and reached into a canister next to a wooden breadbox for a tea bag. After putting the tea kettle on the stove, she leaned against the counter with her arms folded across her chest. As she waited, her eyes traveled to the end of the counter where she spotted a menu from Tony's Pizza on the table. It had been attached to the pizza box David had brought to her house almost three weeks ago.

A week had passed since their return from San Antonio and she hadn't heard a word from David. She had expected him to at least call or drop by unannounced, as was his custom, but so far, he had done neither. Calaine's jaw clenched. She couldn't understand why she was surprised or even disappointed since she knew his track record with women. It was amazing that David had hung around as long as he had. She had known all along he had been after one thing and once he got it, it would all be over. It angered her that she had been so stupid. It angered her even more that she really missed him. He was constantly in her thoughts, and as a result she had been increasingly irritable and impatient at work. It had gotten so bad that Norma had pulled her aside and scolded her for her ill behavior. Calaine later apologized to her staff then retreated in her office to spend the rest of the day still thinking about him. Her body craved his touch. She wanted him holding her, caressing her, kissing her with his full, sexy lips.

"Whatever!" she screamed at the top of her lungs. Enough was enough! She had to do something before she hopped in her car and raced to his house.

Turning off the kettle, Calaine decided to do something she hadn't done in months. She raced up to her room and changed into an old t-shirt and a pair of spandex shorts. Slipping her Nike cross-trainers on her feet, she returned to the living room. She pulled back the coffee table, then popped a Tae-Bo tape into the VCR.

Along with Billy Blanks and the rest of his crew, she kicked and punched for the next half hour. With her hands balled into fists, she swung an upper cut for every year she'd lived a lie. She bobbed and weaved while thinking about how her uncle had lied to protect her. She machine gun kicked her anger at her aunt for turning against her and treating her like an outsider. Her upper cuts she directed at her father for having an affair with a nursing student and getting her pregnant. Her sidekicks lashed at David and every other man she had allowed to use her over the years. Breathing hard and sweating, she worked off her anger.

By the cool down, she felt relaxed. The tension had vanished and her anger had lessened. She even realized that she had no real reason to be angry with David. Even though she had watched him and Chanel kiss, it was no business of hers. She and David weren't committed. There were never any words of love and marriage. David had never promised her anything other than his help and friendship. Despite everything she thought about him, he had been there for her every step of the way. It was no one's fault but hers that she had fallen in love with him. Now she just needed to be strong and get over it. With as many disappointments as she'd had in her life, she should be a pro at handling difficult situations.

The phone rang, ending any further thoughts on the subject. She moved into the kitchen and answered it by the third ring.

"Hello?"

"Calaine Hart, please."

The gruff voice was unfamiliar to her. "This is Calaine."

She heard the man clear his throat twice before speaking again. "Ms. Hart, this is Anthony Conley."

Her lips pursed tightly at the name. No doubt her aunt had asked him to call. "What do you want?" she asked coolly.

He cleared his throat a third time. "I would like to first apologize for your aunt's behavior the other day. It was uncalled for and definitely out of line."

Calaine felt guilty for her immediate attitude. "Thank you. I appreciate it."

"No need to thank me. I should have spoken up then but I did not. Greta has always had a way of intimidating people, even me I'm afraid."

Calaine had to chuckle at that.

"I wanted to reassure you that your mother knew what she was doing when she left all of her assets to you. Katherine came and saw me a week before she was killed."

Her stomach churned. "She did?"

"Yes, she did. She wanted to make sure that her will was iron tight. She told me that even though you weren't her natural daughter she loved you very much and wanted to make it all up to you. I had her sign an affidavit to that effect."

Calaine was speechless. Her mother had done that for her?

"Don't worry about Greta, your future is secure. Katherine made sure of that. I do need your signature on a few documents. How about I overnight everything to your office tomorrow?"

"That would be just fine. Thank you so much, Mr. Conley. You can't begin to know how much this means to me." Tears surfaced and caught in her throat.

"You take care, and if you need anything in the future, please feel free to call my office."

"Mr. Conley?" she asked just as he was about to hang up.

"Yes, Ms. Hart?"

"D-Did my mother ever say anything to you about my…" She paused to swallow the lump in her throat, allowing Mr. Conley to intervene.

"No, Calaine. I'm afraid she didn't. However, she did say she needed to make everything right."

Calaine managed to thank him again, then hung up the phone. She lowered into a chair, unable to move. An unconscious smile was on her face. All these years she had thought her mother resented her when all along she had cared about her. *Maybe she just had a hard time, expressing herself.*

Taking a deep breath, she returned to the living room, switched off the television, then went to the bathroom and took a long, hot shower. As soon as she was done, she made a cup of tea, then went back to her spare room and sat down at her desk. This time the words flowed onto the screen.

David's bed felt as big as the state of Texas without Calaine in it. Each night he found himself rolling from one side to the other looking for her. After only two nights of having her lie in his arms he had grown accustomed to the warmth and comfort of her body curled beside him.

Frustrated, he clicked on the television, hoping to drown out his thoughts. He tried concentrating on the evening news but couldn't. All he could think about was the time they'd spent in Texas. He wished that he could turn back the clock. It had been one three-day weekend he would never forget.

After the drive from the airport, he had dropped Calaine off at her home and had tried to pretend the weekend had never happened, that it had meant nothing to him. Only he couldn't. At night he lay awake wishing she were snuggled up beside him. During the day, he sat at his desk fighting the temptation to drop by her job for lunch. Calaine had said the weekend hadn't meant anything to her, and instead of telling her what it had meant to him, he'd said nothing.

Now he was paying for it.

With a groan, he moved off the bed and headed down to the kitchen, hoping to find something to eat. Rummaging through the refrigerator, he couldn't find anything that appealed to him. A lobster wouldn't have appealed to him. Not even his favorite coconut cake. Not now. Not while Calaine wasn't a part of his life. She made a bologna sandwich appealing, and without her food had no flavor.

He reached in the refrigerator for a beer. Getting drunk might be the only way he would be able to get any sleep tonight, especially when all he wanted to do was hold her in his arms and make love to her again and again.

Gazing out the window, he thought about the woman who had made him laugh, who had made him feel needed. The woman who'd satisfied him in bed. The woman who had grown under his skin.

Calaine had touched him in a way that no other woman had.

Maybe it was only gratitude that she felt for him. After all, she had summed up their time together as nothing more than a brief fling. With a scowl, he had to admit that maybe that had been his intention in the beginning, but now his feelings were emotional as well as physical. He wanted her heart and soul.

With each sip, his anger slowly faded, giving way to a kind of yearning. They were good together. He was good for her. Calaine was good for him. *So why haven't you called her?* a voice asked inside his head.

Stubborn pride stood in his way.

Calaine hung up the phone. Another dead end. She had been trying to find Ursula for two days and after a dozen calls, she still wasn't any closer to finding her. Tossing the list aside, she strolled out to the lobby.

Her interviewer Tyla was busy giving a woman a typing test while another applicant was filling out an application.

"How's it going?" Calaine asked quietly. After Jean's promotion to the sales floor, Tyla had been in that position only a month. Calaine tried her best to make sure her employees had adequate training and didn't feel overwhelmed too early in the game.

Tyla's eyes sparkled as she nodded appreciatively. "Everything is going great."

She was smiling; that was a good sign. "Good. Let me know if you need any help today."

After giving a warm greeting to the other women, Calaine moved out into the hallway to the restroom across the hall. When she returned, she found David standing in the lobby.

Calaine tried to control the rapid beat of her heart. It had been over a week since they'd seen each other. She had done everything to get him off her mind, but found that besides trying to find her biological mother, David was the center of her thoughts.

Her eyes drank in his powerful presence and she realized her memory had not done him justice. The man was as seductive as sin. He looked gorgeous dressed in an off-black double-breasted suit with black wing tip shoes. Only he could pull off the pale pink shirt with matching handkerchief.

A huge smile tugged at his lips as he moved towards her, his stride easy and powerful.

Calaine forced herself to stay composed as she glanced up at him. "David, what are you doing here?"

"Hello to you, too," he greeted in a deep sensuous tone. His gaze then traveled down the entire length of her body, enjoying the way she looked in a two-piece almond pants suit.

Tearing her eyes away from his calculated stare, Calaine turned to find Norma looking at her curiously. She was certain that the fact that she'd had the same man in her office twice in less than a month was going to become office gossip.

"David, please follow me to my office."

She nodded to the group, ignoring their curious looks, then led David down the hallway to her office. As soon as they entered the room, he pushed the door shut.

She'd twirled around, ready to blast him for not calling her when he pressed her back against the door and locked her lips with his. Instead of giving him a piece of her mind, she wrapped her arms around his neck and met each kiss. What a way to end her busy day.

The kiss would have gone on for hours if he hadn't stopped.

David stepped away, then took the seat beside her desk, smiling confidently.

His smug face caused the tingle of his kiss to vanish. Calaine moved around her desk, reached for a Kleenex and wiped away what was left of her lipstick. Looking up at him, her expression darkened. "I would appreciate it if you would call before you decide to drop by my office."

David ignored the comment and reached into his jacket pocket. Removing several folded sheets of paper, he slapped them on her desk. "I found Eunice."

The tongue-lashing vanished from her tongue. "How... when?"

He chuckled softly at the change in her expression. "I found her on the Internet."

She moved around her desk and took a seat, reaching for the papers. Eunice Roberts resided in Wilmington, Delaware. Calaine didn't want to get her hopes up. "She was supposed to be dead. How do you know this is the right person?"

"I found three Eunice Roberts who would have been between the ages of 18-21 in 1975. But only this woman worked as a registered nurse."

She looked down at the paper. Her addresses for the past ten years were public record. She had worked as an RN at Wilmington Hospital. "This information is five years old."

He nodded. "I know. Five years ago she fell off the face of the earth."

"What do you mean?"

"I mean there is no record of her after that. No credit checks, no new address or places of employment."

Her shoulders sagged. "Do you think maybe she died?"

David shook his head. "I don't think so. But it won't be too hard to find out. Her death would be public knowledge."

Calaine dropped down in her chair. Never married. No children. Why? Was it because of me?

David watched the play of emotion on her face. They still weren't sure Eunice was her mother, but they were a few steps closer to finding out the truth.

She glanced at him. "Have you had any luck with the other woman?"

"Dorlinda?"

She nodded.

"Not yet, but I will," he stated confidently.

She stared at him, feeling almost as confident as he sounded. She had never liked an arrogant man but something about David inspired confidence. It was as if he had no boundaries when he wanted something badly enough.

He put a brown bag on her desk. She hadn't noticed him holding anything in his hand. "What's that?"

"Lunch."

She didn't think she could bear to spend an hour with him sitting directly across from her, especially since she knew nothing would ever come of their relationship. "I've got a lot to do. Today isn't a good day."

She was giving him the brush-off again. David's mouth thinned with displeasure. "Tough. I'm already here and the food is in my hand. You've never been one to pass up CJ's wings before."

She took a quick sniff and her mouth watered.

When her private line rang, Calaine immediately picked it up. While she spoke, David reached into the bag, removed two Styrofoam containers and set them on the desk. It didn't take long for him to figure out she was talking to her uncle. He saw the sparkle in her eyes and the smile on her sweet mouth as she spoke into the mouthpiece. Dipping a wing into a container of ranch dressing, he took a bite and watched her while he chewed.

Calaine had swiveled in her chair, giving him a full view of her profile.

By his third spicy wing, David noticed her fingers grip the phone tightly. Her smile sagged and shock was etched on her face. He didn't miss the expression of fear that crossed her face. There was no doubt she was talking about something that had surprised her. She swung around and fumbled for a pen then began scribbling something on a pad of paper. Afterwards she lowered her eyes and he couldn't see what she was feeling. Seeing Calaine's beautiful face distorted disturbed him.

After she returned the phone to the cradle, he asked, "What's wrong?"

She looked up and saw the worried expression on his face. "Uncle Thaddeus found Coletta," she replied in an emotional, throaty voice she hardly recognized as her own.

His eyes grew wide with amazement yet the look on Calaine's face told him she was far from excited. "That's great, isn't it?" he asked as he wiped his hands on a napkin.

It seemed she held his gaze for the longest time before giving him a nervous smile. "I think so."

"Oh course it is," he said, trying to reassure her. David reached across the desk and grabbed the notepad in front of her. "Sexton Road?" he gasped. "She still lives in Columbia?"

Calaine nodded.

"Well then, let's go." He clapped his hands together as he rose.

The noise caused Calaine to jump. "Go where?" There was no mistaking the panic in her voice.

His gaze came down to rest on her puzzled face. "To see Ms. Coletta Ross."

Panic swelled in her throat. "Now?"

"There's no time better than the present. I'll drive while you eat your lunch." Before she could object, he put their food back in the bag. Moving around the desk, he took Calaine by the hand and led her out to his car.

When David started the engine, Calaine put a restraining hand on his arm. "I-I can't do this."

He put the car in park and turned to face her. "Why?"

She looked over and met his probing gaze. "I'm not ready," she admitted quietly.

"What's there to get ready for?" She didn't answer. Seeing her expression, David reached for her hand and squeezed. "Just be yourself. You're going to be fine."

Calaine lowered her eyelids briefly and nodded. David shifted the car into gear. Despite agreeing, terror still sprinted through her. All she could think about was that she was not ready to meet the woman who gave her life, who first held her tightly in her arms. That woman could be Coletta.

"I don't feel so good," she moaned as she lowered her window and proceeded to stick her head out.

David reached over, pulled her back down in her seat and pushed the button, raising the window. "Calaine, the air conditioning is on. Relax, everything is going to be just fine."

She looked down at her hands. They were trembling. "What if she's my mother?"

"Then our search is over." He captured a trembling hand in his. "You will no longer have to go around wondering, because you will finally have answers."

She nodded, knowing he was right. If Coletta was her mother then the mystery was over. If she wasn't her mother, then maybe she might be able to shed some light on several unanswered questions.

"Thanks," she said.

He lifted an eyebrow at her. "I thought I asked you to quit thanking me?"

"I know, but I wanted to say it anyway." She admitted to herself her need for his support. She didn't want to impose on him any further but deep down she depended on his strength.

"What are friends for?"

As they pulled onto Sexton Road, a chill ran through her. She had driven on the street several times before but this time it looked so different. She had never noticed how different each house was structured, as if each had been designed by a different developer. The flow of traffic was constant and with parked cars on sides there was very little room left for two-way traffic.

She took a deep breath and tried to relax. She had come to find out answers about her birth and had mere seconds left to change her mind. The truth. If she dared, she was about to find out the truth.

David slowed his car in front of 403, a quaint brick house on the right hand corner. "This is it," he announced, causing her pulse to dash off in a high chase.

Calaine stared out the window, thinking about all the years she had ridden past this very house without knowing it held the answers to her past.

The house was old but in fair condition. Hanging pots on the porch were filled with petunias, but crabgrass grew freely in a lawn that was overdue for a cut.

"You ready?" he asked.

She flipped the visor mirror down and combed through her hair with her fingers. After another long thoughtful look, she nodded and climbed out the car.

Uneasiness struck her at the sight of children playing in the backyard. Three small girls, one a little taller than the others came to stand against the chain link fence. It was obvious they were sisters. Identical charcoal-colored eyes watched with curiosity as she and David moved towards the porch. The door was open and through the screen, she could hear the television.

Shaking off the melancholy, she pressed the bell.

"Grandma!" she heard one of them yell, "someone's at the door."

Seconds later she heard feet shuffling towards the front door.

Her heart was now lodged in her throat and Calaine was tempted to make a mad dash for the car.

Sensing her uneasiness, David leaned forward, placing a hand to the small of her back. "I'm right here beside you," he whispered, his breath warm against her ear.

A busty woman finally appeared. "Hello, may I help you?" she asked in a sweet voice as she opened the screen and stuck out her head.

Calaine returned the woman's wide smile. "Sorry to bother you, but I am looking for Coletta Ross."

The woman chuckled, drawing attention to a tooth missing in the front of her mouth. "I haven't been Ross in years. I married a Coleman two decades ago."

Calaine took in her ebony eyes, the oval shape of her face and the caramel color of her skin. Was there any resemblance?

Placing a hand to her thickened waist, the woman asked, "What can I do for y'all this afternoon?"

"Uh…excuse me. I'm Calaine and this is my friend David. We…I'm looking…" Her voice trailed off and she looked over her shoulder at David for help.

"She is trying to find her mother and we were hoping you could help us."

Coletta looked at both of them suspiciously. "What makes you think I can help?"

Calaine reached into her purse, pulled out the photograph and handed it to her. Coletta took one look at it and her face drained.

CHAPTER SIXTEEN

Calaine's pulse raced. "You know something don't you?"

Coletta shook her head and handed back the picture. "No, nothing at all. Now if you'd excuse me..."

David stuck his foot out in time to keep the screen door from closing. "Ma'am, please if you know something it would really help."

Coletta's eyes shifted from side to side.

"Please," Calaine pleaded. "I don't want to upset anyone, I just want the truth."

Finally, she dropped her shoulders and said, "Come on in." She pushed open the door.

"Thank you," Calaine whispered as she moved into the living room.

The room reminded her of her paternal grandmother's house. Plastic covered out-of-date furniture and different size pillows were scattered around the room. The room was crowded with photographs of several generations of family.

"Please have a seat."

Calaine moved to the couch and the plastic crackled beneath her as she sat. David sat beside her. Coletta turned off the television then took a seat on a blue recliner.

She held out her hand. "Let me see that photo again."

Calaine handed her the photo. She watched the older woman

stare at it, lost in her thoughts.

"Are you my mother?" Calaine blurted.

Coletta took a moment before she finally looked up and said, "No, I'm not."

The girls dashed in through the back door and into the living room. They stopped in their tracks when they saw Calaine and David and suddenly became shy. They were well groomed, dressed identically in jeans and red cotton shirts. Each had her hair in cornrows and decorated with red barrettes. The littlest one, who couldn't have been older than four, reached for her big sister's hand.

Coletta shifted in her seat and acknowledged the three. Calaine could see the love in her eyes when she spoke. "Yes, girls, what is it?"

"Can you come push me in the swing?" the youngest asked in a soft voice.

"In a few minutes. I have company."

David cleared his throat. "If you don't mind, I'll swing the girls while the two of you talk." He noticed Coletta's slight hesitation. "Don't worry. Ruby raised me well."

Her face lit up. "Ruby Bacon is your mother?"

Nodding, he grinned. "Yes, and she raised me well."

"Well, I'll be. How's she doing?"

"Quite well, ma'am."

"Ain't it a small world? Your mom and I used to be real close. I lost touch with the others over the years but your mother and I kept in touch until we both got so caught up into our own families and just never seemed to have time to keep in contact with one another anymore." She asked David a few questions about his mother before she finally said, "All right. Tiana, Terry and Tabby, this nice man is going to swing you."

David rose and moved to stand in front of the three. When they hesitated slightly, he reached into his pocket and pulled out a roll of lifesavers. The candy was the perfect icebreaker. Within minutes, the girls were pulling him out the back door.

Calaine smiled at the exchange, then looked over at Coletta who was watching them through the window.

Calaine felt she needed to set the scene if she was going to get any answers. "I didn't find out until three months ago that Katherine Hart was not my mother. My father was Geoffrey Hart."

She looked at her with surprise. "Our former mayor?"

Calaine folded her hands in her lap and nodded.

Coletta gave her a sweet, sympathetic smile. "I'm so sorry. I read that he and his wife died in a car crash a couple of months ago."

"Thank you. It's been hard but I'm taking it one step at a time. That's why I need to find out the truth. My mother confessed only seconds before she passed away that I was not her daughter. Now that my family is gone, I don't have anyone I can ask. I found that photo in my mother's drawer and I think that one of those women gave birth to me in 1975."

Coletta rose from her chair and paced across the floor before looking at Calaine again. "There was a baby."

Calaine couldn't breathe as she waited for her to continue.

"Eunice and Dorlinda were inseparable. They had both come up from Mississippi with high expectations and quickly got caught up with partying and hanging out. They were always breaking the rules and Ms. Butler was always on them."

"She was the dorm mother, right?"

Icy contempt filled Coletta's eyes. "The mean old goat! She was so strict that if you were even a minute past your curfew she would take away your privileges for a week."

Calaine looked on with bewilderment. "But all of you were

grown women."

Coletta sadly shook her head and shrugged. "That's just the way it was."

Folding her arms beneath her large breasts, she moved across the floor as she began again. "I remember one night hearing a baby cry. I know 'cause the sound woke me up out of my sleep. I grabbed my robe and went down the hall to their room and there was this baby lying on the bed. Eunice and Dorlinda were sitting there looking scared. They were trying to quiet the baby down before Ms. Butler heard her. Thank the Lord, she was a hard sleeper." Coletta stopped pacing and frowned. "She was colicky. With six younger brothers and sisters, I learned a thing or two from my momma. One thing she taught me was that rocking a baby across your knees helped to soothe the tummy. Sure enough, I had that little angel asleep in no time." Coletta returned to the recliner.

"Whose baby was it?" Calaine asked as she wrung her hands nervously.

"I asked them and they both said the baby was theirs." She gave a laugh of disbelief. "I never could figure out whose child it was. Neither of them had ever looked pregnant so I thought they were lying. They were no bigger than a minute and so pretty. I don't know how either of them could have been pregnant and hid it from the world." She paused and stared off to her left, lost in her thoughts.

Calaine cleared her throat trying to get her attention. "What happened to the baby?"

Coletta looked at her, then blinked several times before she spoke. "For two days they had that baby in their room. One of them would go to class while the other stayed behind. They tried to keep that precious bundle quiet but I knew it was just a matter of time before Ms. Butler found out." She stopped and took a deep breath.

"I remember that night. Wanda and Ursula were at a movie and I was in our room waiting for a phone call, when I heard shouting come from down the hall. I was too afraid to leave my room but I heard a lot of screaming and crying. The next day the baby was gone. Eunice didn't leave her bed for almost a week. I asked Dorlinda what had happened to the baby and she said the little girl was with her father."

Calaine was momentarily speechless as she thought about the photo of her mother holding her wrapped in a receiving blanket.

"Did... did they ever mention the baby again?"

She shook her head. "No. The two became withdrawn and rarely spoke to any of us. I tried cheering them up but nothing worked. I even found Eunice crying a few times. If I had to speculate on whose child it was, I would say that baby had belonged to her."

"Do you know if she committed suicide?"

"Lord, no! Although I wouldn't be surprised. Eunice was truly heartbroken and I can understand why. That little girl was a beauty. I will never forget the distinct birthmark she had on her thigh."

"Birthmark?" Calaine suddenly felt lightheaded.

"Yes, it was shaped like a strawberry."

Her body stiffened with shock just as David entered the room. Coletta rose and said she had to get dinner on the stove before her husband got home from work. Calaine wasn't sure how she found the strength to stand. She thanked Coletta for all her help and hurried out to the car. She felt as if she were suffocating and was thankful for the fresh air.

David came up behind her and reached for her arm. Turning her gently around to face him, he stepped closer and stared deeply in her eyes. "Well, what did you find out?"

"Oh my God...that baby was me." She could barely control her gasps of surprise.

His eyes lit with excitement. "That's wonderful, KeKe, but how can you be so sure?"

"I had my doubts but when she mentioned the strawberry birthmark on my leg I knew it couldn't have been anyone but me. It was me, David! Oh my God, I can't believe this." Tears began to stream down her face. It now felt so real. Her mother was out there; she just needed to find her.

He stroked the back of her head, trying to comfort her. "Are you going to be okay?"

She clung to his middle, absorbing his body heat and nodded. "I think so. It's just so much information to digest."

He held her hand on the ride back and listened as she recounted her conversation with Coletta. Afterwards she asked him to take her home. She was then quiet and he allowed her time to digest the information. David knew that she was dealing with quite a bit and he was determined to be there for her the entire stretch.

When they pulled in front of her house, he parked the car but left the motor running. "You going to be all right?" he asked again.

Her lower lip trembled. "I will never be the same again. Not until I find out which one of them was my mother and why she gave me up." Feeling increasingly depressed, she didn't want to be alone, brooding over what had happened today. "Can you stay awhile?"

David was stunned by her invitation. Deep down he had wanted to stay but did not want the offer thrown back in his face. After all, he was a man and he could only take so much rejection.

He turned the car off and rushed around to open the door for her. He looked down at Calaine still sitting there, lost in a daze.

"KeKe?"

She jumped. "Ooh! I'm sorry." She reached for her purse, then climbed out of the car. David placed a hand to the small of her back and assisted her to the front door. She fumbled around in her purse for her keys and made several ill attempts at opening the door. The set finally slipped from her hands and she began to cry.

David picked up the keys and quickly opened the door. He swept her effortless into his arms and carried her over to the couch where he sat down with her in his lap. She lowered her head against the warm curve of his throat and shoulder. Calaine closed her eyes. She knew she needed to be strong, and silently scolded herself for falling apart. At the moment, she didn't know how she could handle not being with David. There was no way she could leave his warm, strong embrace, not when she so badly needed him.

David pressed his face next to her hair and her body trembled. His hand opened and gathered her protectively against him.

"Sweetheart, it's going to be okay," he whispered as he began to rock her.

She buried her face against his chest. "No, it isn't."

For a long time he simply rocked her in his arms and whispered words of encouragement. The tears increased with his kindness.

She shook her head and asked, "Why?"

His gaze came to rest on her tear-stained face. "Why what?"

"Why did my mother give me up?" she asked in a trembling, choked voice.

"I don't know, baby. But we are going to find out." Leaning forward, he kissed the tears away.

"Why are you helping me? Why would you want to be involved in this mess?"

"Do you have to keep asking me that? Can't you see I'm crazy about you?"

David pulled her even closer. The simple words he had spoken dissolved any apprehensions she'd had about their relationship. Relaxing in his arms, she felt a warm peace she hadn't felt in months. Resting her head on his chest, she heard the vibrant beats of his heart. Everything about him was so male and comforting. "I need you," she whispered. Her mind was in turmoil and she needed to soothe it the only way she knew how.

David didn't want to take advantage of her vulnerability. "You're upset. I don't want to—"

"But I want you," she interrupted as her hand moved to cup him between his thighs.

That was all the invitation David needed. He brought his mouth down on hers, kissing her with an almost desperate passion, taking her lips. With his hand, he gently lifted her head for easy access to her mouth, parting her lips, seeking out the honeyed depths of her mouth with his tongue.

Calaine welcomed him eagerly. She wanted this. Needed it. Regardless of what David might feel for her, she loved him and the only way she could ever show it was in the giving of her body. Tonight they would make love and it would be precisely that for her. She pressed her body deep against his and released a moan.

David broke off the kiss long enough to lift her in his arms and carry her to her room.

They couldn't remove their clothes fast enough. She wanted to touch him, to feel his bare chest against her. With wild impatience, she unzipped her pants and tugged out of her jacket. While he removed his suit, she slid off her pantyhose and threw them across the room. They were two minds with a single thought. David took off his boxers and tossed them in the pile with hers.

Calaine reached for the front clasp of her bra but David stopped her. Swiftly he carried her over to the bed. She moaned softly when he laid her on her back, then straddled her hips. He then pushed her hands above her head before trailing his fingers down the tender flesh of her arms and across her chest, finally hovering at the shadowy cleavage between her sensitive breasts. Instinctively her body arched, inviting him to release the clasp and touch her as she longed for him to do. She settled back with relief when at last he undid the fastening and eased the lacy cups aside. After what seemed ages, yet was mere seconds, his hand moved magically across her breasts, his thumb finding her nipples and caressing first one and then the other with tantalizing possessiveness until they were rock hard. Calaine shifted beneath him, needing more. A whimper of pleasure broke from her as she watched David lower his head and take her right nipple and lavish it with his hot, moist tongue, then move over to give the other equal attention. Unable to lie still, Calaine lifted her hands to the back of his head and clung as waves of ecstasy robbed her of her strength and caused spasms of desire at her wet throbbing core. Then he moved, his lips and hands tracing a scorching path down her body, meeting the barrier of her panties only momentarily as he tugged them down, leaving her naked before him.

"Do you have any idea how beautiful you are?" he murmured. Not waiting for an answer, his tongue skimmed up the insides of her legs to the juncture of her thighs. He parted her trembling limbs and sought out her hot moist center. Suddenly she was overcome by an extraordinary rhythm of release.

"No. Wait," she protested faintly, wanting this to be a shared pleasure. But David had other ideas.

"I want to give you pleasure," he insisted throatily. "Make you forget everything and think only of me and what I'm doing to you." He lowered his head again and began working his magic on her until one last stroke of his tongue sent her tumbling over the edge.

Moans of ecstasy slipped through her lips as her whole body flooded with desire. She lay beneath him with eyes closed, unable to control the outcry of her delight as she exploded.

David came up beside her, planting a kiss to her face. Dazed she opened her eyes, looking like a woman who had been satisfied.

"Brotha, you've got skills," she sighed, her desire momentarily appeased.

He smiled, his fingers tracing the contours of her cheekbones, his thighs rubbing against her hips. "No, I just love the way you taste," he argued, and that brought a spark to her eyes.

"Then it's my turn," she declared, sliding from underneath. In an instant Calaine was straddling him. Grinning mischievously, she met his gleaming green gaze. "Scared? You should be. I'm going to make you feel even better," she promised as her fingers began to explore the taut planes of his powerful chest.

David's teeth flashed. "Just being with you makes me feel good," he retorted. His breath hissed in through his teeth as she found his nipples and lightly teased them with her fingers.

Smiling with satisfaction now that she had his attention, Calaine dropped her gaze to his chest after she saw his eyelids flutter weakly. She loved the way he responded to her, keeping nothing back. A groan escaped his lips and she felt her desire stir to life again as she set about tantalizing him as he had her. Dipping her head, she let her lips find his nipples and her teeth nipped him, bringing forth another moan of pleasure. Then her tongue traced lazy circles before licking back and forth across the sensitive nubs.

She seared a moist pathway down over his firm stomach, feeling the tension grow inside him as she approached his waist. In all his naked glory there was no doubting his wanting her and she felt her own body start to throb with awakened desire.

It was no longer easy to keep her movements slow and tantalizing. Her hands trembled faintly as she ran them over his thighs, getting closer but never quite reaching the place she instinctively knew he wanted her to touch. Finally, she gave in to her own need and her lips encircled him. Stroking the length of him with her tongue, she tasted and teased laving him with her tongue until David thought he would die from pleasure.

He moaned aloud and reached for her. "No more!" he gritted out through clenched teeth as her head came up. She looked at him, meeting the fiery blaze in his eyes. Knowing he could take no more, David clasped her hips, holding her to him as he sought to keep some measure of control.

"David." His name was an ache of longing on her lips and with it his immense control finally broke. He pulled her down and held her so that she stayed locked against him. Then he rolled over so that she was beneath him. Spreading her thighs wide at last, he claimed her with one powerful thrust. His presence inside her made her feel whole again.

"Hold me, KeKe. Move with me."

Calaine clung on, matching his thrust, seeking an ending. Wrapping her legs around him, drawing him deeper inside her, she whimpered his name repeatedly as his body pumped in and out of her.

He sighed with relief when he felt her body begin to climax beneath him. As the last ripple of passion overtook her, David joined her, climaxing with a groan that seemed to be drawn from the very depth of his being. Clinging together, they rode out the stormy seas of passion until at last they washed up on shore, fulfilled and exhausted.

CHAPTER SEVENTEEN

Calaine rose early on Saturday, excited about Donna's impending arrival. After fixing a quick breakfast of toast and coffee, she dashed off to the grocery store. Donna was a country girl who believed in real down home cooking, no microwave or canned meals.

On the way back she swung by and grabbed her dry cleaning, then made the short drive home. She changed into an old t-shirt and black stretch pants, then set out to clean her house from top to bottom. She paused only to go into the bathroom and take her allergy medication before the dust got the best of her.

Going into the guest bedroom that she used as an office, she put away the papers she scattered all across the sleeper sofa. After running her finger across her dresser, she drew her eyebrows together in a frown. Dusting was long overdue. She popped in her favorite CD and hummed along with Mary J. Blige as she cleaned the room and daydreamed about David.

The week had been special to her. They had shared either lunch or dinner together, and after work David would make a mad dash to her house where they spent the evening lying in bed in each other's arms, making love and talking until they dozed off. She wasn't sure how she was going to bear it if the relationship came to an end. All she knew was that the last several weeks would be forever imbedded in her mind.

Calaine put the bottle of furniture polish down and dropped down on the couch. Last night after spending an hour listening to David share his dream of having a large family, she had realized that until she knew more about her family, she was being unfair to David. What if there was some hereditary disease? Maybe she needed to slow things down. She loved David so much, but she wouldn't jeopardize his chance for a family. To drown out the thoughts in her mind, she turned up the volume of her portable stereo and got back to work.

Two hours later, she fell back in a chair in the kitchen quite satisfied. Her house was spotless, if she said so herself. She was exhausted, but the effort was well worth it.

As she drank a glass of water, she heard a horn blow out front. She moved down the hall to the door and opened it just as an airport express shuttle was pulling out her driveway and Donna was coming up the steps.

"Hey girl!" she exclaimed. Putting down her tote bag, she met Calaine halfway.

"I'm so glad you're here," Calaine said as the two embraced.

"I'm glad to be here. I missed my girl."

"I thought you were only here for three days?" Calaine said, pointing to the large suitcase the driver had left at the bottom of the steps. Calaine lugged it up the stairs.

"A girl never knows for sure what she might need."

Calaine chuckled as she suddenly remembered the bag she had packed for Texas.

Donna sauntered into the hallway and turned to look at her host. "I think a little shopping trip might be in order. You look a mess," she offered affectionately.

Calaine realized that she probably did look a sight. Moving over to the hall mirror, she found her hair in disarray and streaks of dust across both cheeks. Feeling increasingly self-conscious, she couldn't help noticing how gorgeous Donna looked. She was tall and graceful and the jeans she wore made her legs look a mile long. Her long, chemically relaxed auburn hair was an artful tumble of curls that fell to her shoulders. Her tawny oval face was delicate and as smooth and clear as ever. Calaine had always admired her naturally long lashes that framed her honey-colored eyes.

Calaine tried to finger her tendrils into place as they went into the living room. Kicking off two-inch pumps, Donna made herself at home.

Calaine flopped down onto the couch beside her. "All right, Donna, what really happened between you and Bruce?"

She shrugged. "A little of this and a little of that. You got any food in this joint? That airplane food sucks."

It was obvious Donna didn't want to talk about it. "Sure, come on."

Calaine went straight for the cabinet and made a pot of fresh coffee. Within minutes, she was whipping up a batch of pancakes while Donna scrambled eggs and fried bacon. Donna was a natural in the kitchen.

Rita Davidson had died of breast cancer when Donna was seven, and after her mother's death Donna became the woman of the house. Her father and her little brothers depended on her so much that her life revolved around them. She never participated in any after school activities and had no dreams of ever attending college.

During her senior year of high school her father remarried, and after a little resistance to losing her title as the woman of the house, Donna and her stepmother formed a strong bond. It was at her insistence that Donna enjoyed her senior year and with her family's support, left home to attend college.

Calaine felt guilty that she hadn't shared with Donna her discovery, especially when she knew that Donna would understand her feelings. While pouring batter onto the electric griddle, she decided she would talk to her after brunch.

"Breakfast was also Bruce's favorite meal of the day," Donna blurted, interrupting her thoughts.

Spatula in hand, Calaine glanced over to the stove where Donna was violently scrambling eggs. She gave her a long, hard stare. "Do you want to talk about it?"

Donna sighed, then dropped one hand to her hip. "All right, if you insist."

Calaine chuckled inwardly. Donna had always had a way of wanting you to twist the truth out of her. She moved from the counter over to the stove and rescued the eggs as Donna took a seat at the table and began to explain their break up.

Calaine found herself only half listening, caught up in the memory of how much Katherine had admired Donna. In fact, her mother had thought Donna to be a positive influence and had even gone so far as to say on several occasions that Calaine couldn't go wrong by being more like her roommate.

"Do you think I was wrong?" Donna asked, breaking into her thoughts.

"About what?" Calaine asked as she reached for a plate and slid the eggs onto it.

Donna blew air between her front teeth. "For wanting to buy a Mercedes."

Calaine blinked as she suddenly realized what they were talking about. Hand resting on her hip, she swung around. "You mean to tell me the two of you broke up over a car?"

Ignoring the implications of her soft voice, Donna whined, "I work hard for my money. If I want a Mercedes, I think I should be able to buy one."

"True, but if the two of you are trying to save up for a home, why can't it wait?"

Donna snorted a laugh. "You're beginning to sound like Bruce."

"Good," Calaine said as she moved over to the table carrying two plates of hot food. "I thought you were tired of dating men who thought only of themselves?"

"I am."

"Then what's the problem?" she asked as she took the seat across from Donna.

"The problem is that Bruce bought an Expedition last month and I didn't say anything, but when I decided it was time for me to buy a car that makes me feel good, he acted a fool!"

"Your priorities are screwed up, not to mention you sound like a spoiled brat."

"I do not!"

"I'm afraid that you do," Calaine mumbled in between bites.

Donna looked down at her plate as she stirred her eggs. "Maybe I do, but I don't think it's fair that he can buy what he wants and I can't."

Calaine shrugged. "Double standard."

Donna chewed roughly on a strip of bacon. "Well, I don't like it." Rising from her seat, she moved to refill her mug just as the doorbell rang. "I'll get it," she offered. Setting her mug on the counter, she strolled into the other room before Calaine could rise.

A few seconds later she heard Donna scream with excitement. Calaine knew it was David even before she heard his voice.

Donna returned to the kitchen with her hips swinging in her slim-fitting jeans. David was behind her. "Look who's here?"

Calaine's brown eyes met his. His expression was intense. Standing in the door, David looked as handsome as ever. He was dressed in black jeans and a white polo shirt that stretched across his broad shoulders. A gold-faced watch hung on his wrist and a diamond stud was in his left lobe. His locs had been freshly twisted. Blood pounded at her temples and heat flowed through her veins. She had missed him.

"You look a mess," he joked, trying to break the tension.

"Who asked you?" Calaine retorted, even though she self-consciously combed through her hair with her fingers.

Donna chuckled as she returned to her seat at the table. "I see there's still no love lost between the two of you. You always did fight like brother and sister."

Brother and sister don't make love.

Calaine's eyes darted over to where David still stood and she could see that he was also thinking the same thing. Heat rose to her cheeks and she thought about the things he had done to her body, the way he had made her feel. The thought caused a heat to pool between her legs. Turning away, she rose and reached for another coffee cup in the cabinet above the stove.

"Take a load off your feet and stay awhile. Here, have some coffee." She slid a mug across the table.

David caught it before it fell off the edge. "Aren't you going to fix it for me?" he teased.

Her lips curled upward despite herself. "Don't push your luck." With that, she escaped to her room. Sitting on the side of the bed, she tried to calm her racing heart. He was affecting her in ways that she didn't want to dwell upon. However, there was nothing she could do to change that, not as long as she loved him.

Brushing aside her thoughts, she moved to the bathroom to shower. Twenty minutes later she was dressed in jeans and a lime green t-shirt.

She returned to the kitchen to find two heads together in serious conversation.

Donna sprang from her seat. "Girl, why didn't you tell me about your mother?" She draped her arms around Calaine's neck and gave her a comforting hug.

Calaine looked over at David and rolled her eyes. He had no right telling her business.

He sensed her anger and nodded apologetically. "I'm sorry. I had no idea you hadn't told Donna."

Donna pulled away. "I can't believe you didn't tell me!" she pouted.

"I was waiting until you got here so I could talk to you in person."

Donna threw her arms around her again. "Oh girl, I can't imagine what you are going through!"

"I'm fine, really," she said as they both moved to the table. "David has been a big help."

David glanced up from his mug and she could tell that he was surprised by her admission.

"Well, David didn't tell me the details. So have a seat and spill your guts."

Calaine refilled her mug before returning to her seat. Then she and David took turns telling Donna about her discovery and how he had come into the picture.

Donna was shaking her head with disbelief. "Unbelievable! KeKe, I would have never guessed."

"I have to thank David. I don't know what I would have done without him," she admitted, not trusting herself to look his way.

"It was my pleasure," he purred.

Donna gave him a curious look before she smiled. "I'm glad you were here for her."

Frowning, Calaine reached for her mug and took a sip of the lukewarm drink. She wondered if Donna had picked up on the sexual tension between her and David. She hoped not. The last thing she needed was to have to share her feelings with Donna, especially when she wasn't sure how her friend felt about David.

Donna was familiar with Calaine's past and the way her parents had neglected her. She squeezed her hand. "I hope you find her."

"I hope so too."

"Let's think positive. Give me the names and a computer and I'll try to track down the last three women before I leave on Tuesday."

"I have a computer at my house with Internet access. Why don't you come by tonight?" David suggested.

Donna batted her eyelashes flirtatiously. "Make it dinner and you've got yourself a deal."

David chuckled, remembering her love of red meat, and nodded in agreement.

Calaine felt a twinge of jealousy but she forced a smile. "You guys have fun."

David glanced across the table at her. "That invitation is open to you also, KeKe."

She shook her head. "No, you two have a lot of catching up to do. I'd just be a third wheel."

"Don't be silly," Donna protested. "It will be like ole times."

Still shaking her head, Calaine declined again. "No, I think I'm going to spend some time at my parents' packing."

Donna's face warmed with concern. "You want me to help?"

"Yeah, me too," David offered.

"No, you go have fun." She rose and put her mug in the sink.

"All right. David, how about we go to Spanky's afterwards for a little dancing?"

David tore his eyes away from Calaine to look at Donna and smiled. "Sounds like ole times."

David and Donna left shortly after they cleaned the kitchen to take a crack at surfing the net before they dressed for dinner. Remembering she was out of milk, Calaine hopped in her car and drove to Walgreens.

Calaine didn't know if she could return to her lonely life before David had made her his own. Not now. Not after she'd discovered what love truly felt like.

The love she felt for David was real. She would never be able to share her heart with any other. Not ever. She would never forget the times they'd spent together. She would never forget what he had done for her.

While moving to the cash register, she heard someone call out her name. She turned around to find Damien Martin moving into the line behind her.

"How have you been?" he asked with a wide and eager smile.

She returned the smile with not quite as much enthusiasm, but a genuine smile nevertheless. "Fine and yourself?"

"Great. Just great."

They had dated briefly before her involvement with McKinley. Damien was a minority recruiter for Mizzou's veterinary school, and because he traveled a great deal their relationship had never gotten off the ground. He was a nice person, always a gentleman, always saying the right things. He was the type of guy a girl would love to bring home to meet her parents, and of course, Katherine had loved him. Unfortunately, Calaine had never felt anything when she was around him.

"Thanks for the flowers," she said as she moved up in line.

"It was the least I could do. Your parents were wonderful people." He offered his condolences again and then they engaged in idle chitchat until she reached her place at the register.

"How about dinner?" he suggested.

Glancing over at him, she was about to decline but before she could form the words, she changed her mind. "Dinner would be great."

His dark eyes sparkled with possibilities. "When would be a good night for you?"

She handed the cashier her money, then suggested, "How about tonight?"

Damien nodded eagerly. "Tonight would be perfect."

CHAPTER EIGHTEEN

David arrived at exactly seven o'clock to pick up Donna. Shutting off the car, he rested his elbows on the steering wheel. He planned to convince Calaine to spend the evening with them. It would be just like old times. In college, the three of them had attended several functions together and usually Donna saw someone she knew and left him and Calaine alone. One time they'd gone to the Boone County Fair and Donna had ditched them to hang out with some of her sorority sisters. He and Calaine had strolled around seeing the exhibits while enjoying the cotton candy. They'd had such a good time. How come he hadn't realized then how much she meant to him? He frowned. Things were getting way out of hand, and if Calaine was going to be stubborn and not admit her feelings, then he was going to have to make her see reason.

Climbing out of the car, he moved up the stairs and rang the doorbell. It was only a few seconds before Calaine came to answer the door. As soon as he looked at her, he couldn't speak. He had expected her to answer dressed in her usual sweatpants and oversized shirt. Instead, she was wearing a short black dress that hugged every curve. The dress ended mid-thigh, exposing a pair of toned thighs and calves. The temperature had reached eighty degrees at lunchtime, so she had opted not to wear hose. She had oiled her legs until their velvety smoothness glimmered. Her painted toes were visible in a pair of black open-toed sandals.

"Where are you going?" he asked, not caring if his tone was sharp.

She rolled her eyes at him. "If you must know, I have a date."

"With who?"

She didn't miss the jealousy in his voice. *Good for him, now he knows how it feels.* "That's none of your business. Now, are you going to come in or not?"

He stepped inside and brushed against her. The scent of her perfume traveled to his nose. She smelled like a bed of roses. He followed her into the living room, not missing the enticing sway of her hips as she moved.

"I thought you wanted to spend the evening going through your parents' belongings?"

She shrugged nonchalantly. "I changed my mind."

David tried to mask his jealousy but knew he was doing a terrible job. The thought of her being with someone else annoyed him more than he cared to admit. He had hoped that if she saw him with Donna that maybe she would finally admit her feelings. Instead, she'd gone out and found a date of her own. *So much for wishful thinking.* For all he knew, she might have already had a date and just hadn't bothered to tell him. Whatever the reason, he didn't like it.

"Don't you look nice," Donna complimented as she strolled into the room.

Turning around, Calaine met her radiant face. "Thanks, you don't look bad yourself."

She was wearing a blue two-piece outfit. The top had spaghetti straps and the skirt stopped several inches above her knees.

"Where are you guys going tonight?" Calaine asked

"I don't know. David hasn't said." Donna turned to him.

He moved and placed a hand to her shoulder. "We'll think of something. Ready to go?" he asked, not trusting himself to look at

Calaine.

"Sure, let me just grab a sweater and I'll be ready." Donna moved back to the guest room, leaving the two of them alone again.

Calaine sat on the couch and leaned her head back against the cushions, closing her eyes. She hoped Donna would hurry up and the two would leave before her date arrived.

"You do look lovely."

Her heart pitter-pattered at the compliment. She opened her eyes and met his warm smile. "Thank you." Giving his pleated slacks and matching rayon shirt a once-over, she replied, "You don't look half bad yourself."

"Where are you going tonight?" he asked.

"I'm not sure either, but I am certain we'll think of something."

He met her direct gaze. Instead of pulling her into his arms as he was yearning to do, he made himself stand several feet away. Tonight he planned to respect her wishes no matter how hard they might be.

The doorbell rang and before she could move, David was already opening the door.

He found himself face-to-face with his competition. The man was a couple of inches shorter but dressed very stylishly. The way he would have expected Calaine's date to look.

The man looked surprised, almost as if he thought that maybe he had knocked on the wrong door. "Is Calaine home?"

David was tempted to tell him no, but he knew with Calaine less than several feet away, it would only anger her further.

"Yes," he said to her date. David knew he sounded guarded and a lot less cordial than he had. Well, it was the best he could do, he told himself resentfully. "Come on in." He stepped aside so her date could pass.

Calaine rose. "Damien, you're early," she said, trying to force a smile.

"I'm sorry. I wrapped up my business a little sooner than expected. If I'd known you'd look this good I would have arrived even earlier though." He openly admired her.

She forced a smile while ignoring the side glances David was giving them and reached for her purse on the table. "I'm ready."

"Where are you two going?" David asked.

"None of your business," she interrupted before Damien could even answer.

The jealousy pulsing out of him made him look like a different person. Something tugged at her inside because she knew that the jealousy was because of her. She had never known a man to show that type of emotion towards her in the past.

"We're going to Outback," Damien offered.

David fumed. He knew that was Calaine's favorite place. He also knew it was childish to resent her date for knowing what she liked. Nevertheless, knowing that did nothing to stop him from resenting her date like hell.

The line at Alexander Steakhouse was out the door with over an hour wait, so the two decided to eat at Boone Tavern. For appetizers, they shared a plate of piping hot Buffalo wings while sipping on margaritas. The two talked over old times and filled each other in on the last decade.

David found Donna to be a wonderful, outgoing person who had blossomed over the years into an even more beautiful woman. Nevertheless, she wasn't Calaine. He couldn't get Calaine off of his mind. He wondered how her dinner was going, and wondered if they were going straight back to her house or to somewhere afterwards.

David tried to cool his anger as he slowly chewed his chicken. He felt betrayed because he hadn't even known she was seeing anyone besides him. He knew that sounded selfish but he had dominated so much of her time over the past several weeks that he'd thought he was exclusive. Now the joke was on him.

Their meal arrived and he tried to focus on carving into his medium rare steak.

"So, when are you going to admit you're in love with Calaine?"

His brow rose at her observation. "Is it that obvious?"

Donna toyed with her potato as she spoke. "Yes. I also know she feels the same way. I don't know why the two of you don't stop playing games and just go for it."

"You're not mad?"

She snorted. "Why would I be mad? Now don't get me wrong. You are still one *fine* brotha, but you know as well as I do our relationship never made it past first base. I really liked you, I still do, but I never felt anything other than friendship towards you." Lowering her fork, she placed her elbows on the table. "I always thought the two of you would make a cute couple."

"You did?" he asked, clearly surprised.

"Sure I did. I also know something was going on between the two of you then. I'm not blind, you know. I saw the way y'all used to look at one another. That's why I used to leave the two of you alone all the time. I also saw it again today."

David leaned back in his chair and chuckled heartily. "I guess you've got it all figured out."

"Yep." Her eyes narrowed suspiciously. "And if you break my girl's heart, I'm going to have to cut you."

Even though she was laughing, he heard the seriousness of her comment. "Don't worry, my intentions are all good." He took a bite of his steak, then asked between chews, "So what about you and what's-his-name?"

She was so surprised by his question that she blushed. "Bruce. I don't know. I love him so much, but he makes me so mad."

"Isn't that what love is about?"

She was still for a moment before she met his gaze. Donna smiled as she responded, "Yeah, I guess it is."

After spending two hours listening to Damien talk about himself, Calaine couldn't take anymore and asked him to take her straight home.

Changing into her favorite two-piece cotton pajamas, she moved into the kitchen and made herself a cup of cappuccino. Sitting at the table, she stirred her mug and felt sorry for herself.

Donna and David were probably out having a wonderful time and instead of joining them as David had suggested, she had gone out with motor mouth. Now she would spend the rest of her evening tormenting herself with thoughts of the two of them together.

She brought the rim to her lips and took a cautious sip as she stared up at the clock on the wall. It was a quarter past ten. The night was too young for Donna to return. She probably wouldn't get in until well after midnight.

Calaine sighed, then rose and moved into the living room, hoping to catch an interesting movie on *Lifetime*. She turned on the television, only to find they were showing a rerun. Dropping the remote, she reached for her mug on the coffee table and took another sip.

She had made a lot of mistakes in her life, but this one was proving to be one of the worst. She loved David. There was no getting around that and she knew he felt something for her. It was obvious, or at least she hoped it was. Why else would he spend so much time helping her? She had to admit that in the beginning she had thought it was about the sex, but even after they had finally made love David still came around and still continued to help her. Then tonight when he saw her with Damien, she had witnessed the dark look in his eyes and the jealousy brewing.

Returning her mug to the table, Calaine rose and headed towards her room. She was being ridiculous. No way was she going to spend the evening feeling sorry for herself. David had invited her to spend the evening with them and she planned to do just that. She climbed the stairs in haste. It would take her only a few minutes to change back into her clothes and join them at Spanky's. She had just reached into her closet for the dress she had hung back up, when she heard the doorbell ring.

Calaine tossed the dress onto her bed and raced to the door. When she opened it, she gasped at what she saw. "David, what are you doing here?"

He leaned against the doorframe, giving her his most irresistible smile. "What does it look like? I'm here to see you. Can we talk?"

Calaine stuck her head out and looked over at his BMW. "Where's Donna?"

"Donna is spending the night at a hotel. I told her I wanted you all to myself tonight."

Her pulse raced, but she needed to be sure before she got ahead of herself. "What about your date?"

David stepped forward until their bodies were touching. Staring down at her he replied, "I'm not interested in Donna. I'm interested in you." Without another word, David tossed his keys onto the couch, swept her up into his arms and carried her towards her room.

"I thought we were going to talk," Calaine challenged as her arms slipped around his neck and her lips found the angle of his jaw.

He didn't pause on his way to her bedroom, "Calaine, sweetheart, I'm like a man dying of thirst and you're the only thing that will keep me alive. I've kept my hands off you since you left my house last night. Don't ask me to wait any longer."

The passion in his voice turned her heart over and emotions overflowed. "I wouldn't dream of it."

Inside the bedroom, David lowered her to her feet and reached over to switch on a lamp beside the bed. Shrugging out of his shirt, he tossed it aside before pulling her back into his arms. She sighed with satisfaction as his strong arms closed around her. When he bent his head to her mouth, she met his kiss, returning it, sensing his need to devour her. It set her heart to racing and her fingers clutched at him, trying to pull him even closer.

This was not like before. There was no slow, sensual build up. They had been apart too long and the need was too great. Their hands dealt feverishly with clothes, discarding them in a staggered trail to the bed where, naked at last, they toppled onto the sheets.

The feel of him against her, the unmistakable evidence of his powerful need thrusting against her belly, scattered Calaine's senses. She moved against him with a moan. One of his knees pushed her thighs apart, allowing him to slip between them and enter her with one push.

Calaine's body arched upwards in pleasure and her legs rose, locking about his hips as she drew him deeper into her. David tried to slow down. She could feel the tension in his body but the desire was too great and with a groan he thrust into her again and again, setting a rhythm she matched, driving them towards the satisfaction they sought so desperately. It came with explosive force, causing them both to cry out and cling to each other as the waves of pleasure tossed them about until finally washing them onto calmer shores where they lay until their heart rates returned to normal.

At last, David raised his head and looked down at her, a sober expression on his face as he brushed sweat-soaked strands of hair from her forehead. "KeKe, I'm through playing games. Without you, my life is a shambles. When I'm not around you I can't think, I can't sleep. You have unlocked my heart and soul... What I'm trying to say is that I love you."

She couldn't believe her ears. He loved her. Her eyes became misty and her throat was dry, making it difficult to speak. She stared up at him leaning over her. There was so much she wanted to say to him.

The phone on her nightstand began to ring, but she was in no condition to answer it. The answering machine clicked on.

"Ms. Hart, my name is Danielle Mitchell. I received a postcard in the mail today addressed to my aunt Eunice Roberts."

CHAPTER NINETEEN

David pulled in front of the Delaware Hospital for the Mentally Ill and climbed out of the rental car. He moved around to the passenger side and opened it for Calaine.

"You ready?" he asked.

She smoothed down the front of her dress, then took his hand.

They strolled up the sidewalk, through the double doors and walked to a reception desk where two middle-aged women were answering a multi-line phone that was ringing consistently.

David scribbled his name on the sign in sheet on the counter and waited until a chunky, blonde-haired woman was ready to assist them.

"Excuse me... Joy." David looked up from her nametag and gave her his most captivating smile. Slowly her large dilated pupils came up to study him.

"May I help you?" she asked, chewing loudly and obnoxiously on a piece of bubble gum. Her eyes traveled from one to the other.

Leaning forward, David rested his elbow on the counter. Quickly, he realized he made a mistake by the chilly look she gave him, and dropped his arm to his side.

Calaine finally found her voice and stepped forward. "I'm here to see Eunice Roberts."

Joy popped her gum between her teeth. "Are you family?"

Was she family? That was a good question that unfortunately

she was unable to answer with certainty. "Yes, I'm her daughter," she blurted.

Joy looked at her over the top of her glasses suspiciously.

David draped an arm around her waist. "Actually Dr. Williamson is expecting us."

She frowned. "Have a seat and I'll page her."

Calaine took David's hand again. They entered a deserted area where a twenty-seven inch television was mounted in the corner. While they waited, David watched the Montel Show and chuckled lightly as the talk show host lectured a brother about fathering five children by four different women. Glancing to his right, he noticed Calaine staring off in front of her.

"Relax, everything is going to be all right," he assured her.

Calaine waited for the butterflies to stop fluttering in her belly. Guilt, tension and fear settled over her like huge dark clouds. Ever since Danielle called two days ago, her life had been in an uproar.

Danielle had never known much about her aunt's past except that she'd had a nervous breakdown long before she was born. Her mother had been appointed by the state as her sister's legal guardian. Danielle and her mother had visited her frequently, and although Eunice sometimes acted like a stranger, Danielle had adored her. When Danielle's mother died three years earlier, Eunice had been placed in a residential facility. Calaine heard the guilt in Danielle's voice when she admitted she had been so wrapped up in her career, she hadn't visited her aunt much, nor had any of the other family members.

As far as Danielle knew, her aunt had never been married and had never had children. She had given Calaine the name of the hospital where she was residing and her physician's name.

Calaine took another deep breath trying to calm her nerves. In a few minutes, she hoped to have answers. It wasn't long before a woman in a white coat came out to speak with them.

"Hello, are you Ms. Hart?"

Calaine rose and walked over to her. "Yes, I am."

"Danielle told me to expect you." She gave Calaine a friendly smile. "Why don't we go to my office and talk in private."

"Sure." She followed her to a room down the hall and took a seat across from her desk.

"You're Ms. Roberts'daughter?"

Calaine laughed nervously. "I don't know. I'm looking for my mother and I think Eunice might be that woman."

Dr. Williamson stared at her for several seconds and saw the sincerity in her face. "It would answer a lot of questions."

Calaine's heart thundered against her chest. "What do you mean?"

"Ms. Roberts has been telling us for years she abandoned a baby girl." She paused when she saw excitement dancing on Calaine's face. "Now please keep in mind, Eunice is a diagnosed schizophrenic. She has a tendency to believe things are happening that aren't even true. Nevertheless, she has been trying to convince us for years she has a little girl."

"Has anyone ever corroborated her story?"

"No. She hasn't had many visitors. I've asked her family but no one seems to know. The only friend she seems to have is a Mrs. Saunders who visits her quite often, and she doesn't know."

Calaine thought about how sad it would be to be locked away for years, unwanted or unneeded by anyone. "I would like to see her."

For a long moment, Dr. Williamson continued to openly analyze her until she saw something in Calaine's face that told her Calaine was sincere. "I must let you know that Eunice also has terminal lung cancer. We're not sure how much longer she has left. But

I have a strong feeling that she has been holding on, waiting for someone."

She rose and they moved through the lobby to where David was waiting. Calaine signaled for him to join her. When he reached her, she looked up at him and whispered, "She's taking me to see her." He squeezed her hand and together they moved to the west wing.

Dr. Williamson took them down a secure wing where several residents were sitting in the lounge watching television while others were sitting at a long table putting puzzles together or playing a game of checkers.

Dr. Williamson stopped in front of a room. "Wait out here a minute while I check and see how Ms. Roberts is doing today." She moved to the desk and spoke briefly to one of the resident supervisors.

David grasped Calaine's shoulder and squeezed. "How are you holding up?"

"I'm so nervous." That door was the only thing separating her from answers.

It seemed like ages before Dr. Williamson returned, opened the door and asked the two to enter.

Calaine shuffled her feet and entered. Dr. Williamson pulled back the curtain. Calaine looked down at the frail woman sitting up in the bed.

Eunice stared up at her with a look of astonishment.

"Ms. Roberts, my name is Calaine Hart and I'd like to ask you a few —"

"Kay? Is that you?" Her eyes narrowed suspiciously.

Calaine went completely still. She lowered into a seat next to the bed. "Y-you know who I am?"

Eunice nodded. Her eyes were brimming with tears. "I always

knew you would come back." She smiled proudly. "Wait until I tell Birdie, she'll never believe this."

Glancing up, Calaine looked over at Dr. Williamson for help. "Who's Birdie?"

"Mrs. Saunders," she answered by way of explanation.

Eunice reached over and squeezed her hand. "How have you been?"

Calaine's eyes misted as she smiled down at her. "I've been fine."

"Did they treat you right? I always wondered if you had a good life."

Calaine nodded, suddenly unable to speak.

Eunice leaned back on her pillow and smiled up at her with adoration. "I always knew you were going to be pretty. You were such a pretty baby. All my friends were so jealous." She chuckled absently as her eyelids began to close.

Calaine smiled down at her warm friendly face. "Ms. Roberts, I have so much I want to ask you."

Her lids flew open in terror. "Where's your father?"

"He's dead."

"D-dead?" Her face softened with relief. Then she began to laugh.

Calaine looked to Dr. Williamson for help.

"Ms. Roberts, Kay would like to ask you some questions."

Eunice continued to laugh hysterically until she started to cough uncontrollably.

Dr. Williamson looked to them with an apologetic expression. "She has good and bad days. Maybe tonight isn't a good time. How about we try again in the morning?"

Calaine gave a robotic nod and allowed David to lead her out of the room just as Eunice began to shriek with hysteria. Moving beside Calaine, David's strong grip steadied her as they walked out to the car.

Eunice Roberts is my mother. She gulped, trying to push back the despair, only this time it was impossible. Not only was her mother mentally ill, she was also dying of cancer.

Calaine held on until they returned to the hotel, but, as soon as they moved into their room, the tears started and then she couldn't get them to stop.

David gathered her in his arms and held her close as the tears overcame her. She slumped against him, her face buried as heavy sobs consumed her. Warm wet cheeks dampened his shirt. His heart went out to her. He didn't know which was worse: her never knowing who her mother was or finding out she was terminally ill.

David sat on the bed, cradling her. His hand stroked her hair as if she were a child while he whispered tender words in her ear until she calmed down. He laid her gently on the bed with her head on the pillow and lay beside her with his arm draped snugly around her as they fell asleep.

CHAPTER TWENTY

Calaine woke up the next morning to find herself in bed fully dressed with David's arm draped across her waist. As she stared up at the popcorn ceiling, thoughts of the night before came rushing back. Her mind spun with bewilderment. She had hoped it had all just been a bad dream. Needing a moment to pull herself together, she slid from under his arm and quietly moved into the bathroom, trying not to disturb him.

After she rinsed out the tub she ran herself a bath, then removed her wrinkled clothes and climbed into the tub before the water had a chance to fill.

She still couldn't believe that she had finally found her mother. Eunice seemed like a nice women with such a good heart. A sob ached at the back of her throat. How she wished things could be different. How she wished she had more time to get to know her.

She looked down into the tub as the water reached her knees, her vision blurred by tears.

She had so many questions she wanted to ask Eunice, so many things she needed to know. Hopefully, today she would have a chance.

Leaning back in the tub, she closed her eyes and tried to weigh the entire chain of events. Anger brewed on the edge and she had to take another breath and try to relax. How could her father have done something like that? She had never truly known her father, of this she was certain , because the man she remembered would have never done such a thing. Why had he taken her away from Eunice? The question hammered at her. She wanted to put together all the pieces and her father was the only one who could do that. Unfortunately, he was no longer here for her to confront for answers. Deciding to raise her as another woman's child was one thing, denying her her maternal right was another thing altogether. She would never have guessed she could feel so much hate and betrayal for a dead man.

Calaine inhaled as the steam began to rise and tried to ignore a cynical inner voice that asked how her uncle could not have known what had happened. After all, he had taught all the women, and her father was his brother. The only connection her dad would have had with the students would have been his brother Thaddeus. Or was it? a little voice asked. She was more certain than ever her uncle knew more than he was telling. Tonight, when she returned from the hospital, she was going to give him a call and demand the truth.

Tormented by confusing emotions, she tried to look at the bright side only to realize there was no bright side. After a long and troubled night of soul searching, she had realized she was going to be forced to make the most difficult decision in her life, to end her relationship with David. What else could she do? With mental illness in her family, the undeniably dreadful fact was that she could never bring a child into the world. In addition, her father's older sister had died last year of lupus, and her biological mother had lung cancer as well as schizophrenia. She couldn't do that to a child and she certainly couldn't do that to David. He deserved to someday have a family. As much as it hurt her, she was going to have to break off their relationship.

She turned off the water and spent the next half hour trying to sort out her conflicting emotions. Lost in her thoughts, she didn't immediately hear him calling her.

"KeKe."

"I'm in the tub," she replied after a moment.

"May I come in?"

David was standing right outside her door. How could she deny him? She hesitated, then invited him in.

He walked in wearing an adorable smile. "How are you feeling this morning?" He lowered the toilet seat and sat down.

She gazed into his waiting eyes and answered quietly, "The same."

"It can only get easier now," he said with reassurance. "It seems that your mother has been waiting all these years for you to come back."

She met his positive smile, tears glistening in her eyes. She was hurting for losing all those years with her mother. She was also hurting for what she had to do. "I have to go and see her," she said in a low, composed voice.

David nodded and murmured, "As soon as you get out I'll take a quick shower and then be ready in a flash."

Calaine looked down and studied her hand. "I want to go alone."

David wasn't sure he heard her right. "What did you say?"

She looked at him. Their gazes held for a moment until she found the courage to say, "I need to do this by myself."

"Calaine, you're in no condition to handle this alone. Let me go," he insisted.

"No." She rose from the tub and reached for the bath towel David offered her. "If I'm going to open this mysterious chapter of my life, I want to do it on my own." Wrapping the towel around her, she stepped out the tub and padded into the other room.

David followed. "All right. I respect that. I'll be here if you need me."

Calaine stopped and turned slowly. David noticed the tension in her face, her lips and her somber eyes. "I don't think that is a good idea. Now that we've found my mother I don't know how long I'm going to be here," she said with sudden anguish.

David shrugged. "I don't care. I want to stay and help you through this." He lowered onto the bed as she reached for her suitcase and opened it on the bed beside him.

"But I don't want you to."

David's pupils grew wide with surprise. He had a sinking feeling Calaine was trying to get rid of him. He shook his head stubbornly. "I'm not going anywhere, you need me."

"No, I don't," she snapped. "I need to sort out my life and I don't need you distracting me." She saw him flinch at her words but she did nothing to soothe him.

Despite her gruff words, a sense of protectiveness lingered in him. He leaned lightly into her, tilting his face towards her. "What are you saying?"

Calaine planted a hand to her hips and spoke with as reasonable a voice as she could manage. "I'm saying that seeing Eunice has made me think a lot about my own life. I still need to discover who I really am, and until I do, now is not the time for a relationship."

"The gratitude is over," he mumbled sarcastically. "I guess that's why you felt compelled to keep thanking me."

"No, I…" She paused. "I'll be forever grateful, but your services are no longer needed. I really appreciated your help but I can handle it from here."

His face stilled. "So you've been using me?"

An unfamiliar look seeped into her eyes. "I didn't use you. You offered your help."

The shock of discovery hit him. It *had* been only gratitude she had felt for him, nothing more.

It hurt her to say those words but it was the only way she could get him to let her go. If he thought for one minute that she was breaking things off because she thought it was unfair to him to give up his dream of having a family, he would never leave. David would sacrifice his own happiness just to be with her and she couldn't let that happen.

"Is that the way you want it?" he asked, puzzled by her change in behavior.

"That's the way it has to be. My priority right now is my mother. Everything else has to come second, including you. I have to find out who I am and I'm going to do that no matter how long it takes."

Rising, David reached out and caught her hand in his. Caught by surprise, she dropped her towel. He wrapped an arm around her naked form, pulling her close against him. "I told you we were in this together. I'm not leaving you until this thing is over."

Calaine wiggled free and lifted her arms to shield her breasts. "This thing is already over," she replied with a ring of finality. "My mother has been found. Now I need to take the time to sort through my life and find some kind of order." Considering the conversation over, she reached into her suitcase and removed matching undergarments, then quickly slipped them on.

David ran a frustrated hand across his face. "What kind of game are you playing? One minute you want to be with me, the next minute you don't. You've been doing this from the beginning."

She shook her head. "I'm sorry, I didn't mean to mislead you."

David was quickly losing his patience with her. He looked up to the ceiling as if asking for strength before his darkened gaze traveled to her again. "Then please explain to me what you do want

263

from me? I put my heart on the line and this is the thanks I get?"

She swallowed. "I'm truly grateful for everything you've done."

"I don't want your gratitude. I want your love," he snarled.

Looking up at him, her heart ached at the pain she saw in the depths of his eyes. She reminded herself that it was because she loved him that she was doing this.

"I know." She paused, trying to find the strength to voice what she was about to say. She kept all expression from her voice and face as she said, "I'm sorry, David, but I can't return those feelings, not now, maybe not ever."

She saw him flinch from the sting of her words and she wished she could start laughing and pretend it was all one big joke, but she couldn't.

"You know what? I'm sick of playing this game with you," he snapped as he reached for his wallet on the nightstand and slipped it into his back pocket.

Calaine stared at him with rounded eyes. "Who's playing? This is my life we are talking about!" she shrieked.

David was silent for the longest time as he slipped on his shoes. Part of her hoped he would come back with a snappy retort, something strong that convinced her she was making a grave mistake.

"Fine," he finally replied. He reached for his room key, then turned to her again, his eyes dark and cold. "I'll be back after you leave to get my things." With that, he turned and walked out the door.

Calaine fell across the bed and cried until her head hurt.

From a distance, behind a curtain, the woman watched Calaine with her heart beating rapidly against her chest. She remembered holding her tiny body only seconds after she was born. She remembered little fingers curled around her thumb while suckling hungrily at her breast. Her heart had been filled with love as she stared down at a head full of curly hair and exotic brown eyes identical to those of the first man she had ever loved.

A lump formed in her throat that she couldn't swallow. It was pride. It was regret because the beautiful woman talking to Dr. Williamson was her little girl. The little girl she hadn't seen since she was five days old. The daughter she had never had a chance to know. Giving Calaine her grandmother's name was the only decent thing she had ever been able to do for her.

An ache swelled in her chest with a longing so profound she almost went to her daughter then. She wanted to hold Calaine in her arms and feel her warm body against her while she begged for forgiveness. She wanted Calaine to tell her that everything was going to be okay.

She dropped her arms to her sides and released a long shaky breath. Regret assailed her. For twenty-eight years, she had been unable to put the pain of something missing from her life to rest. All along, she had known that pain was the loss of her daughter Calaine.

Calaine was on the verge of tears. In a brief visit with Dr. Williamson, she had learned that Eunice's condition had worsened. It was only a matter of days or hours before her death.

It wasn't fair! She had finally found her mother and now she was going to be lost to her again.

265

Taking another deep breath, she moved behind the curtain. Her mother was lying peacefully in the bed without a worry in the world. She stared down at her beautifully aging face. Eunice was on a great deal of medication. The staff was trying to make her last days as comfortable as possible.

Taking a seat in the chair beside her, she took her hand in hers. Eunice stirred and raised her eyelids long enough to see Calaine's face and smile.

"Kay, I'm so glad you came back," she whispered.

"Of course I'm back," Calaine forced around a lump the size of a golf ball.

"I'm so glad, now I can quit worrying, now I can rest," Eunice whispered as she squeezed her hand. "I'm so very tired."

"Rest, we'll talk later."

Eunice nodded her head and drifted off back to sleep. Calaine continued to hold her hand and watch her sleep while tears spilled from her eyes.

"It doesn't matter why you gave me up. All that matters is that we are together now," Calaine whispered. She continued to stroke her hand even after Eunice dozed off. After several minutes, Calaine felt someone watching her. She glanced over her shoulder to find a woman standing at the door.

From the moment she glanced at the lovely woman, she felt an instant tug to her. Was it the look in her eye? Calaine recognized her. She was tall and thin with slanted brown eyes and short salt and pepper hair.

"Dorlinda?"

She nodded. "Hello Calaine." She stepped into the room with a slight smile. "When Eunice told me you were here, I had to see you for myself. I-I feel like I'm dreaming."

"I almost didn't look for her. I-I thought she was dead."

Dorlinda pursed her lips. "No... she is very much alive... for now."

"How come... Why did she...?" She wasn't sure where to begin or what to say. "I would have been here sooner if only I had known."

Dorlinda gave her an understanding nod. "Your being here now is what she'll always remember. You should have seen her face this morning. All she could do was talk about you."

Calaine wiped fresh tears from her eyes. "How long have you been here?"

"Since early this morning."

Calaine dropped her eyes to look at Eunice again. "My mother's dying." She knew Dorlinda was well aware of Eunice's condition, but for some reason, she needed to say the words out loud. Part of her hoped that maybe, just maybe, they weren't true.

"Calaine..." Dorlinda paused, drawing her attention. Stepping closer, she took a deep breath, then replied, "Eunice isn't your mother. I am."

CHAPTER TWENTY-ONE

"What?" Calaine shot up from the chair. It was one thing to think a dying woman was her mother, but this was altogether a different story.

She frowned. Dorlinda looked healthy and well maintained. She didn't appear to have to worry about where her next meal was coming from. Her hairstyle was only from a beauty salon. Her clothes were off a rack at Neiman Marcus. The large, two-carat solitaire on her ring finger indicated that she had married well. In fact, she didn't look like a woman who would have a twenty-eight-year-old daughter. Calaine found it all too much for her to deal with.

Too much.

Dorlinda's top lip quivered. "I've missed you so much."

Calaine shook her head in disbelief. Blood roared through her ears. Her heart thundered in her chest. She wasn't sure her legs would support her. Through misty eyes, she stared at the woman who had just revealed herself as her mother.

Touching her fingers to her lips, Calaine whispered, "How could you…?"

"I know you have so many questions. Please, just give me a chance to explain," she pleaded.

Calaine's eyes turned cold and unfeeling. "Explain what? The reason you abandoned me?" She shook her head vigorously. "I can't talk to you right now. I need time to think."

She rushed out before Dorlinda had a chance to speak. Through a rage of blind fury, she returned to the hotel and found that her pain had just begun. True to his word, David had returned for his things and was gone.

Calaine fell upon the bed with her head buried in a pillow and cried. What was she going to do now? The man she loved was gone.

She cried until no more tears came. When she finally quieted, she forced herself to get up and wash her face. Then she drew in a deep breath.

Her cell phone rang and she reached for it.

"KeKe?"

"Donna?"

"What's wrong?"

"Everything...everything," Calaine wailed, her voice both fragile and shaky.

"Do you want to tell me?"

She could barely lift her voice above a whisper. "Eunice isn't my mother."

"What?" Calaine registered the surprise in Donna's voice. "How did you find out?"

"Dorlinda's my mother. She came by the hospital today while I was visiting."

Donna gasped. "What did she say?"

Calaine snorted rudely into the mouthpiece. "She walked in and virtually said, 'Guess what, I'm your mother.' I walked out of the room."

"Girlfriend, you been waiting weeks for that moment."

"I know, I know. I just got so angry when I saw her standing there looking like a million dollars that I left. How could she have abandoned me like that?"

Donna's soothing voice probed further. "Why didn't you ask

her?"

Sighing, Calaine mumbled, "I guess I should have."

"Yes, you should have. Listen, I spoke to David and he told me... well, he doesn't want you to be alone. Would you like me to fly down in the morning?"

What she really wanted was for David to come back. However, she needed to think and take the time to find out her past and discover what the future held for her. "No... I need to do this alone."

"You're never alone."

"I know, Donna, and I appreciate it. I just need time, that's all."

"I understand. Just remember that I love you, girl."

"And I love you. Can you water my plants before you leave tomorrow?"

"You know I will. Now go and get some rest."

Early the next morning Calaine arrived back at the hospital. Dorlinda was already there sitting on the bed beside her closest friend. Standing at the door, Calaine watched her care for Eunice so tenderly that it brought tears to her eyes. *Why couldn't she have treated me that way?*

She wanted, needed, to put all the pieces of the puzzle together so she could get on with her life. There was only one person who could provide her with answers.

Calaine rapped lightly on the door. "How is she?" she asked as she stepped into the room.

Dorlinda turned at the sound of her voice. "She's been fading in and out." She gave Calaine a nervous smile. "She's been asking for you."

Calaine moved to the other side of the bed and took Eunice's hand. Eunice stirred slightly and gave her fingers a weak squeeze.

"Kay...have you met your mother?" She spoke in a tremulous whisper.

Calaine glanced at Dorlinda. Her face was blank and unreadable. She looked back down at Eunice and nodded. "Yes, we met yesterday."

A weak smile reached her lips. "Birdie's a good person. She's always loved you." Her eyelids fluttered close again. "Take care of her for me."

Calaine simply nodded, then cast her eyes downward.

As Eunice slept, Dorlinda sat on one side of the bed and Calaine on the other, each holding a frail hand. It was quiet except for the faint sounds of the heart monitor and several other machines Calaine found unfamiliar.

"Eunice always thought of you as her own," Dorlinda began, breaking the silence. "She had a biking accident in high school that left her infertile, so you were the child she never had.

"I remember when I first found out I was pregnant. I was so scared. Going home wasn't even an option. My father was a strict Baptist minister who didn't believe in premarital sex. He would have beaten the tar out of me, then thrown me back out into the street. I knew your father would never leave his wife and the scandal would have ruined his career. But I couldn't bring myself to have an abortion, and Eunice supported my decision. I was a weak woman and I fed off her strength. She was so positive. She told me, 'Birdie, we can get through this together.'" Dorlinda smiled as her mind returned to the past. "You weren't due until June. Eunice made plans for us to get an apartment at the end of the semester and I'd had you before we returned to school in the fall. She made it sound so easy that I almost believed it would work." She paused long enough to catch her breath.

"When your father found out I was pregnant, he gave me the money to terminate the pregnancy, and instead I spent it on clothes. Then you came a month early. Eunice and I tried to hide you in the dorm but our dorm mom found out and threatened to have us expelled. I was so scared I didn't know what to do. Therefore, when your father agreed to locate a good home for you, I had no other choice but to agree. I don't know what I was thinking. All I knew was that I couldn't provide for you. I just never thought for a moment that I would never…never see you again." She stopped and took a moment to pull herself together before she began again. "I thought I could finish school, get a nursing job and get you back. Instead, that summer I fell apart. I dropped out of summer school, lost my scholarship and moved to Delaware with Eunice. She enrolled at Delaware State, but I got strung out on drugs. I met my husband when he arrested me for shoplifting. With his love and strength I eventually got myself together."

Calaine shifted slightly. She couldn't speak, only listen.

"Katherine hired a private investigator who tracked me down a week after your twenty-seventh birthday. I was stunned to find out your father hadn't given you away to strangers. Instead, you had always been a part of his life. Katherine wanted to surprise you and had invited me down. I was so terrified you wouldn't understand that I never showed up. Katherine was very understanding. Your father, on the other hand, was furious. He didn't want to see you hurt. He told me to stay away until I was ready to make you a part of my life." Dorlinda turned to make sure she still had Calaine's attention. Finding that she did, she continued, "I underwent counseling for over a year before I finally felt that I was ready to meet you. However, when I tried to contact Katherine in January, I found out your parents had been killed." She sighed. "I wanted to give you time to get over your loss before I tried to step into your life. Two weeks ago, I contacted Thaddeus and told him I was going to tell you the truth. He asked me to give him a chance to talk to you first."

"Wait a minute." Calaine couldn't have possibly heard her right. She rose from the bed, then asked softly, "You spoke to my Uncle Thaddeus?"

Dorlinda looked just as confused. "Uncle? Oh my God! He still hasn't told you."

"What? That you're my mother?"

"No. That… he is your father."

CHAPTER TWENTY-TWO

Calaine's knees buckled. She lowered herself onto the bed just before they gave away.

She was speechless. She didn't want to believe that the only other person she loved had betrayed her. Not Uncle Thaddeus! She dropped her head and closed her eyes before looking back up at Dorlinda, who was watching her.

Dorlinda sighed. "He always did have his own way of dealing with things."

"Apparently, he's not the only one," Calaine murmured sarcastically.

The color slowly drained from Dorlinda's face. "I guess I deserve that."

Calaine rolled her eyes and looked away.

"Thaddeus never promised me anything. I knew he was married but I didn't care."

"He told me he didn't know who my mother was," Calaine said, shaking her head.

"I guess Thaddeus was trying to protect you."

Prolonged silence enveloped them.

"Please, Calaine, say something," Dorlinda urged.

"What is there to say? I've spent weeks dreaming about this moment, only it's nothing like I imagined. Instead of welcoming you with open arms I find out that I have been betrayed not only by you but also the one person I've loved most in the world. I can't understand how you could have known where I was and never bothered to communicate with me."

"I didn't know what to say. I was afraid I would only hurt you more."

"I am a grown woman, not a child! You've had the last two years to tell me you were my mother," Calaine replied with a definite hardness in her voice.

Dorlinda's shoulders sagged. "You're right. There is no real excuse for what I've done. I thought I was doing the right thing. I made a lot of mistakes over the years but I'd like a chance to finally make things right. I-I hope you can find it in your heart to someday forgive me."

Calaine saw tears cloud her eyes and she looked away, not wanting to feel anything for her. However, there was one other thing she needed to know. "Do you have any other children?"

Dorlinda nodded. "I have a son Michael and a daughter Kelly."

Calaine's voice was hesitant. "Do they know about me?"

She gave a sad smile. "They always have."

Calaine returned to her room later that evening with her mind reeling with fresh information. How ironic. She had believed both of her parents to be dead only to find out they were both alive and well.

She slipped a pair of canvas mules from her feet and fell back against the bed. She had kept the "do not disturb" sign on the door. Her bed had not been changed since she had checked in. Bringing the pillow close to her face, she caught the scent of David still on the cotton.

She had been such a fool to send him away. Now it was too late. She had seen the pain on his face and there was no way he would give her a second chance. She couldn't blame him. If anything, the break up was probably a relief to him. Who would want to be a part of a dysfunctional family if they didn't have to be?

Family. She had a family and a history. While Eunice faded in and out, Dorlinda had spent the last several hours enlightening her.

Dorlinda had been raised in the small town of Pace, Mississippi, where everyone knew one another by name. Her father, a Baptist minister, was a respected member of the community. She had been the youngest of seven and with a ten-year gap between her and her youngest brother, she had never been close to the others. The reverend was a strict, no nonsense father while her mother was meek and passive. She met Eunice when she was fifteen and they both dreamed of someday becoming nurses. Her father was dead set against it and wanted her to marry an older member of his con-gregation. For once, Dorlinda stood up to him. However, before she left for nursing school, her father told her she would be forever dead to him. Heartbroken, she set off to Missouri determined to make something of herself.

She fell in love with Thaddeus from the start and despite the fact that he was her instructor and was married; she did everything in her power to get his attention. When she finally did, they had an affair that lasted a month before he broke it off. She had been dev-astated and contemplated suicide before she found out she was pregnant. Thaddeus had confided in her that his wife was unable to have children. Dorlinda hoped her pregnancy would change his mind but it hadn't. As a minister's daughter, she couldn't bring her-self to have an abortion nor could she turn to her parents for help. Thaddeus had been furious but he helped her until Calaine was born. Then he offered to find his daughter a good home. With stubborn pride, Dorlinda refused. She kept Calaine for five days before she realized she was being selfish. There was no way she could raise a child. Calaine saw the torment in her expression when Dorlinda told her that it had broke her heart to give up her baby. Despite her determination to harden her heart, she sympathized with her.

Calaine stared up at the ceiling as she tried to make heads or tails of what she was feeling. She wanted to stay angry but it was hard. Dorlinda was human. Humans were born to make mistakes. If she hadn't become strung out on drugs, there was no telling how much sooner they would have met.

Calaine hugged the pillow to her breasts and took a deep breath. What touched her most was the fact that Katherine had taken the time to track Dorlinda down and had intended to reunite the two. Her gaze clouded with tears. Why had Katherine decided to find Dorlinda? That was one question for which she might never find an answer. She would have to accept the fact that she had loved her in her own odd sort of way.

Rising from the bed, she noticed the red light on the phone blinking, indicating she had a message. She reached over and pushed the button, hoping it was from David.

"KeKe, this is Uncle Thaddeus. I'm sorry. I-I thought I was doing the right thing. I'll be down in the hotel restaurant at seven if you want to talk."

Calaine hung up the receiver, looked at the digital clock, then rose. She had five minutes to get down to the lobby. She reached for her key and headed out the door.

Calaine found her uncle sitting at a small table in the corner smoking a cigarette. It was something he did only when he was nervous. He looked so small and fragile. Had he lost weight since she'd last seen him? Despite every intention of being angry with him, her heart lurched at the sight of the man she had loved all her life.

She remembered all the times her mother had said no and when she wasn't looking her uncle had bought it for her anyway. She remembered all the weekends she'd spent with him fishing or doing anything she had wanted to do. She remembered her sixteenth birthday when her parents had refused to buy her a car, saying that she was too young. Uncle Thaddeus had told them they were wrong and gone behind their backs to buy her a Honda Civic. Neither of her parents had squawked at his actions and she'd never been able to figure out why. Now she knew it was because she was his daughter.

As she reached the table, his sad eyes came up to focus on her blank face.

"KeKe, I'm so glad you came."

She ignored the yearning in his expression and pursed her lips. Taking a seat across from him, she leaned back and waited for him to begin.

"I'm so sorry. I spoke to Dorlinda last night and had to see you."

Calaine shook her head with disappointment and anger all rolled up into one. "How could you?" She choked on her voice.

Thaddeus momentarily dropped his eyelids. "I can't make excuses for my past actions. I was wrong for lying to you but please just give me a chance to explain." When she nodded, he proceeded. "I was young and dumb back then. I was in the prime of my career and on top of the world. I also knew I could have any woman I wanted. Alaina and I were having a lot of problems and instead of trying to work things through, I sought comfort elsewhere. Dorlinda was so willing that I took advantage of her vulnerability. It wasn't until she became pregnant that I realized it wasn't a game.

I was playing with someone's life." He stopped long enough to take a sip from a frosty mug of draft beer. "I asked her to get an abortion but she refused. I was angry but I had to respect her wishes. In exchange for me helping her through her pregnancy, she agreed to give you up for adoption." Thaddeus frowned. "Only when you were finally here, she changed her mind. It took her almost a week before she realized that she couldn't do it alone. She called me and I came over right away. I had every intention of giving you away but when I saw your precious little face, I could not. I remember parking my car in a deserted parking lot with you in my arms gazing up at me with those little eyes. I broke down. I knew there was no way I could give you up." He paused, taking a moment to get himself together. Watching him, Calaine could see how difficult it was for him.

"At the time, my brother, your father, and his wife were trying to have a baby and found it to be hopeless. I confessed to Geoffrey what I had done and he got Katherine to agree to raise you as their child. I was forever grateful to my brother and Katherine for such a selfless act. As long as I never told Dorlinda where you were, they would keep my little secret.

Dorlinda came looking for you when you were almost two-years-old. She was on drugs at the time and I sent her away," he confessed. "She never tried to contact you again." He broke off and paused. "It wasn't until Katherine hired a private investigator that I found Dorlinda had cleaned up and rebuilt her life with another man. We were all going to break the news to you together."

Calaine sat across from him, their eyes locked the entire time. How could she be angry and feel sorry for someone at the same time?

"How come you just didn't tell me the truth when I asked you? I've spent the past month searching for answers that you already had."

Thaddeus swallowed hard and replied, "I was scared of losing you. Everything happened so fast. Your parents were killed, then you started asking questions about your birth and I panicked."

"Does Alaina know?" she asked, cutting to the chaste.

He nodded, looked down at his mug, then back up at her. "I told her yesterday before I flew here. I'm going to be sleeping on the couch for a long time but I just couldn't lie to her anymore. If I had said something a long time ago, maybe things would have turned out differently. If my brother hadn't taken you, I definitely would have had to find a way to keep you, because there was no way I could have given you away to strangers."

"Why did Katherine...my mom decide to look for Dorlinda?"

"Because she didn't find out Mother Graves wasn't her mother until her will was read. She came to me and said she didn't want you to go through the same thing."

Calaine was quiet, unable to speak, needing time to pull everything together.

"Where are you staying?" Calaine asked.

"The Hilton," he answered.

Nodding, she rose. "I need some time to think. I'll call you when I'm ready."

Turning on her heels, she headed toward the door. Calaine had taken no more than five steps when she stopped to glance over her shoulder and found her uncle watching her. Her heart tugged. "Uncle Thaddeus...I still love you."

A single tear rolled down his cheek. "I love you too, KeKe."

David swallowed hard and refused to believe that he had lost her. He almost laughed out loud. Lose her, hell, she had never been his in the first place, at least that's what Calaine had said.

He shut off his computer and prepared to leave for the day. He would then head home for another lonely night in his big empty house. He scowled. What could he do?

Calaine had accepted his help only because he had forced himself upon her. There had never been anything more than a common goal between them, yet somehow he had allowed his mind to believe there was more. Now he was paying for it. He rubbed a hand across his chin. David didn't really believe any of that, but thinking it made it easier for him to understand why she had dismissed him from her life.

It had been over a week since he'd left Delaware. He had done just as she had asked. He had stayed away even though it had been hard. Calaine needed time. Time to figure out who she was and where she was going from here. He just hoped during that time she would realize that he belonged in her future.

David played the events of the last several weeks in his mind repeatedly. The way she moved. The way she talked. The way it had felt being buried deep inside of her honey warmth. It was killing him. He could still feel her cradled in his arms. He could still smell the fabulous scent of her hair. He loved her. There were no ifs, ands or buts about it. Nevertheless, what could he do if she didn't want him or his help?

He tapped his fingers lightly against his desk with irritation. Maybe their relationship had been doomed from the start. He remembered the way she had fought his presence from the beginning, only later letting her guard down and inviting him in.

He had almost forgotten the night she ran into his arms soaking wet, fragile and shaking, needing his strength. She needed him then and as he gave it further thought, he realized that even though

281

she denied it, Calaine needed him now.

He knew deep down in his heart that Calaine cared about him even if she was too stubborn to admit it. What he couldn't figure out was why she had decided to end their relationship. There was something going on that scared her. He didn't know if maybe she was embarrassed about her mother or if she was afraid he would end the relationship and had tried to beat him to the punch.

He rose from his chair and reached for his briefcase. How could he have been so stupid? She was stubborn, which was one of the things he loved about her most. He should have expected complications. She wouldn't be Calaine without them.

Turning off the light in his office, he headed through the lobby and found he was the last to leave. He reached up and punched in the security code and left the building with the first smile he'd worn in days.

CHAPTER TWENTY-THREE

This is the worst birthday of my life, Calaine thought as she stood near fresh dirt and watched as Eunice's body was lowered into the ground. The funeral reminded her far too vividly of the pain and grief of losing both her parents at once.

The last week, though, had been a time for growing and healing.

Dorlinda gripped her hand tightly as the tears fell from her eyes. She had lost her best friend only six months after losing one of her sisters to a brain tumor. Calaine sympathized with her, wishing she could take away some of her pain. She did her best to comfort the woman who had become a good friend during the past several days.

Only a couple dozen mourners gathered at the grave. Calaine's eyes drifted to Danielle. She flew in three days ago and assisted Dorlinda with all of the arrangements.

Calaine glanced over to her sister Kelly, a senior in college. Her face was pale and her brown eyes shone with tears. She rested her head on her brother Michael's shoulder as they comforted one another. They were a handsome pair. Her ponytail and short bangs were adorable, so was her warm and loving personality. Michael was a tall, mahogany-colored man, commissioned in the United States Army. He was everything Calaine could have ever wished for in a brother.

Tears pushed to the surface of Calaine's eyes. The two had

accepted her, their big sister, as if she had always been a part of their lives.

Her eyes darted over to the far left where Uncle Thaddeus leaned against a tree. As soon as she called him to tell him Eunice had died, he hopped on the first plane out. She loved him. Despite all that he had done, he was still her father and the man she would always call Uncle Thaddeus. It would take her a long time, if ever, to forget what he had done, but her love for him allowed her to forgive. Two days ago, she had spoken extensively to her Aunt Alaina over the phone. She wanted to reassure Calaine nothing had changed. She still loved her and was looking forward to her return home.

It wasn't until dirt began to spill on top of the cedar coffin that the crowd began to turn and walk away. Still holding her mother's hand, Calaine moved to where the rest of her family stood.

"Do you have to go?" Dorlinda asked.

She glanced at the woman who had become a major part of her life in such a short time and nodded. "I've got to get back to work. Besides, I have some unfinished business to attend to."

Calaine hugged her new family and bid her goodbyes, then took Uncle Thaddeus' hand and moved with him to the car. Once at the hotel, he waited for her in the lobby while she went up to collect her things.

She went up to the fifth floor and swiped her key in the door. Stepping into the room, Calaine stopped in shock. It seemed that her heart might even forget to beat.

David was sitting on the edge of her bed. His shoulders seemed wider, and his hair appeared longer than when she had last seen him almost two weeks ago.

"How did you get in?" she asked around a large lump that was lodged in her throat.

"I still have my key," he answered in a quiet tone.

Calaine stepped into the room and closed the door behind her. Her mouth grew dry as she stared into his gold-green eyes. She couldn't figure out what he was thinking. Regardless, all that mattered was that he had come back. He stared at her so intensely that she could feel his gaze penetrating her soul. Calaine felt an overwhelming urge to simply throw herself into his arms, but she held back. No, she couldn't do that because she didn't have the faintest idea why he had returned.

"How was the funeral?" he asked, breaking the silence.

Calaine's brow furrowed. "Like all funerals. How did you know?"

"Donna called me."

She should have known Donna would run and blab her mouth.

"Then I guess you also heard about my mother."

He nodded. "And your father, too."

She nodded, then stood there trying to pull her thoughts about him and their relationship to the surface. David also remained quiet, as if he were waiting for her to speak. Brushing her pride aside, Calaine decided to say what was in her heart.

"I had a lot of time to think while we were apart and I realized something," she said in a shaky voice.

David let out the breath he was holding. "And what was that?"

"I never told you that I love you," she confessed as she wrung her fingers nervously in front of her.

"I love you, too." He rose and moved toward her.

She backed up and held up a hand. "Wait. Let me finish."

"All right." David lowered back onto the bed.

"The last few days I have learned I was wrong. Dead wrong. I was never alone. I always had Uncle Thaddeus and then I had you. The love I received from the two of you was enough to fill a lifetime, only I was too busy feeling sorry for myself to see it." She stopped long enough to catch her breath. "Having you in my life was the most wonderful feeling. Without you I can't think, I can't eat, and I can't breathe. You have captured my heart and soul in a way that no other could," she told him as a flood of tears rushed to her eyes. "For once in my life I have the confidence to let go of so many fears and insecurities and live my life to its fullest. I have been blessed again with parents and an entirely new family full of a brother, sister, and lots of cousins," she added with a laugh. "All I'm saying is I'm sorry and if you'll have me, I'd like another chance." She looked over at David as he sat quietly looking at her. He finally rose and moved to cup her face with his hands.

"Only if you'll marry me."

"W-what?" she asked, her expression reflecting surprise... joy.

He smiled and leaned down to kiss her deeply. "I love you, KeKe, even with all your flaws."

"Flaws!" she exclaimed.

"Sweetheart, you're flawless," he murmured.

David drew her into his arms and she felt his heart beating as erratically as hers. Their kiss grew deeper but before things got out of control, she pulled away.

"What a minute, I've got something for you." She moved over to her suitcase.

"So do I."

David pulled something out of his pocket at the same time Calaine removed a greeting card. She had found it in the hospital gift shop and had planned to mail it to David when she got home. If that hadn't worked, she would have parked on his front door until he forgave her.

She swung around and the envelope slipped from her hands as she saw the small velvet box. It was opened and contained a beautiful princess diamond. "What is that?" she gasped.

"What do you think it is?" David replied as he lowered onto one knee and took her left hand in his. "Calaine Renae Hart, will you marry me?"

Before she had time to breathe, she burst into tears. For the first time in months, they were tears of joy. "Yes, yes, I'll marry you."

David slipped the ring on her finger, then rose. He slid his hands down her back, drawing her closer. With a smile, he reclaimed her lips, kissing her softly at first, then urgently, with all the passion that had been pent up for too long. His body was hard and strong, his lips warm and gentle. He lifted her in his arms. Calaine laughed as he carried her over to the bed where he quickly discarded her clothes. When he began removing his own, her eyes grew large and round. "Wait a minute, Uncle Thaddeus is waiting for me."

Humor gleamed in David's eyes. "No, he isn't. I gave him strict instructions to catch the next plane home."

He came to her on the bed, covering her body with his own. Calaine closed her eyes and clung to him as she met another deep thrilling kiss.

Their love was complete.

Mind and body.

Heart and soul.

Other titles by Angie Daniels: Intimate Intention
Imprint: Indigo
ISBN: 158571044X
Retail:$ 8.95

The graceful beauty had relinquished the runways to start her own bridal collection. Unable to finance her dream, she had to walk the runways again. Diva Designs, the family legacy is on the verge of bankruptcy. Just as Terraine begins his new ad campaign, his star model is found murdered and Sasha is hired to fill the dead model's position. Snuggle down and see how this suspenseful romance unfolds.

AUTHOR BIOGRAPHY

Angie Daniels was born on the South side of Chicago, IL but preferred spending her summers running up and down the streets on the West side with her eight cousins, playing softball, roller skating (with only one skate) and jumping double dutch. At night, she would spend hours creating soap operas with her younger sister until the two drifted off to sleep. Angie attended Maria Montessori. During the fifth grade she started the first school newspaper and later went on to write, direct and star in a Christmas play. It was at that time she began spending her summers filling yellow notepads with love stories. During high school she decided to pursue a career in acting and landed the starring role as "Puck" in a "Midsummer Nights Dream." During her sophomore year, her mother relocated to Columbia, Missouri, a small college town, where she landed a role in the musical "The Roar of the Greasepaint, The Smell of the Crowd." Her pursuit of acting was short-lived.

Shortly after graduation, she married and started a family. She later attended Columbia College where she received a Bachelor's of Science in Business Administration and went on to pursue a professional career in Human Resource Management. In 1999, the corporation where she was employed as Personnel Manager went out of business. It was at that time Angela decided it was finally time to return to her love of writing. With her husband's blessings, she took a year off to write her first book Intimate Intentions, which started off as a simple romance novel that later escalated into 542 pages of romantic suspense. After two submissions, Angela was offered a four-book contract with Genesis Press. She currently resides in Wilimington, Delaware with her husband and three children. Read more about Angie at www.angiedaniels.com.

2003 Publication Schedule

January	Twist of Fate	Ebony Butterfly II
	Beverly Clark	Delilah Dawson
	1-58571-084-9	1-58571-086-5
February	Fragment in the Sand	Fate
	Annetta P. Lee	Pamela Leigh Starr
	1-58571-097-0	1-58571-115-2
March	One Day At A Time	Unbreak my Heart
	Bella McFarland	Dar Tomlinson
	1-58571-099-7	1-58571-101-2
April	At Last	Brown Sugar Diaries & Other Sexy Tales
	Lisa G. Riley	Delores Bundy & Cole Riley
	1-58571-093-8	1-58571-091-1
May	Three Wishes	Acquisitions
	Seressia Glass	Kimberley White
	1-58571-092-X	1-58571-095-4
June	When Dreams A Float	Revelations
	Dorothy Elizabeth Love	Cheris F. Hodges
	1-58571-104-7	1-58571-085-7
July	The Color of Trouble	Someone To Love
	Dyanne Davis	Alicia Wiggins
	1-58571-096-2	1-58571-098-9
August	Object Of His Desire	Hart & Soul
	A. C. Arthur	Angie Daniels
	1-58571-094-6	1-58571-087-3
September	Erotic Anthology	A Lark on the Wing
	Assorted	Phyliss Hamilton
	1-58571-113-6	1-58571-105-5

October	Angel's Paradise	I'll be your Shelter
	Janice Angelique	Giselle Carmichael
	1-58571-107-1	1-58571-108-X
November	A Dangerous Obsession	Just An Affair
	J.M. Jeffries	Eugenia O'Neal
	1-58571-109-8	1-58571-111-X
December	Shades of Brown	By Design
	Denise Becker	Barbara Keaton
	1-58571-110-1	1-58571-088-1

Other Genesis Press, Inc. Titles

A Dangerous Deception	J.M. Jeffries	$8.95
A Dangerous Love	J.M. Jeffries	$8.95
After the Vows	Leslie Esdaile	$10.95
(Summer Anthology)	T.T. Henderson	
	Jacqueline Thomas	
Again My Love	Kayla Perrin	$10.95
Against the Wind	Gwynne Forster	$8.95
A Lighter Shade of Brown	Vicki Andrews	$8.95
All I Ask	Barbara Keaton	$8.95
A Love to Cherish	Beverly Clark	$8.95
Ambrosia	T.T. Henderson	$8.95
And Then Came You	Dorothy Elizabeth Love	$8.95
A Risk of Rain	Dar Tomlinson	$8.95
Best of Friends	Natalie Dunbar	$8.95
Bound by Love	Beverly Clark	$8.95
Breeze	Robin Hampton Allen	$10.95
Cajun Heat	Charlene Berry	$8.95
Careless Whispers	Rochelle Alers	$8.95
Caught in a Trap	Andre Michelle	$8.95
Chances	Pamela Leigh Starr	$8.95
Dark Embrace	Crystal Wilson Harris	$8.95
Dark Storm Rising	Chinelu Moore	$10.95
Designer Passion	Dar Tomlinson	$8.95
Eve's Prescription	Edwina Martin Arnold	$8.95
Everlastin' Love	Gay G. Gunn	$8.95
Fate	Pamela Leigh Starr	$8.95
Forbidden Quest	Dar Tomlinson	$10.95
From the Ashes	Kathleen Suzanne	$8.95
	Jeanne Sumerix	
Gentle Yearning	Rochelle Alers	$10.95

Glory of Love	Sinclair LeBeau	$10.95
Heartbeat	Stephanie Bedwell-Grime	$8.95
Illusions	Pamela Leigh Starr	$8.95
Indiscretions	Donna Hill	$8.95
Interlude	Donna Hill	$8.95
Intimate Intentions	Angie Daniels	$8.95
Kiss or Keep	Debra Phillips	$8.95
Love Always	Mildred E. Riley	$10.95
Love Unveiled	Gloria Greene	$10.95
Love's Deception	Charlene Berry	$10.95
Mae's Promise	Melody Walcott	$8.95
Meant to Be	Jeanne Sumerix	$8.95
Midnight Clear	Leslie Esdaile	$10.95
(Anthology)	Gwynne Forster	
	Carmen Green	
	Monica Jackson	
Midnight Magic	Gwynne Forster	$8.95
Midnight Peril	Vicki Andrews	$10.95
My Buffalo Soldier	Barbara B. K. Reeves	$8.95
Naked Soul	Gwynne Forster	$8.95
No Regrets	Mildred E. Riley	$8.95
Nowhere to Run	Gay G. Gunn	$10.95
Passion	T.T. Henderson	$10.95
Past Promises	Jahmel West	$8.95
Path of Fire	T.T. Henderson	$8.95
Picture Perfect	Reon Carter	$8.95
Pride & Joi	Gay G. Gunn	$8.95
Quiet Storm	Donna Hill	$8.95
Reckless Surrender	Rochelle Alers	$8.95
Rendezvous with Fate	Jeanne Sumerix	$8.95
Rivers of the Soul	Leslie Esdaile	$8.95

Rooms of the Heart	Donna Hill	$8.95
Shades of Desire	Monica White	$8.95
Sin	Crystal Rhodes	$8.95
So Amazing	Sinclair LeBeau	$8.95
Somebody's Someone	Sinclair LeBeau	$8.95
Soul to Soul	Donna Hill	$8.95
Still Waters Run Deep	Leslie Esdaile	$8.95
Subtle Secrets	Wanda Y. Thomas	$8.95
Sweet Tomorrows	Kimberly White	$8.95
The Price of Love	Sinclair LeBeau	$8.95
The Reluctant Captive	Joyce Jackson	$8.95
The Missing Link	Charlyne Dickerson	$8.95
Tomorrow's Promise	Leslie Esdaile	$8.95
Truly Inseperable	Wanda Y. Thomas	$8.95
Unconditional Love	Alicia Wiggins	$8.95
Whispers in the Night	Dorothy Elizabeth Love	$8.95
Whispers in the Sand	LaFlorya Gauthier	$10.95
Yesterday is Gone	Beverly Clark	$8.95
Yesterday's Dreams, Tomorrow's Promises	Reon Laudat	$8.95
Your Precious Love	Sinclair LeBeau	$8.95

Order Form

Mail to: Genesis Press, Inc.

1213 Hwy 45 N
Columbus, MS 39705

Name _____

Address _____

City/State _____ Zip _____

Telephone _____

Ship to (if different from above)

Name _____

Address _____

City/State _____ Zip _____

Telephone _____

Qty.	Author	Title	Price	Total

Use this order form, or call 1-888-INDIGO-1	Total for books _____ Shipping and handling: $5 first two books, $1 each additional book _____ Total S & H _____ Total amount enclosed _____ *Mississippi residents add 7% sales tax*

Visit www.genesispress.com for latest releases and excerpts

Order Form

Mail to: Genesis Press, Inc.

1213 Hwy 45 N
Columbus, MS 39705

Name _____

Address _____

City/State _____ Zip _____

Telephone _____

Ship to (if different from above)

Name _____

Address _____

City/State _____ Zip _____

Telephone _____

Qty.	Author	Title	Price	Total

Use this order form, or call 1-888-INDIGO-1	Total for books _____
	Shipping and handling: $5 first two books, $1 each additional book _____
	Total S & H _____
	Total amount enclosed _____
	Mississippi residents add 7% sales tax

Order Form

Mail to: Genesis Press, Inc.

1213 Hwy 45 N
Columbus, MS 39705

Name _____

Address _____

City/State _____ Zip _____

Telephone _____

Ship to (if different from above)

Name _____

Address _____

City/State _____ Zip _____

Telephone _____

Qty.	Author	Title	Price	Total

Use this order
form, or call
1-888-INDIGO-1

Total for books _____

Shipping and handling:
$5 first two books, $1 each
additional book

Total S & H _____

Total amount enclosed _____

Mississippi residents add 7% sales tax

Visit www.genesis-press.com for latest releases and excerpts.